MW01124554

THE PALACE
OF SINNERS
AND SAINTS

A Novel

AMMAR MERCHANT

SIMON & SCHUSTER

New York   Amsterdam/Antwerp   London
Toronto   Sydney/Melbourne   New Delhi

Simon & Schuster
1230 Avenue of the Americas
New York, NY 10020

This book is a work of fiction. Any references to historical events, real people, or real places are used fictitiously. Other names, characters, places, and events are products of the author's imagination, and any resemblance to actual events or places or persons, living or dead, is entirely coincidental.

First Simon & Schuster hardcover edition May 2025

SIMON & SCHUSTER and colophon are registered trademarks of Simon & Schuster, LLC

Simon & Schuster strongly believes in freedom of expression and stands against censorship in all its forms. For more information, visit BooksBelong.com.

For information about special discounts for bulk purchases, please contact Simon & Schuster Special Sales at 1-866-506-1949 or business@simonandschuster.com.

The Simon & Schuster Speakers Bureau can bring authors to your live event. For more information or to book an event, contact the Simon & Schuster Speakers Bureau at 1-866-248-3049 or visit our website at www.simonspeakers.com.

Interior design by Wendy Blum

Manufactured in the United States of America

1   3   7   9   10   8   6   4   2

Library of Congress Cataloging-in-Publication Data has been applied for.

ISBN 978-1-6680-6758-1
ISBN 978-1-6680-6760-4 (ebook)

PROLOGUE

AHMAD HAIKAL WAS AFRAID of wolves. He'd never seen one in person. They weren't native to the island of Borneo, and he had never left the Sabah region of Malaysia or wandered far from his small town of Beaufort.

When he'd been a boy, however, he had seen a horror movie that featured the beasts. It left him scarred. His mother comforted him by promising that because of where they lived, he'd never actually come across the fearsome creatures.

For over thirty years, her words had been true.

Then the stranger walked into Ahmad's tiny, failing roadside restaurant.

He was tall and had shoulder-length, unkempt black hair with hints of gray. His eyes, under thick, sweeping brows, were dark. A shaggy beard covered a face that was . . . well, Ahmad was not one to be unkind, but this man was not pretty. His features, like the rest of him, seemed to be carved out of stone, which was a great thing for muscles but not so great a thing for a nose.

He wasn't Malay, likely hailing from India or Pakistan or Bangladesh, which wasn't unusual in this part of the world. What was unusual was his height, his bulk, and the menace he radiated.

Ahmad stepped back, moving away from the massive wok in which he was deep-frying bananas. A moment passed before he realized what he'd done, after which he shook his head. There was no reason to be afraid of the man.

At least that's what he tried to tell himself, but the primal part of his brain, which recognized a predator when it saw one, would not stop crying wolf.

Reminding himself that he had recently gotten used to being around dangerous men, Ahmad called out a greeting. Not knowing whether his new customer spoke Bahasa Malaysia, he used some of the little English he had.

"Hello, sir."

The stranger didn't respond. Instead, he stood by the entrance and surveyed the place, taking in the cheap, plastic furniture, the rickety oscillating pedestal fans in every corner, and the white concrete walls with their peeling paint. Eventually, his gaze found the other seven men present.

They were former members of the Abu Sayyaf group—part terrorists, part pirates. They were also the reason Ahmad's business had cratered. They'd fled to Beaufort from the Philippines and had taken an unfortunate liking to his food. A few of them seemed to always be around, and as a result other locals now avoided his establishment.

Driving them off was out of the question. Attempting to do so would mean his life. Since their arrival four months ago, several tourists had been held for ransom, there had been shootings and robberies and a few murders. Killing was their work, and they seemed to like their jobs.

They were there that afternoon, hunched over their usual table, cackling over crass jokes while waiting for their food. They paused to study the stranger when he strode in, like hyenas hungry for a bite. Instead of harassing him, like they did everyone else, they looked away quickly and went back to their conversation, speaking now in more subdued tones.

Smiling a little at their reaction, Ahmad called out again. "Order here, sir."

The stranger ambled up to the counter and, with bandage-wrapped hands, reached into the back pocket of his worn jeans. He pulled out a folded article cut from a newspaper. It was in some language Ahmad didn't know, but there was a picture of a smiling young woman on it he recognized.

Cilek Osman was one of the first foreigners who'd disappeared after the "retired" Abu Sayyaf men had set up in Beaufort. She had been a nineteen-year-old with dreams of becoming a travel vlogger. She'd come to nearby Kota Kinabalu to snorkel.

Her body had been found floating through town on the Padas River. There had been no ransom demand in her case. Ahmad had heard the Abu Sayyaf men laughing as they talked about what they'd done to her.

When he saw her face now, Ahmad couldn't help but look in their direction.

The stranger noticed, nodded, and said, "The furniture here looks cheap."

Ahmad, who had been expecting him to ask about the girl, started. "Yes, cheap food. You eat?"

"I was talking about your stuff. You didn't spend a lot of money on it. It won't be a big loss if it gets broken."

Ahmad shrugged.

"Just start a tab."

"What is 'tab'?"

"Keep a record of your damages."

"No order?"

The stranger sighed and started undoing the bandage on his right hand. His knuckles were skinned raw and bruised purple. "What's good?"

"Nasi lemak ayam with sambal very good. Spicy okay?"

"Sure. You work on that." The stranger gestured toward the former Abu Sayyaf men with his head. "I'm going to talk to them."

"Sir," the restaurateur leaned forward and whispered urgently, "they dangerous, yeah?"

"I'm dangerous too."

That was easy to believe. Still, Ahmad wanted him to understand what he was about to start. "They hurt people."

"So do I."

"You came for . . ." Ahmad fumbled around for the word "revenge," couldn't find it, and decided to do without. He gestured toward the picture of Cilek Osman. "Your daughter?"

The stranger's expression darkened and for a moment it seemed like the guess was accurate, but he eventually shook his head. "Her father hired me. These guys are the ones who took her, right?"

Ahmad swallowed, licked his lips, then told him the truth: "Yes."

"Good." The stranger pointed at the bananas Ahmad had been frying, which he'd forgotten about, and which were now starting to burn. "I'll take those too."

"I make new. How many—"

The stranger's left hand darted out and grabbed the huge wok by one of its handles. Lifting it effortlessly, he marched to the Abu Sayyaf table. All seven men there looked up at his approach. He swung the wok, spraying them with boiling oil. They screamed as it hit their faces, sizzling as it burned their skin and seared their eyes. Howling and clutching their heads, they rolled out of their seats.

The stranger grabbed the pirate closest to him by the hair, held him in place, and slammed the hot cast-iron wok on the man's nose with staggering force. Blood sprayed everywhere. The stranger did this again and again and again, until the criminal dangled in place limp and lifeless, like a puppet without strings.

He turned his attention to one of the men rolling on the floor next to him. He pinned his quarry in place by putting a heavy boot on his chest, then dropped the wok on top the man's face, so that it muffled his screams. Then the stranger stomped on the wok viciously, repeatedly, until there was a crack and his target's cervical spine snapped.

A terrorist who'd been spared the brunt of the initial assault came at the stranger with a knife. The stranger stepped aside and tossed him toward Ahmad, who shrieked and ducked behind a counter.

From where he was hiding, Ahmad saw the stranger hold the terrorist's face above his stove. The sick smell of burning hair and flesh filled the air, joined by cries straight out of hell.

Ahmad closed his eyes, cowered in a corner, and listened to punishment being meted out. Minutes later, there was silence, followed by the sound of running water.

Ahmad slowly got to his feet and saw that the stranger had taken the bandage off his left hand too and was washing blood off of himself.

Seven bodies lay on the floor of Ahmad's restaurant. A crowd had gathered outside and was looking on in silence. In the distance, the call for the Asr prayer started.

The stranger looked around for a towel, found none, considered his own gore-covered clothes, then walked over to Ahmad, grabbed the restaurant owner's shirt, and used it to dry his hands.

When he was done, the stranger took out his wallet, counted out a thousand ringgit, and dropped them on the counter. "To fix up your place," he explained. "And for the meal. I think I should take it to go."

"To go?" Ahmad echoed dully.

"It's time for Asr and then I have a plane to catch."

"You kill, then you pray?"

The stranger shrugged. "It's when I need forgiveness most."

Ahmad stared at him.

The stranger tapped at his left wrist, at an imaginary watch that wasn't there.

"Okay. Nasi lemak ayam with sambal. You said spicy, yeah?"

"Yes."

Still trying to process what had happened, Ahmad drifted back into his kitchen. "Can I get a name for your order?"

"Mirza," the stranger said.

Part One

THE COST OF CONSCIENCE

ONE

PRINCE MAHMUD IBN HABIB fidgeted in his seat, staring at every passenger who boarded their small Air Asia flight, trying to determine if they were a threat.

His fiancée, Renata Bardales, knew it was a useless exercise. Mahmud wouldn't be able to pick an assassin out of a church choir. She suspected that in his imagination they looked like bad guys out of movies—dressed in black, dripping with malice, the evil in their hearts writ large on their faces.

That just wasn't true. Professional killers—the good ones, at least—often weren't easy to spot. A smiling waitress or air hostess could hand you a poisoned drink. Your life might end in a fatal car accident caused by an innocuous, exhausted-looking man in a wrinkled suit. Just about anyone you came across could be a merchant of death.

Ren didn't point that out to Mahmud, of course. He was more than anxious enough already. There was no reason to take him further out of his depth.

He was royalty after all, and had been raised like all Aldatani princes were, flying around in private jets, attending prestigious schools, ensconced in a cocoon of privilege and safety alien to most of the planet. He didn't know how murderous the world could be.

Ren, who had grown up in an "orphanage" where she'd been trained to fight and kill, was much better equipped to deal with being prey than he was.

So, even though being patient took some effort, she decided not to be irritated by his wide-eyed antics. Instead, she reached over, took his hand in hers, and gave it a reassuring squeeze. "Relax. It'll be fine, habibi."

Renata's use of the Arabic endearment, which had stopped feeling foreign on her tongue, made him smile a little. It wasn't a sight she saw very often these days.

"Inshallah," he said. "I am just worried we stayed in Chiang Mai too long. We should have moved right after my last piece went to print. What if my cousin has found us? I'm sure he's looking for me more intently than ever before."

"Well, kings don't usually appreciate attempted coups. Quien siembra vientos, cosecha tempestades."

Mahmud raised his eyebrows. "What does that mean?"

Ren didn't translate the proverb for him. She didn't tell him it meant that "whoever sows the wind, reaps the storm," because even though he'd never said it, she knew Mahmud felt terrible that his decision to oppose the tyranny of the Aldatani throne had completely altered the kind of life they'd expected to have together.

A year ago, when his father had called for massive democratic reforms in Aldatan, including the provision of rights like free speech and fair elections, Mahmud could have disavowed him.

Mahmud wouldn't have been a hunted man then. He would've been a hero to his government, but he wouldn't have been someone she could love.

As it was, Mahmud—though abroad—had joined his father's cause and launched a social media campaign against the oppressive regime of his paternal cousin, King Nimir. He'd also published several exposés in Western newspapers detailing exactly how Aldatan surveilled and blackmailed its citizens, forcing them into either silence or submission.

His last article had been particularly incendiary, as it revealed the hypocrisy of his cousin, who pretended to be a pious Muslim because Aldatan used religion to control its people. The truth, however, was that the king was fond of succumbing to his baser instincts.

It was sure to have earned Mahmud his monarch's renewed wrath, which was no trivial thing. Many who supported Mahmud's father, Habib, had been jailed, killed, or disappeared. Habib himself hadn't been seen or heard from in ten months. The Aldatani journalists with whom Mahmud had worked in the past were all corpses now. Mahmud himself had almost been kidnapped twice in Cairo.

He and Renata had been on the run since then, moving from city to city, country to country, trying to escape the reach of the Aldatani sovereign.

As she saw him scan the onboarding passengers with terrified eyes, Renata could see that the strain of it all was getting to him.

"Remember there's help waiting for us in Bangkok," she assured him.

"Your brother might try to help us, but he's just one guy. What can one man do against the might of an army and the weight of a crown?"

Renata shrugged. "That depends on the man, don't you think?"

Renata didn't know much about Bangkok, but the drive from Suvarnabhumi Airport to the hotel where her "brother" was staying was enough to make her understand just how crowded a place it was.

They arrived late at night, but the city was still congested. She'd been to Los Angeles and Paris and London, and none of those cities could compete with the rush on the roads of Thailand's biggest metropolis, where bikes wove through traffic and cars seemed to get impossibly close to each other as they attempted to inch toward their destinations.

As their luxury cab neared the Al Meroz Hotel, however, it began to pick up a little speed, and Renata realized they were heading away from the city center and the kind of glitzy places at which her fiancé liked to stay. Irfan Mirza seemed to have picked an establishment a little removed from the action that attracted so many to Bangkok. She wondered what that said about the kind of man he'd become.

She had seen him three years ago, at a "family" reunion, but they hadn't spoken much. Mirza's body language had made it clear that he did not want to be there. She figured he had only attended because the gregarious Finn Thompson, another "brother" of hers, had insisted.

Ren had never understood how the taciturn, dour Mirza and the cheerful, extroverted Finn had become close. It was like midnight befriending noon. It shouldn't have worked, but it did.

She didn't know Mirza well—few people did—but when she found herself in trouble she couldn't get out of, his was the first name that came to mind.

This wasn't entirely rational. Some part of her, she knew, was still the weak little girl who had been kidnapped, trafficked, and purchased by the General. When she had arrived at his "orphanage," where she'd be forced to train to become a soldier, she'd been beaten and bullied. Other, stronger kids had taken her food and forced her to do their chores. It was the survival of the fittest.

She had soon noticed that other children like her, those in need of protection, found it in Mirza's shadow. She was safe when he was around, as was everyone else who needed help.

It was strange, in that he wasn't their friend, he wasn't sweet or warm or thoughtful. He was just . . . there, an iron shield when needed, completely indifferent otherwise.

Now, decades later, in flying herself and Mahmud to Bangkok to meet him, she knew she was engaging in a ritual she had learned when she'd been young. Like an atheist turning to prayer when faced with a calamity, she was seeking Mirza out because she didn't know what else to do.

"You're very quiet, habibti," Mahmud noted beside her.

"I'm just thinking."

"About?"

"My first trip to Aldatan."

"When we met," he remembered with a smile. "That was a good day."

"The best," she agreed. "I wouldn't have been there if it weren't for Finn and his obsessive need to keep everyone from our orphanage connected."

"You don't talk about it much. The orphanage, I mean."

"No. I don't."

Mahmud started to say something or ask something maybe, but then reconsidered. He knew she didn't like talking about her past, and he was too kind to insist.

She smiled. After a lifetime spent among hard, rough men, she had chosen this slender, gentle, cultured bookworm with whom to spend her life. Presented with a world full of killers, she'd picked someone who would struggle to hurt a fly.

Sometimes—usually after a close brush with the Aldatanis hunting them—she couldn't help but think about how reassuring having a partner who could hold his own in a fight would be. In those moments, she wondered if she'd made the right decision.

But she knew that they would have demanded answers from her in a way that Mahmud didn't. He didn't demand anything from her really. He was happy to just exist where she existed and this, she figured, was love or at least something close to it.

"What is it?" Mahmud asked when she continued to study him with her light-brown eyes.

"You're good company."

That earned her a broad grin. "An actual compliment? Are you feeling all right, señorita?"

Renata nodded as the car began to slow down. From her window, she could see that they'd arrived at a hotel with an array of flags flying outside it. She recognized the ones belonging to Kazakhstan, Algeria, Indonesia, Saudi Arabia, and Morocco.

"It's like the UN," she joked.

"More like the OIC," Mahmud corrected, and at her confused look added, "the Organization of Islamic Countries."

He got out and held the door open for her before the taxi driver could.

Renata followed and looked around at their surroundings as Mahmud reached for his wallet. Her wandering gaze picked up the bright headlights of a van heading in their direction.

She instinctively knew something was wrong. It took her a moment to realize what. The large vehicle wasn't slowing down as it got closer to them. It was, in fact, gaining speed.

Then its driver-side door flew open and a man jumped out, while the van kept barreling toward them.

Renata screamed and launched herself at her fiancé, pushing him out of the way. As they tumbled to the ground, Renata heard the van smash into their cab in a violent collision that shattered glass and crushed steel.

TWO

IN HIS ROOM AT the Al Meroz in Bangkok, Irfan Mirza pulled his rough, bruised hands out of a bucket of ice and stared at them. The swelling and discoloration around his knuckles, which had been getting better before his recent encounter with the Abu Sayyaf men, was worse. The skin there, often abused, had torn again. His joints popped as he made a fist, his fingers stiff because of the cold he'd drenched them in. He wasn't able to entirely stifle a grunt of pain.

On the laptop screen in front of him, Omen Ferris winced on his behalf.

Mirza had no definition for their relationship.

They could be called business partners, except they weren't really. There were times when his work as a mercenary and her work as an "acquisitions expert"—that was to say, a professional thief—overlapped. It made sense for them to cooperate in those circumstances, but they didn't usually split profits or make a habit of collaborating.

He could fairly introduce Omen as his newest friend. They had met a year ago and had gotten so close that they'd started having weekly video calls, like the one they were on now. Mirza wasn't sure exactly how this routine had formed, but he was not at all inclined to break it.

But that was a platonic label. Using it despite his desire for her was

15

a bit like calling a wild, desperate, ravenous timber wolf pacing in a cage just a dog.

The fact that he was still married to someone else—even if they had been separated for a decade and their divorce was pending—made being more accurate about his feelings, however, entirely impossible.

Without acknowledging Omen's sympathy, he asked, "Are you still in Hanoi?"

"Yeah. I already have what I came for though. I'm going to head to Da Nang soon. You should meet me there if you can."

"What's in Da Nang? A new gig?"

"No. A beach. Come on. Look at you. You obviously need a vacation."

Mirza grunted and began wrapping fresh cotton bandages tight around his bruises, hoping that the compression would help him heal faster. Even though he took meticulous care of it, his body no longer recovered from the punishment he routinely put it through as quickly as it once had. It'd been the primary tool of his trade all his life. It was the sledgehammer with which he broke people for money. Sometimes— almost always, in fact—their bones tried to break him back.

No one had managed it yet, but it seemed less impossible than it once had.

"At least think about it," Omen urged.

He met her bright-green eyes and smiled without meaning to. "I will."

"I guarantee you'll have a good time."

"We have very different ideas of what that is."

"Yeah, yeah." The redhead rolled her eyes. "Big, bad Irfan isn't happy unless he's bashing someone's skull in. I know. From the look of your hands, you had a blast in Kuala Lumpur."

"I wasn't in KL."

"You said you flew in from Malaysia."

"They have other cities."

"I'm American," she joked. "I can't be expected to know these things."

When that didn't draw a reaction from him, she added, "Was it at least a well-paying job?"

"No."

"When I tell my friends about you—"

"Why would you—"

"—they assume," Omen pressed on, "you make bank. Apparently, mercenaries can get a small fortune if they're with the right PMC."

Mirza nodded. That was true for private military companies based in the West, especially the United States. He, however, lacked the necessary security clearances to work for the best of those.

The PMCs he had been employed by in the past had been less than reputable, and they'd been contracted by governments with standards that weren't as exacting as those in the more developed parts of the world. Their pay, by extension, wasn't as good either, though it was still more than he earned solo.

Even so, Mirza preferred the freedom he had now, the freedom to choose his own clients, even if it meant leaving money on the table.

"I'm just saying," Omen added, "your life could be easier."

Mirza grunted. "I'm not interested in that."

"What are you interested in?"

There was something about her tone when she asked that question that made him pause before answering. Turning his full attention to her, it struck him, as it often did, how stunning she was, with her silky, copper-red hair and delicate features. It was enough to make him wish he were a different man—handsome, gentler, more romantic.

But he was who he was—the human version of a baseball bat wrapped with barbed wire—and there was no help for it. So, instead of giving her the first answer that popped into his mind, he said, "I'm trying to do some good in the world."

"By beating people up?"

"That's the only way it's fun."

Omen shook her head. "You're ridiculous."

That wasn't entirely untrue, so he just shrugged.

"Anyway, let me know if you can make it. Though I guess that'll depend on what your sister wants. Have you met up with her yet?"

Mirza thought about correcting her but didn't. As far as he was concerned, the children he had grown up with weren't his family. Saying they were felt like hiding from the truth that he simply hadn't had one of those when he was young.

Well, that wasn't exactly true. He'd had parents once. That was unavoidable, but his mother had died when he was six, and his father had disappeared shortly thereafter. He'd spent his early childhood as an urchin in Karachi, begging, stealing, fighting, and hustling to survive.

That had changed when he'd caught the attention of the General, a retired Turkish military officer who had the grand dream of assembling a specialized, private army of operatives whose skills he could put up for sale.

Mirza had been taken to Turkey, where he grew up training with other lost, forsaken, or vanished children from all over the globe.

It had been a mad, imperfect plan that had ultimately failed. Telling them they were siblings, that he was their father, hadn't made the children under the General's control love him. They weren't loyal to him and slowly, over time, they stopped returning from the missions they were sent out on.

Some had gone on to try to build regular, mundane lives for themselves and had cut themselves off from their "family." Others—mostly those who were still soldiers of fortune—stayed in touch with each other. Finn Thompson, Mirza's closest friend, kept them all connected as best he could. He'd even gone so far as to arrange a reunion once and had gotten Mirza to attend only after a great deal of cajoling.

Finn was the one who'd connected Mirza to Renata Bardales, who needed help keeping her fiancé safe. Mirza didn't know what the details were, exactly, but he wasn't looking forward to the assignment. He'd considered turning it down and would have done so, in fact, if Finn hadn't insisted he take it on.

"I haven't seen her," he told Omen. "They're flying in from Chiang Mai. I'm meeting them for breakfast tomorrow."

"You could sound more enthusiastic about it."

"I can't. It's a protection detail."

Omen chuckled. "And you hate those."

"I'm wasted on defense."

"That's not it. You like having the initiative. When you're guarding someone, you're forced to be reactive. You don't enjoy it because you love being in control."

"Who doesn't?" he asked.

"You'd be surprised. People have all kinds of kinks."

Mirza was still trying to figure out how to respond to that when he heard a faint scream followed by a loud crash.

THREE

RENATA'S SKULL SLAMMED AGAINST the edge of a sidewalk as she fell. Something in her vision shifted, like the world had gone out of focus for a moment. She clutched her head. It felt wet. When she pulled her hands back, they had red on them.

Mahmud peered over at her, concern etched on his face. He didn't seem afraid. It hadn't registered with him that someone had just tried to injure or kill them. He seemed to have assumed it was an accident. She had to warn him of the danger they were in.

Ren forced herself to sit up and groaned.

"Stay still," Mahmud insisted. "I will ask them to get you a doc—"

Squealing tires cut his words off. A second van came up to the Al Meroz and five men wearing balaclavas poured out. Renata could tell from the way they carried themselves, by how imposing they were, that they weren't civilians or even simple thugs or amateurish mercenaries. They moved like professionals.

Her suspicions were confirmed when she saw that one of them had pulled up the sleeves on his shirt. On his forearm, she saw the tattoo of a roaring predatory cat, its ears up and eyes wide.

Her heart seemed to falter, like it would stop beating at any moment.

Leopards.

King Nimir had sent his legendary death squad for them.

"Fuck," she whispered.

At least they weren't carrying guns. They had likely followed them to Bangkok from Chiang Mai and hadn't had time to obtain weapons. Thailand had strict laws regarding firearms. It wasn't easy for foreigners to procure them quickly.

Not that it mattered. These men were more than lethal enough unarmed. Even at the peak of her fighting ability, Renata knew she would've struggled to match even one. Now, after a decade of rust, five . . . no, six—the driver of the first van had run over to join them—Leopards posed impossible odds.

Mahmud, still focused solely on her, protested as she struggled to her feet. He remained oblivious to any danger until two of the men jogged up to each side of him, grabbed him by his arms, and yanked him away from Renata. His expression shifted from confusion to annoyance to outrage to panic as he realized what was happening.

"Let him go!" Renata shrieked. The words wouldn't have any effect on their assailants, but a crowd had started to gather outside the Al Meroz as employees and guests were drawn out by the commotion. She hoped some of them would intervene. With the force of numbers, perhaps even the deadly Leopards could be subdued.

No one moved to help.

Mahmud was dragged closer to the waiting van, its engine still running.

Left without a choice, Ren launched herself at the closest Leopard.

She aimed a blow at his neck. He ducked out of the way and delivered a swift counterpunch to her chest. It sent her stumbling back. There was a gasp from the onlookers.

She recovered as best she could and tried a kick at his abdomen. He caught her leg and brought a heavy chop down on her shin, causing Renata to cry out and limp back as he released her.

One of the men dragging Mahmud away called out, "Bring the bitch. Just for fun."

Laughing, the Leopard grabbed at her. Renata shoved his hand away and managed to strike his right cheek. He seemed shocked for a second, then growled and reached for her again. She wasn't able to stop him in time, and he got ahold of her hair. Renata cried out and he . . . released her.

A titan had planted himself between the Leopard and the van into which Mahmud was being loaded. Despite the fact that she hadn't seen him in years, despite the long hair and beard he now sported, Renata instantly recognized the intense dark eyes and mighty frame of Irfan Mirza.

He stood before the Leopard, fists clenched, so obviously a threat it was no wonder the solider had felt compelled to let Renata go.

"Who—"

The Leopard never got to finish his sentence. Mirza's left fist collided with the man's solar plexus faster than Renata would have imagined he could move.

Mirza followed up with a headbutt, then a swinging elbow to the side of the staggering Leopard's face.

The Aldatani soldier retaliated, catching Mirza with a kick to his right thigh, then one to his left shoulder. That seemed only to drive Mirza to move faster, to hit harder, with more brutality. As the two men fought, Renata saw her brother for what he was. A berserker who happily took damage to inflict damage, using his pain to spur his body to its limits.

It wasn't smart, but it seemed to work.

It was over in less than a minute, with a member of one of the world's premier assassination squads lying unconscious on the ground. A grinning Mirza, bleeding from the side of his mouth and from a cut above one of his eyebrows, turned to face the other five Leopards. He extended an arm and gestured for the men to come at him.

"You're insane," one of them said.

Renata had to agree. What did he think this was? A kung fu movie?

"I am."

"You'll die here," another Leopard warned.

Mirza cranked his neck, then shook his arms, as if trying to shed the hurt he was experiencing, like a great hound trying to dry itself, and promised, "Not alone."

The Aldatanis glanced at each other as if not quite sure what to make of the response. Then two of them stepped forward to fight.

Renata looked back at the bystanders, who were watching in hushed silence. No one seemed any more willing to get involved now than they'd been before. She couldn't blame them.

She couldn't let Mirza fight alone though. So she stepped forward, leg still aching, and stood next to her fellow janissary.

He glanced over at her and grunted, either in disapproval or appreciation, she couldn't tell.

Then, without warning, Mirza charged the Leopards.

It caught her by surprise.

It caught them by surprise too. Mirza speared the chest of one of the men with his shoulder, sending the Leopard flying back like he'd been gored by a bull.

This left Mirza's flank exposed, and the second soldier caught him with a palm strike to the side of his face.

Mirza fell back a little, snarled, and turned toward the attacker.

They were polar opposites in terms of build. The soldier was wiry and toned. Mirza was all bulk and sinew. He was quick for someone his size. That was how he'd caught his first opponent off guard, but he wouldn't have that advantage this time, and there was no way he was going to be agile enough to match this man.

They circled each other for a while, Mirza falling back toward the wrecked cab as the Leopard feinted and advanced.

Police sirens began blaring in the distance.

"Stop playing," one of the other Aldatani operatives called out. "Finish him and let's go."

Even though two of them had gone down, Renata could hear the complete confidence in the man's voice. They thought they were toying with Mirza. They knew that given enough time, they would win. Their skill and their numbers ensured it.

The Leopard complied, coming at Mirza with a flurry of blows that fell like lightning, zipping past Mirza's defenses, connecting with his jaw, his sternum, his gut and driving him back and then down to his knees, bruised and wounded.

Chuckling, the Leopard stepped back, looking down at the mercenary he'd felled.

Renata started to move forward, but Mirza held a hand out, commanding her to stay where she was.

His other fist closed at his side.

She could see it was bleeding but couldn't figure out why.

Then Mirza lunged to his feet, opening his hand as it neared the Leopard's face. Shards of broken glass from the car accident flew forward. Some got into the eyes of the Leopard, who screamed, his hands darting up belatedly to protect his face. Mirza drove a vicious boot into the man's right knee, then his left, leaving him broken on the ground.

Renata shook her head.

Mirza had planned that. He'd moved himself closer to the ruined cars intentionally, absorbed the punishment necessary to make his quarry believe he really had fallen. Then he'd played the ace up his sleeve. It was—

Her thoughts were cut off at the same time as her breath.

She kicked helplessly against the sudden, relentless pressure that was being applied to her windpipe.

The world was already fading to black in the few seconds it took for her thoughts to catch up with what was happening. While she had been distracted by Mirza's display, a Leopard had slipped behind her. His arm was now wrapped around her neck in a perfectly executed chokehold.

She croaked, trying to call out to Mirza for help, but words seemed impossible to form, and she wasn't sure she would be able to make a sound before the world plunged into darkness.

FOUR

ANOTHER LEOPARD CHARGED AT Mirza. This one had armed himself with a lug wrench.

As Mirza squared up to face the attacker, the gathered crowd, which had been mostly silent so far, began to scream and point. They wanted him to turn around, to look behind him, but there wasn't time for that.

Mirza swayed out of the way of an overhead swing, grabbed the Leopard's hair, and yanked his head back hard. Then Mirza struck the soldier's throat, once and again and again and again, in succession, until his trachea fractured under the barrage.

All fight left the man. He staggered back, wheezing, his eyes frantic as he struggled to breathe. Mirza shoved him to the ground, where he lay writhing and gasping.

By the time Mirza saw what had excited the crowd, the van holding Mahmud was peeling away. He looked for Renata and didn't see her. A few people around him called out that she'd been taken too.

Cursing under his breath, Mirza scanned his surroundings for cars or motorcycles he could give chase in. There were no viable options in sight, just the two wrecked vehicles that had been part of the crash that had drawn him out.

The driveway at the front of the hotel did lead to an underground parking structure, but by the time he got to it, commandeered something, and got back, his quarry would be long gone.

He clenched and unclenched his fists, taking deep, calming breaths.

Despite the fact that there was no immediate danger left, no one approached him. In fact, the crowd shrank from his dark gaze. A few brought their phones up in front of themselves, as if they were priests wielding holy crosses and he a fearsome demon who needed warding off.

Ignoring them and the fact that they were recording him, Mirza strode over to the luggage lying by the taxi that had been rammed. He figured it had been hired by Renata and her fiancé.

There were two suitcases beside it, along with a fancy burgundy leather briefcase. Picking up the latter, he carried it to the hood of the cab and—making sure it was pointed away from the witnesses—popped it open.

There was a large tablet inside, but it was secured via a passcode, along with a laptop. There were a few pens, a couple of books, and a USB stick.

He pocketed the drive as surreptitiously as he could.

He would've liked to take the other devices too, but the cops would quickly find out if he did. Anything he was seen removing from the scene they'd want returned as evidence.

With an exaggerated grimace, he shut the case, trying to make it look like he'd found nothing in it all.

An intrepid manager broke away from the pack, wringing her hands as she made her way over. "Are you okay, sir? You're hurt, no? You need a doctor?"

"I'm fine."

"Are you sure? You don't look good."

"That's a preexisting condition," Mirza said. Making his way over to the last attacker who'd come at him, he began a thorough search.

Like all the others, this man was dressed entirely in black, which Mirza thought was cliché.

There was no identification of any kind, no money, no clues at all. Not that Mirza had expected any. Whatever else these people were, they weren't amateurs.

"They're not Thai," the manager observed from over his shoulder.

That was obvious, so Mirza didn't reward her with anything more than a grunt of acknowledgment.

He spotted the tattoo of a roaring predatory cat on the man's arm and frowned. The symbol was vaguely familiar, but he couldn't place it, not without context. Pulling out his cell, he photographed it.

"You don't have to do that, sir."

"No?"

"The authorities will take care of it. The kidnapping of farang, that's the kind of thing they investigate seriously." The manager said this in a tone that was meant to be comforting and would have been if she weren't shaken and harried. "You don't have to worry. I'm sure they'll find your . . . I'm sorry, were those two people your friends?"

"Not really." Mirza rose to his feet. "But they were my responsibility."

"I don't understand."

"Don't worry about it."

"What I'm saying is that in this kind of situation, there's not a lot ordinary people can do."

"True," Mirza replied. "But I'm not ordinary people."

FIVE

MIRZA WAS QUESTIONED AT length by the Royal Thai Police's tourist bureau, which had been designed to deal specifically with foreigners. It was a special division that existed because the rank and file of the force was so corrupt that the government feared exposure to them would sour visitors on their country. Thailand couldn't afford that.

So the locals lived with the moral rot of the authorities placed over them, while foreigners were given a cleaner, more bearable experience.

They made sure Mirza was given medical attention, most of which was focused on extracting a few small shards of glass still embedded in his left hand and stitching up the cuts there. Then he was interrogated. It took an hour and a half. It was wasted time in his opinion.

There were plenty of witnesses to corroborate his story that he'd stepped in to prevent a kidnapping in progress. It was indisputable he'd acted in defense of a third party. Video footage, which was already getting traction online and in the news, backed him up as well. There was no case to build against him.

Even so, they seemed hesitant to just let him walk. He had, after all, wounded four men, two of them seriously. The cops seemed to think that ought to have consequences.

By the time he was back in his hotel room, he had several texts from

Omen, who was wondering what had happened after he'd run off. He messaged her back, saying there was no reason to worry, and then dialed Finn Thompson.

His childhood friend from the "orphanage" listened in silence as he was brought up to speed, then said, "That's a sudden, heavy rain you're dealing with. Sorry, mate. I convinced you to walk out into this storm and now you're stuck out in the cold on your own. These are dangerous people."

"I figured."

"Have you managed to identify them?"

"Not yet," Mirza admitted.

"Mahmud is—What's that sound?"

"My phone's buzzing. Omen's calling me."

"Conference her in," Finn suggested.

"Why?"

"This is an investigation now. It's brain work and . . . well, hers is bigger than yours. She might be able to help us."

Mirza scowled but did as he was told. As Finn caught Omen up, Mirza went to the worn duffel bag he traveled with, pulled out a couple of pain pills, and chucked them.

"As I was about to tell Irfan," Finn said, "Renata is engaged to Prince Mahmud ibn Habib of Aldatan, cousin to King Nimir, who got the throne around five years ago."

The tattoo he hadn't been able to identify earlier flashed in Mirza's mind.

"Leopards," he said.

"Right," Finn confirmed.

"What're you guys talking about?" Omen demanded.

Mirza walked over to the complimentary bottles of water the staff had left in his room and popped one open. "King Nimir has a unit of commandos he uses for wet work. They're the ones I fought tonight."

"Think assassins," Finn put in. "Excellent ones. Trained by American

Special Forces, in fact. They're used to silencing any dissenting voices in Aldatan. Rumor has it that they're behind the death or disappearance of many prominent critics of the throne. It's said they recently murdered a journalist in Azerbaijan."

"That's what I love about my country," she said. "Always making the world a better place."

"What does Nimir want with Renata and Mahmud?" Mirza asked.

"With Ren? Nothing. Her boy, though, the king has been hunting for a while. Mahmud is a dissident. His father, Habib, called for a revolution here, for democracy, elections, all of that. Almost had enough military support to topple Nimir. Aldatan would've become a republic."

"Wait," Omen said. "What do you mean 'here'? Where are you?"

"Finn has led the security detail for Aldatan's Culture Minister for . . . how long has it been? Five years?"

"Just about. So, obviously, when Ren came to me and said her fiancé was in trouble, I agreed she needed Irfan. I pushed him to help her because I couldn't. Not only do I already have a job, but I also work for the very government her fiancé wants to overthrow. I didn't know the king had let his Leopards loose, though. If I had, I would've—"

"What could've been doesn't matter," Mirza cut in. "All that matters is what is. My protectees are missing. I'm going to get them back."

"They are more than just clients," Finn protested. "Ren is family."

"Doesn't change the mission. What I need now is a location. We have to figure out where the Leopards are keeping them."

"If they're alive at all," Omen interjected. When silence met her statement, she muttered, "Sorry."

"No. That's fair play," Finn told her. "It's a possibility we have to consider."

"If the Leopards wanted Mahmud dead, they could have killed him right here." Mirza shifted his cell to his left ear. "I wouldn't have been able to stop them. Taking him means they want him alive."

"Makes sense," Finn conceded. "Those bastards like to play with their food, though. Could be they took him somewhere to chop him up. That's what they did to the reporter I told you they killed. They cut him into little bits. Used a dull ax."

"That's just a scare tactic. They want people to fear them."

"You should," Finn advised. "They're the best."

"I took four down."

"There are fifty of them, Irfan."

"Forty-six."

Finn sighed.

"Okay," Omen broke in. "All this machismo is super sexy and all, but it's not an actual plan. Do either of you have one of those?"

No one said anything for a few seconds.

Eventually, Finn spoke. "Bangkok has CCTVs, right? The local shades should be able to track the vehicle the Leopards used, at least."

"I don't think the Thai police are going to share that footage with me."

"Not voluntarily anyway," Omen said. "I could call Bey."

"You have a bae? I thought you and Irfan were—"

"She's talking about a hacker we know," Mirza cut in.

"I think she could help," Omen explained. "We could try to get access to the cops' computers. See if they've gathered any clues. They're going to interrogate the soldiers Irfan took down and write reports. Those might have useful information too."

"Do it," Mirza said.

"Please," Finn added wryly. "Any other ideas?"

"Do you have pictures of Ren? Or Mahmud? I could put them on social, ask if anyone has seen them. I'm guessing Irfan is already trending locally for the fight. I could piggyback on that."

Mirza grumbled, but it was unintelligible.

"I'll see what I can find and send them to you," Finn decided. "Thank you, Omen."

"No worries. I'll get in touch with Bey right now. Night, Irfan."

Mirza grunted in acknowledgment, and she rang off.

"You know," Finn declared after a moment, "you were right."

"About what?"

"That thing you said about not assigning fault. I don't want you to—"

"I don't blame myself," Mirza assured him.

"Good."

"I blame Renata."

"What?"

"She should've fought better. She's out of practice."

"Not everyone punches people for a living," Finn reminded him.

"Pity for them."

Finn let out an exasperated breath. "Just . . . never mind. I'm going to do some digging of my own in these parts. I don't hear a lot about troop deployments. My client runs the Ministry of Culture. He does film festivals and shit. This kind of thing is beyond his ken. But I have friends at Dandarabilla. It's possible they've heard something."

"Dandarabilla? The private military company?"

"They're entrenched here. Who do you think trains the Leopards now that Nimir's human rights record is a little spotty? Not Western governments. Dandarabilla's collection of former US Marines and soldiers has taken over that role now."

"Really?"

"They're huge in Aldatan. The king keeps them on retainer as security consultants. That's how I got my gig. Nimir started a fad. It's a status symbol in the court to have foreigners guarding you. There are always two or three of the blokes from Dandarabilla around the palace. Nasty fuckers. Fun to drink with, though."

"I thought alcohol was illegal in the Kingdom."

"Nothing is illegal anywhere if you've got enough guts and gold."

Mirza nodded.

"If Omen's right and there's video of your fight with the Leopards online—and it will be because everything is—I can start a natural conversation with them about it. Maybe after we've all had a few, they'll let something slip. You know how it is. When the wine is in, the sense is out."

"Try it. Make sure Omen tells the internet who took Mahmud and Ren. No one will know they're Leopards otherwise, and Dandarabilla will wonder how you figured it out."

"Will do. I'll have more for you soon."

"Okay. I'm going to rest up."

"Good. And, Irfan?"

"Hmm?"

"I meant what I said. Them getting taken, it wasn't your fault, brother. There was nothing more you could have done."

"You don't know that," Mirza said. "You weren't there."

"I didn't have to be. I know because I'm a man of faith."

Mirza chuckled. "Are you? When did you start believing in God?"

"I believe in you. You will get Ren back. I'm certain of it."

"That . . . that's the worst thing anyone has ever said to me."

"Too much weight on your shoulders?"

"Just a bit," Mirza confirmed.

"You can handle it. Now hang up so I can go find you something to hit. In the meantime, stay out of trouble."

33

SIX

THE PRESSURE IN THE hotel shower was excellent, the temperature exactly how Mirza liked it—a little too hot to be entirely comfortable. Leaning with his back against the stall, head bowed, he let water crash into him like he was a mountain under a monsoon rain.

He stood there for a long time. Past when the grime of travel and the sweat of combat had washed off of him, past when the aching of the fresh bruises on his arms, torso, and legs had soothed a little. In the billowing steam, he hid for a while from the day that had been spent, the task that was ahead, and the world that was waiting.

Eventually, he grabbed a towel, dried off, changed, prayed, and sat down with his laptop to see what was on the USB he had retrieved from the crash site downstairs.

The drive had his dried blood all over it, but it worked fine. It contained an article—along with a collection of supporting notes and documents—about King Nimir's rule.

It was a lengthy think piece, the kind of thing Mirza never would have read voluntarily. In an age when everyone always seemed to be talking, he didn't care about the opinions of other people.

No one ought to, as far as he was concerned. It was a position his fifteen-year-old daughter, Maya, despised. It meant she wasn't allowed to have any social media accounts. He wanted her to be as independent of the critique or praise of other people as possible. That was true freedom.

Given the circumstances, however, Mirza made an exception and read the op-ed. It outlined Mahmud's perspective on his king's reign.

After coming to power, his cousin and childhood friend Nimir had immediately gone on a charm offensive in the West. The Aldatani monarch had been in magazines, papers, and television shows everywhere, claiming he would create a new, more secular Aldatan, a modern and progressive nation in the Middle East. For a while, as he began to reform some of the more archaic laws of his country, it had looked like he would deliver on the promise.

Spring, however, was short-lived in the desert, and soon the true colors of Nimir bin Daleel had shown themselves. The Machiavellian royal moved quickly to consolidate power and build his own wealth. People who spoke out against him, whether conservatives upset that the strict laws of the Kingdom were being softened or liberals who thought Nimir's reforms did not go far enough, began to disappear. Whispers of a large secret prison gripped his nation's imagination.

His brutality came to international attention with reports of vicious crackdowns on refugees fleeing north into Aldatan from Yemen. Nimir defended his policies, initially swearing that his government was only going after criminals and terrorists to protect national security.

Later, when images of Aldatani forces beating innocents, including women and children, and forcing them out of cities and into the desert, were broadcast, he argued that he was trying to protect the economic interests of his citizens from desperate, foreign leeches who would eagerly suck the blood out of his country if he let them.

The stories Mahmud recorded about the treatment of these refugees were wild. He wrote about girls who were separated from their families and never heard from again. He relayed the misery of some men who were sent to labor camps while others—and this, Mirza thought, had to be a tall tale—were forced to fight like gladiators for the amusement of Aldatani royalty.

Local journalists who dared cover any of this were murdered. Citizens who called for democracy or freedom were beheaded after being accused of blasphemy or heresy. The access Aldatanis had to the internet was severely curtailed and monitored.

As his image soured, an increasingly paranoid King Nimir, worried about a potential coup, rounded up his country's elite. Anyone who might pose a threat to him was imprisoned, their properties seized, their bank accounts frozen.

After Aldatan's leading Islamic cleric, Ehsan bin Ghiath, spoke out against this oppression, he was made to vanish as well.

When Imam Zayd, a contemporary and friend, demanded Ehsan be returned, he was banished to a small, insignificant mosque in one of the capital city's impoverished neighborhoods.

It was around this time that Habib, Mahmud's father, raised the banner of revolt. He was arrested shortly afterward. Rumor had it that Habib, Ehsan, and all other high-value detainees were being held in a secret prison.

Mirza looked away from his computer when his phone vibrated.

It was a text from Omen.

Omen: Put on the news.

Mirza reached over and grabbed the remote to the hotel room's television. It took a minute for him to figure the thing out. He hadn't used it before in any of his stays at the Al Meroz. He finally got it to work, only to realize that the reporting was all in Thai.

It didn't matter. He didn't need to understand the words to know something had gone terribly wrong. The video being played told him enough.

The screen was split in two. One side showed a hospital on fire, the second a police station. First responders scrambled around both buildings, trying to put the flames out, hoping to save lives.

Omen: Explosions at the locations the Leopards you captured were being held.

Omen: They're dead.

As was, Mirza realized, any information about Mahmud's whereabouts or the Leopards' local base that they might have had.

An hour later, Mirza was on the phone with Omen and Bey. The hacker was, as always, disguising her voice. She sounded a little garbled and mechanical. Still, her irritation came through loud and clear. "This project was a waste of my time, wasn't it?"

"Yes," Mirza admitted. Even if the police had somehow managed to get leads out of the Leopards he'd taken down, they simply wouldn't have had the time to write up reports that Bey could hack into their system to read. "It's a dead end."

"Literally," Omen muttered.

"I have to be paid regardless," Bey insisted, "for the time I've already put in."

"You know we're good for it," Omen said.

"Yeah. Okay. So that's all you want? For me to stop trying to access the Thai police system? Just text me like normal people next time."

"We still need help," Mirza said.

"With what?"

"Omen told you what we're dealing with, right?"

"Yeah. Aldatan and its Leopards. I know."

"Can you get into their system?" he asked.

"You want me to compromise the cybersecurity of a foreign military's top commando unit? What do you think this is? *The Lord of the Rings*? Speak 'friend' and enter?"

Mirza threw a hand up in the air. He had no idea what the hacker was talking about.

Omen apparently had the same problem. "What do you mean?"

Bey sighed. "It's just that sometimes you normies act like what I do is magic. There isn't an obvious secret code. Governments take this stuff seriously, and they spend lots of coin on it. It's not simple."

"Is it impossible?" Mirza asked.

"I didn't say that. There's a key for every lock. For this kind of thing, though, the first step is to find the right door. It's very difficult."

"So maybe tech isn't the answer. Maybe we go with HUMINT this time."

"What's that?" Bey asked.

"Human intelligence. Information gathered from an actual person on the ground."

"You've got someone in Aldatan?"

"His brother provides security for the Minister of Culture there," Omen explained.

"He's going to meet with some guys who train the Leopards," Mirza added. "They're a private army called Dandarabilla. He's going to get them drunk and try to get them to talk."

"Are you kidding?" Bey demanded. "That's fantastic."

"It may not work."

"No. Don't you see? That's the way in. If he's physically there, I can have him run a program on a Kingdom PC that'll give me access to their network. And if he is close enough to these Leopard trainers to have their cell numbers, I might be able to get into their phones."

38

"That'd be amazing," Omen said.

"No guarantees we'll get what we need," Bey cautioned.

"Let's try," Mirza urged.

"Done deal. By the way, you guys do know about my foreign language surcharge, right?"

"Your what?" Omen asked.

"I don't read Thai, and I don't read Arabic. Running everything through a translator slows me down. I'm going to charge you for it."

Mirza grimaced. He had taken on this job because Finn wanted him to, but he hadn't had the chance to agree to a fee with Renata or her prince. He had no idea how much he was going to get paid for this work or when.

Any expenses he racked up now would have to come out of his own pocket. That wouldn't be a problem in the long term. He was sure they would reimburse him. In the short term, it wasn't great. He wasn't exactly swimming in cash, not after his recent series of satisfying but financially unrewarding gigs. But there was no help for it. The information Bey might provide could be critical.

Grudgingly, he told the hacker, "Don't worry about the cost."

"Nice."

"I'll send Finn's contact information over to you," Mirza said.

"No need. I'm getting it off your cell as we speak."

Mirza frowned. "I've told you to stay out of my phone."

"What can I say? I keep my friends close. So, it's still evening in Aldatan, right? I'll reach out to this Finn of yours now. You're sure he'll help?"

"Yes," Mirza said.

"How do you know?"

"Because for him this is a family thing."

SEVEN

AS ALWAYS, WALKING THROUGH Gozel, Finn Thompson couldn't help but appreciate the capital of Aldatan. The city was a striking sight, especially when there was a full moon. The posh neighborhoods near the royal palace, where the king lived, seemed to glow in its silver light. This was an illusion created by the pearly white paint the law required all buildings in the area use because it was Nimir bin Daleel's favorite color.

The city center, in particular, was exquisitely planned. Large swaths of ancient Gozel had been demolished and rebuilt with oil money. The streets were clean, wide, and laid out in perfect grids. The architectural language used was modern and sleek. Gleaming skyscrapers made of steel, concrete, and glass dominated a rapidly evolving skyline.

There were still a few places where the chaotic, organic metropolis that had once existed on this land persisted, but these were increasingly on the outskirts of town, far from the towering prosperity at its heart. The port and beaches to the west were the closest remaining examples of what the capital had once been, though plans to gentrify these areas had already been drafted.

The poor lived in the south, and beyond their modest homes, slums had sprung up to accommodate the foreign laborers who had actually built Gozel. No one seemed terribly interested in improving their lot.

King Nimir's declared intention was to make this a new Paris.

Finn didn't think Gozel would ever have the kind of cultural ca-chet that'd require. He could, however, see it turning into a cheap copy of Vegas or Dubai, which was still an achievement for a small, often overlooked nation like Aldatan, sandwiched between Saudi Arabia and Yemen.

The crown had taken to hiring influencers to burnish the country's image, and tourism had recently picked up, driven by the insatiable appetite of YouTube travel vloggers for new content.

The closer Finn got to the Ministry of Culture, the heavier the tiny flash drive in his pocket felt. He would likely be able to enter unchallenged. The guards there all knew him because he led the minister's private protection detail.

But he had no reason to be there at this hour and, worse, he had no reason to interact with any of the computers in the building. There were cameras everywhere. It was possible that what he was doing would be seen.

The drive in his possession was special. Mirza's Bey had emailed Finn a link that directed him to a website that let her commandeer his laptop. She'd used that access to program the device he now carried. She'd tried to explain what it was supposed to do, and he'd pretended to understand, but it was all inscrutable nerd magic as far as he was concerned.

Finn did understand his task. It was his job to insert the drive into a port on a powered-up computer connected to the Aldatani government's network. Bey would take over the operation from there.

She had warned him, however, that her program might be detected by the Kingdom's cybersecurity experts before they had what they needed. If that happened, it wouldn't be difficult for the Aldatanis to figure out that they'd been breached from inside the Ministry.

They would be able to identify which machine had been compromised and, if he was still in the vicinity, well, that'd be the end of him unless he could fight his way out of the building. Nimir bin Daleel was not known for being merciful to traitors.

If this weren't about getting Ren back, Finn doubted he would risk it. As it was, he had no choice.

Taking a deep breath, he entered a towering building, which housed both the Ministry of Media—responsible for censoring all the content coming into Aldatan, blocking websites, and monitoring public morality in the arts—and the Ministry of Culture. They had previously been one government entity—the Center of Information and Propaganda—but their functions had been split and their names changed to be more palatable to the West once King Nimir had risen to power.

Cool air greeted him as he left the warm night behind. Four guards sat behind a desk, under a large portrait of the king that had to be displayed in every building to which the public had access. Not only was the king's picture up in every government building, but also in every restaurant, every shop, and outside every mosque. It was impossible to forget that this was very much his country.

The guards had an array of around twenty CCTV monitors in front of them. The video feeds they were watching changed periodically, cycling from one location to another.

In other parts of the world, these men would be hidden in a remote corner of the building, away from the public eye. In Aldatan, the government wanted you to know you were being watched.

The guards nodded as Finn marched in. One of them stepped forward with a pad to have him sign in. "Working late, Mr. Thompson?"

"Just a little."

"The minister can't be coming in. It's almost nine."

"No. I'm just here to get some memos for him."

The guard frowned. "Seems like a waste of your time. Anyone on your team could have done this."

"Yes," Finn said. "But the minister sent me."

The man seemed to find this perplexing, which was understandable. The Ministry of Culture was currently working on getting the WWE and the NBA to perform in Gozel. Those organizations had a history of kowtowing to oppressive regimes for profit. The minister had publicly reasoned that there was money to be made in Aldatan and, therefore, the Americans would come. Their morality was never as strong as their dollar.

The Ministry's work, in other words, wasn't exactly top secret. The guard was clearly wondering what material in the minister's office was so sensitive that Finn had to be personally dispatched to retrieve it.

Finn shrugged. "We do as we're commanded even if we don't understand why, right?"

This made the guard chuckle. "That is true, sir."

Finn strode over to the nearest set of elevators and rode up to the twenty-second floor. Once there, he made his way to the Minister of Culture's office. When he had been hired to oversee the man's safety, Finn had familiarized himself with the security system at his employer's place of business.

As with every other state building, those who worked here had no privacy. Even the ministers, who were all royalty, had cameras in their workspaces. The only concession made to their station was that their offices had only one camera, which was directed at their desk in such a way as to not show what was on their computer screens.

This was a practical courtesy. After all, some department heads supervised truly classified projects. The Kingdom couldn't give ordinary guards the ability to look over their shoulders.

It was a weakness in the system Finn intended to exploit.

The minister's office was decorated in a maximalist, gaudy manner common to most official buildings in Aldatan, with an emphasis on the use of burgundy velvet and elaborate woodwork. Everything that could be gilded was gilded, creating a sharp contrast with the staunchly modern exteriors of the city's structures. This, in Finn's opinion, was an indication that while Aldatanis feigned a love for modernity, their hearts were still deeply old school.

When Finn got to the heavy cherrywood desk that dominated the room, he saw the minister's computer was running but dormant. A screensaver showing the Aldatani state seal—a silver horse galloping on golden desert sand—was on display.

He reached over and picked up a stack of documents. He had no idea what they were, as they were written in Arabic, but he made a show of studying them as if to make sure they were what he had been sent to retrieve. Then he dropped them, apparently by accident. Shaking his head, he bent down to pick them up.

As he did so, Finn reached into his pocket, pulled out Bey's flash drive, and inserted it into the PC tower. Then he took out his phone, stood up, and pretended to answer a call, leaving most of the papers still lying on the floor.

A quick glance showed that the computer screen had changed, and now a wall of code was rapidly zipping across it.

Bey had said the process would take around three minutes. So Finn had an animated conversation with no one about nothing, waving an arm around and generally looking like he was frustrated about something.

Then his phone buzzed for real.

Bey: I'm in.

Erasing the text, Finn went back to picking up the documents he'd dropped, retrieved the drive, and walked out, already wondering if what he'd done would be discovered and whether his life and his employment status were about to dramatically change.

EIGHT

CONSUMING ALCOHOL WAS ILLEGAL in Aldatan, but "the forbidden refreshment," as the locals called it, could be purchased in the heart of Gozel, in places that common people could not afford.

The Pyramid, a swanky hotel owned by Nimir bin Daleel and named after its unusual shape, was exactly such a place. Just below the penthouse at the apex, which was forever reserved for the king's use, a bar poured out spirits from all over the world, offering something for every taste.

Finn was there to meet Myers and Price, two former US Marines who now made an excellent living serving in Dandarabilla. They had started drinking without him.

He smiled as he joined them at their table. "Sorry I'm late, gentlemen. Got delayed at work. You understand."

As the men brushed aside his apology, Finn waved down a waiter and ordered himself a Fat Frog. The first time he'd come to the Pyramid, he'd had to explain how the bright-green drink had to be made with WKD Blue, Bacardi Orange, and Smirnoff Ice. Now every bartender in the place knew how to mix it.

"The video you sent us on WhatsApp didn't work," Myers said. He was lean with keen eyes and thin blond hair. It was clear from the slight slurring of his words that he'd already had more than was wise. "What was it?"

"Didn't it?" Finn asked. "That's a shame. It was a recording of an absolute monster demolishing four of your cats in Bangkok. Thought you guys should see it."

It was also, he didn't mention, embedded with a malicious code Bey had provided, which gave her access to their phones. This wasn't a new tactic. The Kingdom itself had used it on foreign leaders and tech CEOs, though those attempts had eventually been discovered. Finn figured Dandarabilla would realize the devices had been compromised sooner or later as well. Hopefully, that wouldn't happen until after he had some actual information on Ren and Mahmud's whereabouts.

"We've seen it," Price groused. He was short and deceptively baby-faced. "Haven't we, LT?"

Myers nodded. "Fucking disgraceful, fully trained Leopards getting beat by some thug."

"Do you know who he was?" Finn asked.

The men shook their heads.

"I suppose that makes sense. The footage is dark and the camera work is shit. Still, the king must be raging."

"That's well above our pay grade," Myers said.

"But LT said it was good for us. Didn't you, LT?" Price chimed in.

That earned the younger man a scowl. "Just a thought. I didn't mean for you to share it with the world. Sorry, Finn."

"No bother. But Price is right. It shows the king that he needs you around, that his own squad isn't up to dealing with all threats yet. Keeps Dandarabilla relevant."

"We're entrenched here in Aldatan," Myers said. "That's the fact of the matter. What the Leopards can or cannot do doesn't make a difference. Still, I have to admit this little show didn't hurt. It's like the Quran of these people says: Reminders are good, even for believers."

Finn blinked. "You've read it?"

"We had to. It's required. Leadership says hunters should try to understand their prey."

"I skimmed most of it, to be honest," Price admitted. "Religion's not really my thing."

Finn steered the conversation back to a track likely to get him actionable intel. "On the other hand, I suppose all this could look bad for Dandarabilla in a way. I mean, His Highness might blame your company's training for his Leopards being banjaxed. Failing a mission in public like that—"

"They didn't fail. Tell him, LT. They got the package they were after. They're flying it out to Atlas Boss as we—"

"They didn't fail," Myers cut in. "But they did look like fools. They should have waited and properly prepared for the mission while keeping the target under surveillance. Instead, they jumped the gun. At least they had the sense to clean up after themselves."

"Atlas Boss?" Finn asked.

"You must've heard of him. He's the big man. Dandarabilla's his show."

"Of course. I just haven't seen him around the palace in ages. I thought he wasn't in Aldatan anymore."

"Well, he is. What I'd like to know, Finn, is why all the questions? It's not like you."

Finn paused to let the waiter serve him, took a sip of his vodka, then said, "Just trying to get the lay of the land. I might be looking to make a move soon."

"You're leaving the Minister of Culture?"

"Thinking about it," Finn corrected. "Don't get me wrong. It's a sound gig. Very easy. I'm not here giving out. At the same time, I have to say, nothing ever happens. I miss being in the thick of it sometimes. I see a video like the one I sent you, and I think, *Give me a lash of that*, you know?"

"Hmm," Myers said thoughtfully. "Well, you'd be welcome for my part—"

"And mine," Price put in.

"—but I don't rightly know if we have any non-Americans working for us. Not that we have anything against the Irish, mind. But I don't know if we could take you. Boss is in the desert as usual, but—"

"Where in the desert?"

"At a classified location," Myers said.

"He loves it there," Price added. "Doesn't like to leave, not even to come here. Better him than me. Works out this time."

Finn waited for either one of them to elaborate on that last statement, but no explanation was forthcoming.

Eventually, Myers shrugged. "Anyway, we'd be glad to have you. I'll call Boss and ask if that's something that can happen. What say you to that?"

Finn raised his glass. "Sounds grand to me."

NINE

MAHMUD WOKE TIED TO a chair, naked. He was in a bright room with ancient, worn stone walls. The space was lit by halogen lamps designed for outdoor use. Orange wires connected to them ran out past a large wooden door, probably to a generator converting petrol to electricity. He could hear its constant hum and smell the smoke it was spewing out.

A man with a long, narrow face and sharp features stood in front of Mahmud, not just bald but completely hairless, with no eyebrows and no eyelashes.

Mahmud's heart got frantic as he realized who this was. He could hear it beat loudly in his ears, like a child caught out in a violent sandstorm pounding on a door, begging to be let in. He noticed then that it was warm, that he was sweating hard.

He had never met this man before, but he'd heard descriptions of the puppeteer who ran one of the most infamous private militaries in the world.

Mahmud had been told Dandarabilla's leader suffered from alopecia, was very tall but remarkably thin, and insisted on dressing in white turtlenecks even in the desert. He invariably had on shoes made from the skin of inland taipans, one of the deadliest snakes in the world, the aboriginal word for which he had as a name for his organization.

No one called him by whatever name he'd been given at birth. It wasn't clear if anyone even knew it anymore. At some point in his life, he'd had it changed, and now everyone addressed him by the title he'd chosen for himself: Atlas Boss.

"Welcome, Ibn Habib," Atlas said in a quiet voice, a small smile on his nearly colorless lips. "You led us on quite a chase."

Mahmud closed his eyes and bowed his head, giving himself some respite from Atlas's dead, gray stare. A second later, the man's warm, damp breath was on his ear, his lips grazing Mahmud's skin as they moved, causing the captive prince to shudder.

"I enjoyed hunting you down," Atlas whispered. "I am rarely challenged, which is tragic. After all, what is genius if it is not tested? In this dull, boring world you gave me sport. That deserves a reward, I think."

Mahmud felt a dry, scaly hand reach between his thighs and touch his penis. He jerked back, but his arms were bound, his shins strapped to the legs of the chair, and it was impossible to move.

Atlas sighed. "Stop resisting or I will make you watch while I skin your woman alive."

"Ren? Where is Renata? Don't you dare—"

"Ssshh. Enjoy this very special moment. I want you to be present with me and fully experience what is about to happen. It is no less than what you have earned."

Atlas cupped Mahmud's testicles in his cold hand and squeezed with all his might, pulling all the while, as if trying to rip them off the prisoner's body.

Mahmud screamed.

Atlas grinned, then dipped his head forward and bit Mahmud's ear, trying to tear that away from him as well.

Mahmud's cries of agony and anguish echoed for hours that night through the black site where he was now a captive.

TEN

A FEW HOURS LATER, Mirza was up again, having a spartan breakfast of black coffee and OxyContin in the hotel's café when Finn called to brief him. The news that the Leopards were flying "the package" out to Aldatan was good. If they'd already made a corpse out of Mahmud, they would've likely disposed of him in Thailand. The fact that they were going through the trouble of transporting him suggested he was still alive.

It didn't tell them anything about Renata's fate, but it was reason to hope, at least.

Knowing that Mahmud was being delivered to Atlas Boss at some desert location didn't help narrow things down, though. Yes, Aldatan was a relatively small country, about the size of Jamaica, Gambia, or Qatar, but it was mostly sand. More than enough sand to lose two people in.

They'd need a more precise location before any sort of rescue could be mounted, but it was obvious that whatever was going to happen wasn't going to happen in Bangkok.

"I'll take the next flight out to Gozel," Mirza told Finn.

"You should, but I don't know if you can."

"Why not? Visa issues?"

"No, you can get those online right away. They're just a moneymaking scheme."

Mirza nodded, remembering now the cursory application process visiting Aldatan had entailed. Turkey, where he'd made his home, had a similar system. Visas were processed instantaneously online, and seemed to exist only so that the government could collect fees from foreign nationals. "What's the probem?"

"We have two. Videos of your fight are circulating around here. The Dandarabilla lads I spoke to had already seen them. That means other people might have too. Some might work at the airport, maybe even in immigration."

"And you're worried they'll detain me if they identify me."

"They'll do more than that," Finn said. "But you're right. You could have trouble when you land. I mean, the footage wasn't great, but you don't exactly blend in to the herd."

"I'll disguise myself."

"That'll take a lot of sheep's clothing."

"Trust me."

Finn was silent for a while, then let out a long breath. "I do, of course. It'd just be nice if we didn't have to take the risk."

"Risk is what we do." Mirza waved for the check and a waiter, catching sight of him, nodded. "What else?"

"You've got to wait for the cavalry."

"What are you talking about? I am the cavalry."

"You're part of it. I got you backup."

Mirza scowled. "What?"

"I hired Omen on behalf of Ren. She's flying over to you."

Mirza sighed.

"Stop pretending. I know you love it when she's around."

"I don't like it when she's around danger. You said yourself that these Leopards mean business."

"She's aware. She wants to help anyway. She knows family is important."

"How is Omen part of the 'family'?" Mirza asked.

"She's not now, but maybe she will be one day."

"What are you talking about?"

"Get up outta that. You know exactly what I mean."

Mirza grimaced. "I'm married, Finn."

"How much longer are you going to hold on to that grenade? It's been ten years since she—"

"I know what she did. Doesn't change the fact that I made a promise."

"Well, regardless, your divorce should be final in a week, right?"

"Something like that."

"Then you should be grateful I'm sending your red bird to you. She'll be around when you're free."

Mirza let out a grunt, which served both as a response for Finn and an acknowledgment of the bill his waiter had brought to his table.

"Anyway, we can talk about all that once we've put the world back in order," Finn said.

"Or we can not talk about it."

"Fine. All that matters right now is that Omen is an asset. She has strengths where you don't. Use her."

"Fine." Mirza took out his wallet. Pulling out a handful of baht, he placed them under his coffee cup. "I'm going to go prepare for the mission now."

"By doing what?"

"Shopping."

Mirza bought a pair of thick, square, vintage-looking eyeglasses to put on. Then he looked up an English-speaking barber and, for the first time in forever, went to get a haircut.

While waiting for his turn, Mirza studied the peculiar art in the neat, small shop. It featured a sequence of three paintings. The first showed a man with hair down to his back fighting a lion with his bare hands. The second depicted a woman chopping his hair off as he slept. In the last one, the same man was pulling down pillars as a building collapsed on top of him. Beneath them was a sign that read: "What a bad do can do to you."

A very fashionable young man noticed Mirza's interest and asked, "Clever, huh?"

Mirza shrugged.

"You know the story? It's Samson from the Bible."

"I don't."

"He was a powerful warrior blessed by God." This information was delivered with the practiced air of someone who had given the same speech many times. "The catch was that he had to keep very specific vows, one of which was that he'd never cut his hair. When his wife found out, she betrayed him and went snip snip one night. Because of that, Samson lost all his might and ended up being taken prisoner by his enemies. But he prayed, and even though his word was broken, God gave him the strength to bring the castle or whatever down on the bad guys, killing all of them and himself."

"Okay," Mirza said.

"So? What do you think?"

"I think I'd like to get this over with."

The young man sighed like he was in the presence of a philistine, then studied Mirza's long, unkempt hair and beard. Struggling to keep derision out of his voice, he demanded, "How do you want it?"

"Different."

"Uh . . . okay. We have a look book here for you to go through if you want to pick out a style and—"

"Do whatever you think is best."

The man raised his eyebrows. "You sure?"

"Yes."

"Well, we're losing a lot of the beard for sure. And I mean a lot. As

54

for the rest . . ." He reached over and patted Mirza's face. "You've got a square jaw under there. How would you feel about a nice, clean disconnected undercut?"

Mirza tried not to grind his teeth. "I don't know what that means."

"I can show—"

"Don't tell me. Just do it."

The barber held up his hands in surrender—a gesture Mirza was used to seeing in his line of work—before picking up an electric trimmer. "I swear, you're going to look like a whole new man by the time we're done."

"I'm counting on it."

Forty-five minutes later, Mirza was glowering at a reflection of himself that was substantially younger and more stylish than the one he was used to seeing.

He looked nice . . . at least nicer than before, but also less wild and dramatic.

"You look good," the barber declared. "Well, not . . . I mean, not 'good' . . . It's just that you're . . . distinguished."

Ignoring the babbling, Mirza asked, "People will still be scared of me, right?"

"Um, God yes."

"It's all right then," he said, rising to his feet.

Back in his hotel room, Mirza changed and picked up the worn, camel-brown leather duffel with which he'd been traveling for over a decade. After checking out of the Al Meroz, he left for the airport.

He tried not to look down at his left hand, at the wedding band that was no longer there, as his cab took him to international arrivals, where he'd meet Omen before boarding a plane to Jeddah. They'd connect to Gozel from there.

Despite his best efforts, his mind took him back to a time when he and Caroline had been engaged, like Renata and Mahmud were now. They'd been in love. At least, it had seemed like love. Mirza hadn't realized then that she thought his experience of the world had left him broken, that she believed he needed to be put back together, and that she could do it.

Caroline had the soul of . . . not a healer, exactly, but a restorer. She was attracted to damage and so he, as a young man, had seemed irresistible.

Before Caroline, Mirza had never had anyone be intensely invested in caring for him—no one he could clearly remember, anyway—and being around her had been the first time he had felt valued for more than his martial prowess.

Eventually, he'd figured out that the kind of man she wanted to make him—a domestic, intellectual, settled man who didn't need adventure and preferred the company of her academic peers to the sound of bullets—was not someone he could become.

She'd grown frustrated with him, with how restless he was at Oxford, where she would eventually go on to become a professor. If he would just give the life she wanted to live a chance, she was sure he'd come to love it.

Affection had become bitterness, and bitterness anger, and anger betrayal—at least on her part, a way to punish him for his long absences.

Now, all these years later, it was hard to even understand how starting a life together had seemed easy and effortless. Maybe such naiveté was a cursed gift the world only allowed young people to possess.

As for Omen . . . He shoved thoughts of her away. He was still bound by the promise he'd given Caroline. He'd never broken it, and he would not break it now. The worth of a man's word, after all, was the worth of the man.

By the time he got to the airport, Omen was already waiting for him, pulling a small carry-on behind her. She was wearing a white button-down shirt over blue jeans. Her copper-red hair was pulled into a ponytail. Her eyes widened when she saw him.

"Whoa," she said.

Mirza couldn't keep himself from grinning. Bowing his head a little, he put his right hand on his heart in greeting.

Omen ignored the gesture, walked up to him, put her hand behind his neck to pull his head down, stood on her tiptoes, and gave him a peck on the cheek. The scent of vanilla and lavender washed over him. He took a deep breath and fought off the urge to wrap his thick arms around her slender waist.

"I mean, dude . . . you actually look civilized," Omen said.

"That's a little insulting."

She studied him for a while longer. "I could get used to this."

"Don't."

"I like the glasses. They make you look like a professor."

"A professor?" he asked. "Of what?"

"Ass kicking, mostly."

Mirza grunted.

"Don't tell me this is all for my benefit."

"Finn thought I might get recognized from the fight videos."

"Ah," Omen said. "Smart, I guess. What about your passport photo? An immigration official will still see it."

"We'll have to roll the dice on that."

She nodded.

"Look, Omen, seeing you is . . . good. But—"

"What am I doing here?"

He nodded.

"Finn said you needed help, so—"

"I don't."

"Awesome. I'll just get paid to watch you work, then."

Mirza scowled.

"Don't make that face. We're doing this together. Unless you honestly don't want me around."

"That's not what I'm saying. It's just . . . death could be waiting for you in Aldatan."

"Only for me?" Omen teased. "Not you?"

"I'm ready for it. The Reaper and I are old friends."

She rolled her eyes.

"I'm serious," Mirza insisted. "I don't want you to get hurt."

"Sweet but chauvinistic. I guess you can take the boy out of Pakistan, but you can't take Pakistan out of the boy." Before he could respond, she went on. "I've managed to stay alive for a good thirty-two years without your help. I can take care of myself."

"You're thirty-three."

"Yeah, well, I'm not denying that you've saved my bacon a couple of times since we met. Now can we get a move on, please?"

He waved for her to follow him to the departures hall. "We're flying all night. Finn will meet us at the airport in Gozel in the morning."

Omen fell in step beside him. "Do we know where Renata and Mahmud are being held yet?"

He shook his head. "Bey is on it."

"What happens if she can't find anything?"

Mirza shrugged.

"Do you know what I love about working with you? All of your brilliant and carefully constructed plans."

"We'll find her," he assured her.

"Them."

"Hmm?"

"We're looking for Prince Mahmud, too, remember?" Omen said. "You meant to say we'll find them."

"Right."

She studied him for a moment, then asked, "You okay?"

"A little bruised. Nothing I can't handle."

"I meant emotionally."

Mirza slowed down a little as he glanced at the overhead signs telling them where to go. Without meeting her gaze, he countered, "Why wouldn't I be?"

"Ren was taken in front of you. She is your sister."

"She's not. We endured loss and pain and misery together for a long time. That doesn't make us family, no matter what Finn says."

"You know," Omen told him, "I'm actually not sure that's true."

ELEVEN

IT WAS ALMOST DAWN by the time Atlas Boss strode out of the Greeting Room, leaving an unconscious Mahmud ibn Habib slumped over in a chair behind him. The heels of his polished snakeskin boots struck the rock beneath them as he walked, causing his footsteps to echo around him.

Atlas smiled. The acoustics of Mahmi Castle, the twelfth-century medieval fortification built on the orders of the Ismaili Shia sovereign Arwa al-Sulayhi, the first queen regent of the Muslim world, were a thing of beauty as far as he was concerned.

Noise traveled far throughout the structure. Screams in the room he'd just left, in particular, seemed to echo and reverberate delightfully through large parts of the sandstone building.

This was because significant portions of Mahmi's walls were hollow by design, riddled with clandestine passages to allow the Queen and a select few among the nobility to move around the fortress undetected. It was natural for sound to bounce off the dense walls in these enclosed, empty spaces. The high, arched ceilings of the castle did not help.

The Queen's veiled routes, by themselves, were not at all unusual. The Alhambra in Granada, which had been built around a hundred years after Mahmi, had miles of covert tunnels. Krak des Chevaliers in

Homs, which was of a similar age, famously had not only escape routes but also hidden chambers built into its thick walls.

Other places roughly contemporary to Mahmi, like the Tower of London and Windsor Castle in the United Kingdom, the fortress of Masyaf in Syria, Predjama Castle in Slovenia, and Muiderslot Castle in the Netherlands, all had similar secrets. Even later constructions like the Palace of Versailles in France, Topkapi Palace in Turkey, and the allegedly haunted Egeskov Castle in Denmark had carried on what was essentially a tradition.

What distinguished Mahmi was not the presence of furtive corridors, but the extent and auditory effect of them.

Sound leaked into these passages not just because the interior walls of the castle were thin, but because each room had at least one—the larger chambers had up to three—unique brick installed.

These bricks had small, parallelogram-shaped holes in them. The Queen had planned to have these filled with shining crystals, so that Mahmi would be called Qal'at Al'Anvar, or the Fortress of Lights.

But her shipment of crystals never made it to Mahmi, ambushed on the way by raiders, and because of the significant cost involved, this plan had to be abandoned.

It was said that every echo in the castle was its lament for the loss of its beauty.

For Atlas, the effect was useful. He wasn't the first one to think so. There was a time when what he called the Greeting Room had been used to give the *adhan*, the Muslim call to prayer, so that it would get projected far and wide.

Atlas was using it to "meet" new prisoners when they were brought in, like he'd just met Mahmud ibn Habib. The tortured shrieks of those who had just arrived served to remind his other captives what kind of agony any defiance or disorder would result in. It kept them frightened and timid.

Two Leopards—of the five King Nimir had assigned to Mahmi—were waiting for him in the corridor outside. One handed him sanitizing wipes, which Atlas used to clean his hands. Then he was given a napkin, with which he delicately dabbed Mahmud's blood off his lips.

He glanced down at his turtleneck and grimaced. There were red splotches on it. Perfectly good cashmere ruined. Now he would have to go all the way up to his room and change. Unfortunate, but cares were the cost of every pleasure, and he'd had such a delightful time with Prince Mahmud that he wasn't in a position to complain.

The second Leopard held out a satellite phone, which Atlas took. He didn't need to ask who it was. Nimir bin Daleel had taken a very personal interest in Mahmud's case. The royals had, from what Atlas had heard, been very close growing up. The sting of his cousin's betrayal had been fierce for the Aldatani king.

"Your Majesty," Atlas drawled by way of greeting. "I hope you are well."

"You have assumed custody of Mahmud." It wasn't a question. King Nimir knew his statement was true. The Leopards, despite having been trained by Atlas's Dandarabilla, reported to him directly.

"Yes. We spent the night together."

Atlas imagined he could hear the smile in his employer's tone. "We hope you had fun."

"I am content. For now."

"Just remember not to do any permanent damage. We still have uses for him."

"I'll make sure he lives," Atlas promised, gesturing for the Leopards to attend to Mahmud, before walking away from them.

"We need you to do a little more than that."

"You have a new assignment for me?"

"If you can handle it."

Atlas chuckled. "When has Dandarabilla ever disappointed you?"

"Have you not seen the videos that have come out of Bangkok? The world saw four of the Leopards you trained fall. Members of our elite strike force went down to one fighter. One. Now you dare pretend that you have never failed us?"

Atlas clenched and unclenched his free hand but kept his tone civil and subservient. Customer service was the worst part of his job. "We did train your men, but the ones you dispatched to Thailand had graduated long ago. Dandarabilla has not been responsible for them for quite some time. It is unfair to blame us, don't you think?"

"Excuses," King Nimir hissed.

"I would also point out that there is no actual proof that the soldiers in those videos were Leopards. That is just social media speculation which has snowballed. I wouldn't worry about it."

"People who matter know it is the truth. The whole thing makes us look weak. Beatable."

Atlas tried to come up with a counter for that argument, failed, shrugged, and then offered the monarch some consolation. "At least the mission was a success."

"Was it? Who told them to bring the woman along? Renata Bardales is a Spanish citizen. She is not one of our own. The international pressure that is about to follow . . ." King Nimir took a deep breath. "You are not to touch her. Not until we have had a chance to confer with our foreign minister. Can you restrain yourself?"

Atlas got to the stairs leading to the North Tower and started to climb. It was the structure in which the queens and kings had once lived. It now held the warden's office—his office—and the rooms he had claimed for himself. Everyone who worked for him was housed here as well, but obviously closer to the ground floor, well below him. "Yes, of course."

"Good. Here is your task. Now that you have Mahmud, use him to break our uncle, Habib. He is the highest-ranking royal still in open rebellion. His name remains a beacon for those who share his views.

Get him on video admitting that his opposition to us was motivated by a thirst for personal power. Better yet, get him to admit he was colluding with a foreign power. The world needs to see him as a malicious actor, not a hero."

"And my prize for completing this task?"

"One you have long desired. We will send Dandarabilla into Yemen to help secure our national security from the terrorists that place breeds. There you will be powerful enough to be a sovereign in everything but name."

Atlas's thin tongue darted out to wet his lips.

"Is that not a kingly reward?" Nimir asked, his tone tinged with amusement. "Are we not generous?"

"Absolutely, Your Majesty. And don't worry. I will personally make sure your will is done."

TWELVE

THE RINGING OF HIS phone woke Finn Thompson. Grumbling, he reached for it and looked at the screen. He saw a sequence of rapidly shifting digits where the number for the incoming caller should have been.

Glancing out the window, he saw that the sun was up. It was probably around seven. His alarm would've likely woken him in a few minutes anyway. He was supposed to go pick up Mirza and Omen at the airport.

He yawned and answered, "Go for Finn."

A voice that was clearly being electronically altered said, "Look what I found."

"What are you on about?"

"I just sent you pics," Bey said.

Finn rubbed the sleep from his eyes and browsed over to his messaging app. He saw a satellite image that showed what appeared to be a massive fortification.

As he flipped through the pictures, it became clear that he was looking at a keep of some kind. It looked old to his untrained eye, like something that had stood for more than a thousand years.

"What is this?"

"Mahmi Castle. Remember those two Dandarabilla guys you spoke with?"

"Myers and Price? I think I can stretch my mind that far, yeah."

"You said they told you that their leader was in the desert," Bey reminded him. "They also said he was going to receive Mahmud from the Leopard people."

"Uh-huh."

"Well, they called his SAT phone to talk about how you want to join them. I had to get into his service provider's system, which was a pain. But once I managed that, I was able to get a pretty good idea of where he was."

"And Atlas Boss is at this . . . Mommy Castle, was it?"

"Mahmi," Bey corrected. "But yes. And it gets better. I cross-checked all Aldatani government records for mentions of that castle. Buried in a bunch of boring reports is the fact that the Interior Ministry has been paying for regular supplies of food, water, and fuel to be sent there, like clockwork, every two weeks, for like five years."

"So, just after King Nimir took power," Finn noted. "Around when whispers of a secret prison where he keeps important prisoners started."

"I think Mahmi is it."

Finn frowned. "This seems . . . too easy."

"And that seems like something Mirza would say."

He smiled. "It really does."

"I haven't slept, you know."

"Still."

"Okay. Fine. You want me to admit I got lucky? Yeah. I got lucky. I had you to get me access," she said. "And if the Dandarabilla head guy didn't happen to be there, I'd never have—Oh no. Shit. Shit. Fuck!"

"What's wrong?"

"They found me."

He jumped to his feet, though he knew that wouldn't do Bey any good. "The Aldatanis? They're at your location?"

"No. Virtually. They're . . . I have to deal with—"

Finn yanked the phone away from his ear as he heard a series of car doors closing in rapid succession. Hurrying over to the window of his seventh-floor apartment, he looked out to see armored officers of the Gozel police force, armed with assault rifles, pouring out of black SUVs with the universal blue and red flashing lights of law enforcement. They'd kept their sirens off.

Finn ran for his pistol. Aldatan wasn't an easy country to get weapons in, but he was allowed to keep a firearm because he led the security detail for the Minister of Culture. His German SIG Sauer P226 didn't exactly represent overwhelming force in his situation, but it was something.

He heard Bey shouting his name on the phone.

"They're here," he told her. "Not virtually. For real."

"Damn it." Even through the electronic distortion she was employing, he could hear the tearful desperation in her voice. "I'm sorry. I'm so sorry."

"Make sure you're somewhere safe," he told her. "Now."

"What about you? What are you going to do?"

Finn hung up on her and loaded his weapon.

He didn't want to tell her he didn't know.

THIRTEEN

"BE NICE," OMEN WHISPERED to Mirza as they made their way toward immigration at Gozel's King Abdul Rahman Airport. It was a relatively short queue. Nimir bin Daleel's aggressive campaigns to attract tourism to Aldatan were having only moderate success. The nation's reputation as a strict Islamic state was still entrenched in the Western imagination.

"Nice?" Mirza asked.

"Just . . . smile, okay? Everyone likes people who do that."

"I don't," he said. "Anyone who smiles too much can't be trusted."

"I smile all the time."

"And you're a thief."

Omen rolled her eyes at him but didn't seem to have a comeback.

Mirza started to pull out his phone, noticed a sign prohibiting the use of cellular devices while in line, and slid it back into his pocket. "We'll go to separate agents. If this goes badly, pretend not to know me."

She nodded.

"Find Finn. He'll get you to safety. Don't try to go get Ren without me."

Omen seemed amused by his instructions.

"What?" Mirza demanded.

"You seem to think you can order me around and I'll just listen."

"This is my mission. You play by my rules, or you don't get to play at all."

She sighed. "Whatever."

A gate agent—a thin, sly-looking man in his late fifties—glanced over. His gaze lingered on Omen before he reluctantly signaled Mirza over.

Mirza stepped up, dropped his duffel bag to the ground, and slid his passport and e-visa documentation over to the man.

"Are you sick?" the immigration officer asked.

"No. I just can't sleep on planes. Haven't gotten more than a few hours in a while."

"I was talking about your hands. What's with the bandages?"

Mirza held them up in a helpless gesture. "A skin condition."

The agent grunted and flipped the Turkish passport open to the page with Mirza's picture on it. He stared at it, then looked up at Mirza. He glanced back at the picture before looking up again, a frown on his face.

Mirza studied his surroundings. He had counted four airport security officers in the vicinity. There would definitely be more nearby. If this man recognized him from the video of his brawl with the Leopards and a fight ensued, it was unlikely it'd end anywhere but in jail for him.

He likely wouldn't survive to see a trial.

"You look very different than you did when your passport was issued," the agent said.

"Yes."

The agent made a disapproving sound and flipped through the document.

"I got a divorce," Mirza added.

"Sorry?"

"My wife and I, we separated. So . . ." Mirza pointed up to his face and gave a little shrug. "I'm making an effort."

That drew a smile from the agent. "Good luck to you."

"Thanks."

"There are lots of beautiful women in Türkiye. What are you doing in Aldatan? Here they all cover themselves and don't like to speak to strange men. You will have a much harder time."

It was disguised as a joke, but Mirza recognized it as a routine question asked of people crossing international borders all over the world: What is the purpose of your visit? "I saw ads about the beaches here. They didn't make it seem like that."

The immigration agent's eyes found Omen again. "Yes, well, this country is improving all the time." He reached for a stamp and slammed it on a random page of Mirza's passport. "Gozel is beautiful. Enjoy yourself."

"I will," Mirza said.

He'd taken maybe three steps when the agent yelled out something behind him.

It was in Arabic, so Mirza couldn't really understand. Still, he slowly turned around.

In English, the man said, "Don't forget your bag."

Mirza relaxed, went back, and retrieved his duffel.

Omen met him on the other side, and they walked through the surprisingly small, utilitarian, run-down airport toward the exit. Plans to build a new one had been announced many years ago, but the project was obviously not a priority. The massive oil wealth of Aldatan was primarily being used to build a formidable army and state apparatus, improve the capital, and enrich those who ran the Kingdom.

Mirza watched Omen pull out her phone, check it, and frown. "A few missed calls from Bey."

As she called back, he checked his cell. It showed that Bey had tried to reach him too. He had a text message from her. It was short and not altogether helpful.

Bey: I'm compromised. Finn's in trouble.

"She's not answering," Omen said.

Mirza showed her his screen.

"Damn," she muttered. "I didn't know someone could do that to her. I thought she was too good."

"Governments have pretty tight cybersecurity."

"Do you think Finn is all right?"

Mirza nodded. "I'm sure he's got things under control."

FOURTEEN

FINN HAD SECONDS TO formulate a plan. The unit dispatched to come get him—the Special Ground Forces—was equivalent to the Garda ERU in Ireland and SWAT teams in the United States. Except the Aldatanis weren't known for taking prisoners. In around 78 percent of SGF missions, a suspect died. They shot first and shot to kill.

The Directorate of Security claimed that this was because they were only sent out to deal with high-level threats, which tended to be violent. But quiet murmurings were that the Kingdom was using the SGF to stage "encounters," where undesirables were said to be resisting or fighting back when they weren't.

They were executioners, not officers.

He doubted they intended to take him in.

Finn considered his options.

There was no fire escape. If there were building safety codes in Gozel, no one paid attention to them.

A jump from the seventh-story window to the ground wasn't an option. It was likely he'd die. Even if, by some miracle, he survived, he'd be too injured to run away after. Besides, his apartment directly faced the entrance to the building, which was where the cops were. He'd land right in front of them. That was no good.

If he went up to the roof, he could try to jump to the adjoining complex. It had been built very close. The distance was short. He figured around ten feet. He could make it.

At thirty stories high, would the wind be a factor? He imagined so. He hadn't tried anything like that before. This seemed like a bad time to start.

Deciding the leap had to be made from a more reasonable height, Finn rushed out of his apartment and sprinted across the carpeted hall. The sounds of police boots striking concrete echoed in the stairwell. He realized that he was wearing only the boxer shorts he'd slept in just as his shoulder collided with his neighbor's door. He exploded into her apartment with a crash and a shower of splinters.

The elderly Arab woman whom he'd passed by a hundred times but whose name he'd never bothered to learn gaped at him as he scrambled to his feet, paused in the act of knitting something.

Then she screamed, which was reasonable.

She reached down to pick up her slippers to throw at him, which was reasonable too.

Finn ran through her flat, aiming his 9 mm at her window and blowing it out. He kept firing as the glass exploded, destroying the window in the adjoining building as well. There was panicked shouting everywhere as people tried to make sense of the sudden chaos.

He heard someone call out to him in Arabic, looked back, and saw that an officer had reached the landing.

Finn punched at the remaining glass of the window in front of him to clear it away. Then he climbed on the sill, snarling as pain shot through his feet as they were cut open by the shards still there, and launched himself into the air.

A volley of automatic gunfire opened up behind him before he could make it to the next building. Two bullets tore through him, one striking the top of his left shoulder, the other just below the scapula.

He was leaking blood and barely paid attention to the cowering family that watched him land in and stumble through their home, his left arm dangling almost uselessly by his side. The blood on the soles of his feet was making it difficult to walk without slipping.

Finn got to the elevator and slammed his fist into the call button, willing the lift to come quickly. There was no way he was going to make it down the stairs in his condition.

When it arrived, he saw that it was full. It took a moment for him to realize why. The residents had seen the cop cars next door and heard the gunfire. They knew to fear the authorities and were trying to get away.

Finn grabbed the nearest man by the throat and yanked him forward, pulling him out into the hallway. He protested until he saw the pistol in Finn's hand. That shut him up.

"Keys!" Finn yelled at the others in the lift as he stepped in, facing the crowd. Looking over his shoulder, he saw that they were already heading down to the underground parking structure. They stared at him blankly, clearly terrified and unsure of what to do. He tried to remember the words he was looking for. "Mafatih. Mafatih alsayaara."

He didn't get what he wanted, so he pointed his weapon at a niqabi woman near him who shrieked. "Mafatih," he demanded again, "al-fucking-sayaara."

A couple of hands came forward, offering him their car keys.

Finn studied them for a moment. Then, gritting his teeth, he forced his left hand up to grab one that stood out to him because of the racing silver pony on the key fob. "Cheers."

No one said anything else.

Pleasant, light Muzak played in the background.

The elevator dinged, and the doors opened behind Finn.

He hit the button for the penthouse, and he backed out of the lift. No one objected.

When he finally turned around, he saw a few vehicles leaving the parking lot. He pressed the remote-start function on the key he'd taken, and a red Mustang a few feet away roared to life.

Finn smiled.

It wasn't subtle. But it would do.

FIFTEEN

"HE'S STILL NOT ANSWERING," Mirza told Omen as their cab pulled up to the hotel Finn had booked for them. It was a towering, impressive structure next to some kind of fancy pyramid. Like every other building in the heart of Gozel, it was painted white. It looked entirely too rich for his blood, but it was probably the kind of place Finn had gotten used to over the years.

Omen, who'd been trying Bey, made a face. "Same."

He cursed under his breath as a doorman walked up to the cab to open Omen's door and help them with their luggage.

"What's the plan?" Omen asked.

Mirza shook his head. He didn't have one.

They walked into a vast lobby, which had marble floors and what looked like real crystal chandeliers hanging from a domed roof. A hijabi woman at an expensive-looking, shiny wood counter greeted them warmly.

"Checking in?" she asked.

Omen nodded. "Yeah. This place is amazing, by the way."

"Thank you, ma'am. May I please have your travel documents and marriage certificate?"

"I'm sorry?" Mirza, who'd only been half listening, asked. "What?"

"Your marriage certificate, sir. Without one, a man and a woman cannot check into the same room in Aldatan. It is the law."

"That sucks," Omen said.

"It's a Muslim country, ma'am."

"Still."

"It's fine," Mirza told the front desk clerk. "We're not together."

That earned him raised eyebrows from both women.

"I mean," he clarified as he handed over his passport, "we're not . . . We are just business acquaintances."

"Wow," Omen muttered under her breath.

"Close business acquaintances," Mirza amended. "We're staying in separate rooms. This is Omen Ferris. I'm Irfan Mirza."

"Very good, sir. Would you prefer that your rooms be on the same floor?"

"Sure," Mirza answered.

Omen's phone began to buzz. She excused herself and stepped away.

"Are you flying in from Istanbul?" the clerk asked.

"Bangkok," he said.

"I've never been. How is it?"

"Hot and humid."

She smiled. "We only have one of those problems here."

Mirza nodded, then listened patiently as the woman explained the four restaurants they had on-site, the locations of the gym and the pool, before finally handing over two key cards.

"I'll get someone to help with your bags," the clerk said.

"I've got them," Mirza said, grabbing ahold of his duffel along with Omen's carry-on.

"Are you sure? Your hands look like they're hurt. It's no trouble."

"I like to do things for myself," Mirza told her.

The clerk smiled uncertainly, as if not sure how to respond to such a bizarre sentiment, before wishing him a pleasant stay.

Mirza walked over to Omen and heard her say to the person on the other line, ". . . how long do you think before you're online again?" She mouthed "It's Bey" when she saw him approach. "That's good. Yeah, I'll tell him. No, it's not your fault. We all know the risks. Let's just find Finn, all right? Good."

She hung up, turned to face him, and said, "Bey says she'll be back in the game soon. No word on Finn yet. She was talking to him when they came for him. He hung up, and she hasn't been able to get in touch since."

"All right. Come on. We're this way."

"She feels bad. She isn't sure how they realized she had access to their system, but—"

"It doesn't matter now," Mirza said.

"There is some good news," Omen said as they made their way to the elevator. "Bey thinks she's found where Mahmud and Ren are being held."

"How?"

Omen shrugged. "Computers?"

"Where is he?"

"Some place called Mahmi Castle."

Mirza nodded and hit the button for the twenty-second floor.

Omen reached over to touch his arm.

He glanced down at her.

"He'll be fine, Irfan."

"Right."

"I mean," Omen went on, "he's as good as you are, right?"

"No." Mirza managed a tight smile. "But it's close."

SIXTEEN

FINN RESISTED THE URGE to peel out of the underground garage as fast as he could. He drove calmly but with purpose, trying not to think about the way his hands were shaking or about the blood seeping out of his bullet wounds, warm and slick down his chest and back.

Once on the street, he turned left, away from the small convoy of Special Ground Forces SUVs in front of his apartment complex. In the rearview mirror, he could see heavily armed officers pouring into the building he'd escaped. Soon, they would secure the garage and, eventually, would hear from the residents which car the wounded, nearly naked Irishman had stolen. They'd use the Mustang to track him down.

To evade capture, Finn needed to find another car and, if he lived long enough, he decided he would. His immediate priority had to be to get medical attention. Easier said than done. Any hospital he went to would report him.

He bit his lip and glanced at the clock built into the car's radio. Mirza and Omen had already landed and were, hopefully, through immigration by now. He could go see them. But if he showed up at a fancy hotel in this condition, it'd cause a scene. The authorities would show up faster than a speeding bullet.

Finn thought about calling them so they could come up with a plan together, but realized that he'd dropped his phone in his mad dash to escape his own apartment.

He slapped the steering wheel, then got on the freeway, letting his instincts guide him. They were telling him to get as far away from the center of Gozel as possible. If there was salvation for him, it'd be away from the heart of the city, on the outskirts, where the metropolis faded into the desert.

It was hard to think, hard to focus. His mind was awash in pain, leaving him confused about what to do next. It was, he realized, a symptom of his condition, just like his dripping sweat and the clamminess of his skin. He pulled down the visor and looked at himself in the mirror. He was losing color fast.

"Fuck," he growled. "Come on, Finn. Find a way out."

No ideas came to him.

He kept driving until his vision started to darken. There was solace in the fact that he'd managed to put some distance between himself and the Special Ground Forces.

When he felt like he couldn't go farther, he pulled over and stepped out of the car, breathing hard.

He looked around the deserted freeway. He was just past the edge of the city. There was nothing here except for the slums where legal and illegal migrant workers lived, the invisible, unacknowledged hands that had built the luxury the wealthy in Gozel enjoyed.

Finn wondered what they would do if he wandered into one of their camps.

Would they turn him in?

Maybe. Maybe not.

They wouldn't want any trouble with the law by giving him aid.

On the other hand, they also wouldn't want to attract the attention of the authorities, especially because it was likely some of them were out of status—that was to say, they were in Aldatan on expired visas and work permits.

Voluntarily becoming modern-day wage slaves to earn a few dirhams was better than going to their home countries, where there was no work to be had at all. They wouldn't want to be deported. They couldn't afford it.

Finn hated bringing trouble to the door of people already desperate and afflicted.

There was, however, no choice. They were his best chance.

Leaving the Mustang at the side of the road, he shuffled toward the slums of Gozel.

Part Two

THE MIDNIGHT LEAGUE

SEVENTEEN

IT HAD BEEN HOURS since Mahmud's screams had stopped reverberating through Mahmi Castle, but Renata could still hear them. They felt like they'd sunk into her bones and were echoing inside her, as if she were as hollow as the walls around her.

Even when she managed to stop thinking about the pain being inflicted upon him, she found no respite. Her mind kept returning to the fight outside the Al Meroz and her own part in it. She'd been ineffective. If Mirza hadn't shown up when he did, the Leopards would've accomplished their mission essentially unchallenged. All she had managed to do was get herself captured.

"Did you get any sleep?"

Ren looked over at her cellmate, Dina Malik, and shook her head.

They were in the South Tower, where female prisoners were kept. Renata had been told that she could not leave it. This dictate appeared to be unique to her alone. During the day, at least, everyone else seemed to have free run of Mahmi.

What Ren did have was permission to wander within the tower. If she didn't like Dina, she could go sleep somewhere else. It seemed like there were around fifty or so women around—she hadn't had the chance to get an accurate count—and there was still plenty of space.

Ren did like her, though, even if they hadn't spoken much. Dina was the only one who had bothered to console her when she'd cried through a large portion of the night. Everyone else had seemed largely unmoved. Tears were common in this place, and everyone had their own to shed.

"The first nights are the hardest," Dina said, her voice quiet and haunted. "Then you learn how to make things bearable. You get used to it. At least, that's what you pretend."

"How long have you been here?"

Dina shrugged her bony shoulders. "Maybe three years? I kept track in the beginning but . . . What's the point?"

"Has anyone ever gotten out?"

"Not alive, no."

Renata closed her eyes and exhaled.

"You're the only foreigner I've seen in Mahmi. What did you do?"

"Loved the wrong person."

"Oh," Dina said sympathetically. "I'm sorry. Didn't anyone tell you it's not legal to be gay in Aldatan?"

"No, that's not—"

"It won't matter to him. He'll still call you. It's inevitable. It happens to everyone. I've heard he spares the older men, but—"

"Who?"

"Atlas Boss." Dina whispered the name. The weight of it seemed to make her voice waver and almost break. "Just remember . . . don't fight him. He enjoys that. The more you resist when he . . . when he claims you, the more often you'll have to live through it. No one told me that when I first got here." She wrapped her arms around herself. "I . . . I've learned. I just lie there, and now he doesn't show much interest anymore."

Renata shuddered.

Dina was very pretty, maybe in her midtwenties, though the right side of her face was badly bruised and swollen.

Ren gestured to it. "Did he do that?"

"What? Oh." Dina chuckled. "No. That was me."

"Why?"

"I was an actress. I was almost famous. Before . . ." Dina waved her hands to encompass the medieval fortress around them. "The guards, they . . . If I hurt myself, if I look like this, they mostly leave me alone. Otherwise . . ."

"This place is an atrocity," Renata said.

Dina shrugged. "Not everyone here is terrible. Adam with the sad eyes said he would bring me to his room tonight. You know you're safe for sure when that happens. He just talks about his pregnant wife and the Komrad she gave him."

"What does that mean?"

"It's what he calls his gun. Komrad." Dina started to speak, then hesitated. "I wish I was good enough to let you go in my place, but . . . I'm too selfish. I'm sorry."

Renata managed a little smile. "Don't worry about me. I can take care of myself."

Dina looked at her with skeptical eyes, and Ren couldn't help but admit—at least to herself—that those doubts were entirely justified.

The women Renata found herself with were an eclectic group.

A handful were royal, condemned to this place not because of anything they had done but because their fathers, sons, or brothers had challenged Nimir bin Daleel.

"Radicals" made up the largest percentage of the prison's female population. These were firebrands who had marched for equality, for the freedom to choose what they could wear, and even for the ability to have a driver's license.

It wasn't that King Nimir was unsympathetic to these causes. He had, in fact, bestowed many of these rights on Aldatani women later in his reign, after his power had been solidified and religious hardliners tamed.

These activists weren't being punished for believing the wrong things, but for daring to protest against the crown. Civil dissent was their real crime and that was still illegal. Subjects could not be allowed to demand things from their rulers. They were only permitted to beg and receive, because their government was neither for them nor by them.

The last significant group were media personalities, such as news anchors, journalists, and social media content creators who had offended the throne.

Dina was one of their number. Her offense was turning down the role of the king's third wife in a proposed biopic glorifying Nimir. She'd publicly said she didn't want to be part of producing state propaganda, and for that statement, her life had been completely altered.

Most of the women stayed near the base of the tower because it was convenient. Renata climbed to the top and found an empty chamber of a decent size. *A good place*, she thought, *to train*.

Her combat skills had never had the kind of serrated edge that Mirza's did, but there was no doubt they had dulled from what they'd once been.

More accurately, Ren had allowed them to dull. When she'd turned her back on a life of violence, she'd assumed she wouldn't need them anymore. Long, painful, intense drills and sparring sessions had given way to a casual interest in fitness, Pilates, and yoga and the occasional hike.

She still knew all her katas, though. She knew how to become a bared blade again.

Ren promised herself she would, not because she had any realistic expectation that she could escape on her own, but because she believed that eventually—weeks or months from now—her deliverance would come. Irfan Mirza and Finn Thompson would find her.

When she stood shoulder to shoulder with them then, it'd be as an equal, not someone who couldn't fight her own battles.

And if her faith was false and her brothers failed and she was never found, if she was destined to live here and die here and be buried in the sands outside, she'd extract a price from anyone who dared touch her.

Renata walked to the center of the room and took a deep breath.

It was time to embrace the life she'd once been deliriously happy to leave behind.

EIGHTEEN

MIRZA PACED THE LENGTH of his posh hotel room as if it were a cell. From the massive windows overlooking Gozel, he could see that the sun was starting to fall. Most of the day was spent, and they had precious little information about Finn.

Local news had been their best source. It had reported on a raid carried out by Special Ground Forces on one of Gozel's downtown apartments. They were looking for Finn Thompson on a plethora of charges, including stealing state secrets.

There was a brief clip of a visibly worked-up elderly woman, waving knitting needles around dangerously, screaming at the camera in Arabic as she attempted to explain what had happened. The police steered her away and issued a statement saying they were not releasing any details at this time.

Mirza knew there would be no follow-up. There was only one news channel in the Kingdom, and it was operated by the government. Unsurprisingly, it wasn't exactly known for hard-hitting journalism.

The knowledge that Finn had managed to escape the initial assault was reassuring, but he had no explanation for why his old friend hadn't tried to contact him yet.

At least they had a possible lead on Renata and Mahmud's location.

Bey—after finding a place to hide and buying a new PC—was back online. She'd sent over images of Mahmi Castle, which were still on display on Omen's tablet.

Mahmi was around 600 kilometers away in his language, which for Omen was roughly 370 miles. It was deep in the desert, with no towns or villages nearby. Except for the occasional bedouin tribe passing by, traveling between the few scattered oases in the region, it was completely isolated.

Due to the flat, nearly lifeless terrain, there was no way to approach the castle without being seen. Any vehicle headed toward it would be spotted. Exhaust and the spinning of wheels would send sand billowing into the air, meaning that a cloud of dust would follow you if you went there. That wouldn't go undetected.

Mirza had suggested that he could drive most of the way, then walk to Mahmi in the dead of night. Omen had pointed out that even if he got there without being spotted, he didn't have the skill set to breach a guarded medieval fortification. The thing had been built to withstand a siege. It wouldn't have easy points of entry for enemies to exploit. That'd defeat its entire purpose.

He parked himself in front of Omen, who was perched on the edge of his bed, watching the news in case any word about Finn came through.

She raised her eyebrows and asked, "Yes?"

"I don't like this."

"Really? I couldn't tell."

He scowled. "I'm serious. Help me talk through the problem. There has to be a way into that castle, right?"

"There always is," Omen agreed.

"How would you do it?"

"Well," she said, crossing her legs and leaning back a little, "I spend most of my life making sure I don't end up inside a prison, so this feels weird to say. But honestly, I think I'd get arrested."

"Arrested?" Mirza repeated.

"Yeah. Just let the bad guys toss you in there. Seems like the simplest way."

He shook his head. If Bey was right, then Mahmi was a black site where Nimir bin Daleel held VIPs. Given how casual his regime was about committing murder, these had to be people the king either couldn't execute or didn't want to execute, either because they were part of his family or had powerful allies. It was meant to hold scholars and royals and ministers and thinkers and artists, not random thugs off the street. "Wouldn't work. I'm just a regular person who'd go to regular jail."

"Right." She drummed her fingers on her knee, thinking for a while. Then she got up and walked over to look at her tablet. Flipping through the information that their hacker had sent, she asked, "Didn't Bey put something in here about how they're supplied?"

"Supplied?"

"It's in the middle of nowhere, right? People need food and water and clothes and shoes and all kinds of stuff."

Mirza nodded. "She said the Interior Ministry takes care of that. They send a convoy every two weeks with—"

"There it is, then."

"There's what?"

"The way in. Mahmi Castle's remote position is a strength, yeah, but that means that it relies on a bunch of stuff coming in from the outside to keep it habitable. You just have to be part of the next convoy."

"And how am I supposed to do that?"

She shrugged. "I don't know, but I'm sure you'll figure it out on your own. It's like you said at the airport. This is your game. I'm lucky you let me on the field."

"I didn't say it like that," he protested.

"How'd you say it?"

"I was nicer."

Omen crossed her arms and gave him a flat stare.

"I meant to be nicer," Mirza amended. "I didn't mean to be . . ."

She waited for him to finish.

He sighed. "I'm sorry. You know I don't play well with others."

"It's okay. You're always hard. I like that about you." She paused, grinned, then added, "See, that's your cue to jump in with a sex joke and defuse the tension."

"Pass," Mirza said, though he did smile. Then, he turned to look at the television, which was still on behind him. "Finn might know something about the convoy."

"Sure. Having a local—or even quasi-local—contact would be awesome right now."

"Has Bey found—"

"She's working on it," Omen said. "Give her some space, okay? She's still beating herself up about how things went south. I can't even comfort her. I mean, was there another, better program she could've put on the USB she gave him? I don't know. So, when I tell her she's not to blame, I'm not even sure if I'm—"

"Wait." Mirza spun back to face her. "What'd you say?"

"Uh . . . just that because I don't have the technical expertise to know if Bey did something wrong, I can't—"

He shook his head. "No. You mentioned a USB."

"Right. I mean, you knew that's what she had Finn use to get access to the Aldatani government system."

"Sure. I just forgot about the other one."

"What other one?" Omen demanded.

"Just . . . keep working with Bey to find Finn." He walked over to grab his wallet and put it in his back pocket. He decided to leave the fake eyeglasses he'd gotten in Bangkok behind. "I'm heading out for a bit."

"Where are you going?"

"To make a new friend."

———

Being a freelancer, Mirza often didn't have access to the kinds of information-gathering apparatus available to government agencies and their proxies or even operators working for large corporations. He usually worked for small-time clients on small-time jobs, so he had to gather his own intel or he had to find sources he trusted.

In countries like Pakistan, where he'd had repeat gigs, Mirza was well connected. In Aldatan and other places where he rarely did business, he didn't really know anyone.

Luckily, he understood how one finds allies among strangers.

When she had first started going to boarding school four years ago, his daughter told him she was having difficulty making friends in a new environment. Mirza let her know what he always did in such situations.

"Find your enemy's enemy."

"I don't have any enemies," the eleven-year-old Maya had pointed out.

"Not sure what to do about that," he'd admitted. "I've never had that problem."

Now he was taking his own advice.

Mirza hadn't thought much about the flash drive he had retrieved from Mahmud's briefcase in Bangkok or the article it contained. It felt like it hadn't given him any leads, just a description of the terrible political situation in Aldatan.

He'd realized that wasn't true when Omen had mentioned a USB in the context of finding a local to help. It had dawned on Mirza then that he had read about one man who had an ax to grind with the Aldatani throne.

In his think piece, Mahmud had recorded the disappearance of Ehsan bin Ghiath, a world-famous Islamic scholar. He'd also said that Ghiath's colleague and contemporary, an Imam Zayd, had spoken out against the extrajudicial arrest, because of which Zayd had been banished to a mosque in one of Gozel's poor neighborhoods.

Finding out where Zayd was preaching had required nothing more than a Google search followed by the perusal of a Reddit thread. Even Mirza, Luddite though he was, was capable of such feats.

He now approached a tiny, dilapidated mosque, very much unlike the grand venues of worship the Kingdom had sponsored in the city's affluent areas. This was a common place for common people, much too humble for someone of Imam Zayd's stature. The Ministry of Virtue, which decided who would be given what pulpit, had clearly transferred Zayd here to send a message, not just to him but to any other holy men considering stepping out of line.

Mirza joined the worshippers for Maghrib on a threadbare carpet, under a rickety, low-hanging fan. Once the prayer was over, he went over to see the imam.

Zayd was small, thin and slight, and looked to be over sixty. A kind smile lit his face when Mirza greeted him. The imam shook his hand and asked a question in a language Mirza didn't understand.

"I don't speak Arabic."

Zayd nodded slowly, then declared, "It would be better for you if you did."

"I keep meaning to learn, but I never have the time."

"What do you occupy yourself with?"

Mirza, used to speaking the truth, started to say "violence" but stopped himself. "I'd like to speak to you, Sheikh."

"Then it seems that you are doing what you like."

"I mean, can we talk alone? I have a problem you might be able to help with."

"We cannot talk alone," Zayd said, "for Allah Subhanahu Wa Ta'ala is with us. What we can do is talk away from other people. Walk with me."

When they stepped out of the mosque, Mirza took a deep breath, relishing the fresh, warm air, then told the preacher, "My name is Irfan."

"A good name. It's from the Quran. Do you know what it means?"

"Wisdom, right?"

The imam nodded. "It means one possessing the ability to recognize what is good and true in thoughts and deeds. A bold claim."

"Not one I made," Mirza pointed out.

The older man chuckled. "Yes, well, no man gets to name himself. Anyway, tell me, Irfan, who are you and why are you here?"

"A couple of nights ago, a young Aldatani prince by the name of Mahmud ibn Habib was kidnapped in Bangkok." The mercenary took out his phone, pulled up videos of the incident, and showed them to Imam Zayd. "I tried to stop it from happening, but I failed."

Zayd took hold of one of Mirza's arms and pulled him farther into the dark, even though there was no one around. Whispering, he asked, "What do you want from me?"

"The woman Mahmud is engaged to is . . . some people say she's my sister." Seeing the older man's brow furrow, he added, "It's a long story. The point is that she was taken as well. I want to bring them both back."

"Many disappear in the crown's shadow. None are ever seen again. I fear what you intend to do is not possible."

"I have reason to believe Mahmud is still alive. I'm hoping that means Ren is too."

"You are probably right. The government has been very reluctant to execute members of the royal family." The imam offered a wan smile. "I believe they are worried it would give people ideas."

"My only problem is finding out where they are being held."

Zayd snorted. "That is not your only problem."

"Fine. It's my first one. I still have to solve it. I read that your friend Ehsan bin Ghiath was abducted too. There are whispers of a secret prison—"

"So much more than whispers," the holy man interjected. "It is something of a cacophony now. What you are looking for, we in Aldatan call

Qasr ul-Uthama'i wal-Qiddiysin. It has grown into something of a myth. People live in fear of it, but none knows where it is, which is good for the king. I swear, if believers knew where Ehsan bin Ghiath was held, where lights of our religion like Wahab ibn Bahri, Abu Amara, or Ubaydah ibn Khalid are being kept, they would descend upon that place like a swarm of bees seeking out pollen with which to make honey. The powers of this world would not be able to stop them."

Mirza doubted the last bit very much, but he didn't say so. He hadn't before wondered why King Nimir kept the location of his political prisoners hidden, though. Hearing what Zayd had to say made it make sense.

The sovereign didn't want to turn those who opposed him into martyrs, but he also had no desire to give their supporters a place to rally and congregate. That would look bad on the international stage—especially if force became necessary for crowd control. He wanted to be seen as a reformer, not a despot.

Mirza considered telling the imam what Bey had learned about Mahmi Castle. The idea of causing Aldatani authorities grief appealed to him. It'd be payback on Finn's behalf.

He held off. If Mahmi Castle's true nature became public and the citizenry reacted like the sheikh was predicting, it would cause heightened security there. Reinforcements would be called in. The eyes of the world would turn in that direction, and getting in would become an even more daunting proposition than it already was.

"I don't know anyone in Gozel," he said instead. "That is why I came to find you. I thought you would sympathize with my cause, and I need information."

"I should turn you in," Imam Zayd pointed out.

"You won't."

"How can you know that?"

Mirza shrugged. He didn't want to confess to the priest that he would physically stop that from happening. It wasn't likely to get him the co-operation he was looking for.

Zayd didn't wait for an answer. "Even if I were inclined to help you"—he glanced around them again to make sure there still wasn't anyone in earshot—"and I'm not saying I am. Even if I were, I don't see what I could—"

"I've learned that the Interior Ministry has been sending a convoy full of supplies to King Nimir's black site for years. Have you heard anything about this?"

The preacher stroked his beard, thinking, then shook his head.

"Where would such a caravan leave from? Would it be from the capital or someplace else?"

"How would I know such a thing?"

"You haven't heard rumors? Anything might help."

"No," the imam said. "Nothing."

Mirza ran a hand over his face, but reminded himself that this wasn't really a dead end. Imam Ehsan bin Ghiath was not the only man who'd been disappeared by Nimir bin Daleel. Many others had been affected. He had come here first because of Mahmud's article, but in time he would be able to find others who might be able to help him.

"Thank you for talking to me," he said. "If you could keep this conversation to yourself, that'd be good."

"There is no one I wish to tell. You can be assured of that. But what are you going to do now?"

"I am going to keep searching. Someone has to know something."

Imam Zayd smiled. "Allah knows everything."

"Sure. But conversations with him are pretty one-sided."

"And, of course, the Interior Minister would have the answers you seek."

Mirza chuckled. "Right. Do you happen to have any idea how someone like me would get to him?"

"Actually," the preacher said, serious again, "I do."

"What?"

Zayd hesitated. "I like you, Mr. Wisdom."

"But?"

"If I give you the answer you seek, if you keep walking down the path you are on, I fear you will not live long. It is not my wish to be the cause of your demise."

"We all end, Sheikh," Mirza said. "I'm not afraid of dying. I just want to make sure it's worth it. So tell me what you know and let the Angel of Death come for my soul if that is God's command. Inshallah, he will not find me unprepared."

NINETEEN

IMAM ZAYD REFUSED TO speak further standing out on the street and insisted Mirza walk home with him, so they could talk without the fear of being overheard.

Zayd, who had once lived in a lavish home paid for by the Aldatani government, had now been relegated to a cottage not too far from the mosque. His neighborhood was made up of small, poorly maintained homes, with garbage lining the streets. There was a hint of a stench in the air from a distant open sewer. The narrow roads they took were broken and needed to be paved again.

From a global perspective, Mirza knew this wasn't all that bad. When you had seen Cairo's Garbage City and been to the largest favela in Brazil, when you had tracked down a target hiding in a slum to the west of Nairobi, where families lived on less than a dollar a day, you had some perspective on poverty. When you had marched through war zones in Yemen and Syria and witnessed what shelling and drone strikes did to a population, the way you looked at the world changed.

The contrast between how the rich lived and how the poor lived was striking, yes, and it was a symptom of the moral decay of Aldatani society, but it was still better than the difference between Skid Row and

Beverly Hills in Los Angeles or Dharavi and Malabar Hills in Mumbai. This was humanity, ugly as often as it was beautiful.

Zayd's home itself was neat, and the preacher made them both cups of green tea over which their conversation resumed.

"The Interior Minister, Waqif ibn Khaleef, what do you know about him?"

"Almost nothing," Mirza said.

"You haven't heard of his scandals?"

"No."

Imam Zayd threw up his arms in amazement. "People here think the world knows."

"The world is a big place, and everyone has their own troubles. Tell me something that will help me, Sheikh."

"Waqif has always been notorious for being very . . . what is the English word for it? A man who revels in the pleasures of this world. Hedonistic, yes?"

"Sure."

"One of the famous stories about him is from when he was in school. He used to pay some boys to beat up other boys. One of the children he had attacked was an Italian citizen, so the incident was widely covered by the foreign media."

Mirza frowned. This wasn't helpful. He wasn't interested in the man's history, just his location. Even so, he let Zayd go on, hoping the preacher would say something he could use soon.

"Waqif goes to every execution and public punishment we have in the city. Every time a killer loses his head or a thief loses his hand, Waqif is there. He was asked about this, you know, because it is not part of his duties. He says he does it because he believes in justice and wants to see it carried out. It is closer to the truth, I think, to say that he likes watching people hurt each other. He likes being a witness to pain."

"What makes you say that?"

Zayd answered with a question of his own. "Did you know there is a homelessness problem in Gozel?"

Mirza tried not to sound impatient. "Not really."

"It has gotten very bad in recent years and not just because of Aldatani problems. The war in Yemen goes on, and Saudi Arabia has closed its borders, so refugees cross the desert into Aldatan and stay. Many find their way to this city, looking for work and to rebuild their lives."

Mirza nodded. Istanbul, where he lived, had seen an influx of refugees from Syria, and Karachi, where he was born, had seen the same thing happen during the Soviet invasion of Afghanistan. If peace, safety, and the hope of prosperity were taken away from people, they had no choice but to chase after those things. It was the pursuit of happiness or, at least, the pursuit of a tolerable existence.

"Waqif has found a use for these people. He makes them fight."

"Fight who?"

"Each other, of course," Imam Zayd explained. "He and his friends gamble on who will win."

"Tell me more."

"Waqif's men round up people who have nowhere to go, and they are given a choice. They either fight in what he calls the Midnight League— for which he pays them personally—or they are imprisoned and forced to work for the government."

"And the government doesn't pay them?" Mirza asked.

"It does, but only a little. Around four dirhams an hour. That's—"

"A dollar, right?"

Zayd nodded. "Meanwhile, Waqif pays them a hundred dirhams to fight, and whoever is left standing at the end gets five hundred more. Besides, going to jail means no longer being able to see or support your family. It means being separated from parents and siblings and kids. No one wants that."

Mirza grimaced. "I understand. How do you know all this?"

"I am now the imam of the poor here. They told me. Some want to know if God will forgive them for what they did when compelled to fight. Others want permission to participate."

"They volunteer?"

"Wouldn't you?" Zayd demanded. "If you were in their place?"

Mirza bowed his head.

"Yes," the preacher went on, "the young, the desperate, the reckless see the Midnight League as an opportunity. I advise them not to, of course. Setting religion aside, the truth is that I have presided over enough funerals of bruised and battered beggars to know exactly what they risk."

"I understand," Mirza told him.

"But you will still go, won't you?"

"Yes."

The imam sighed. "So be it. I will tell you where you will find it. Please remember that only a few ever go there willingly. Most people are forced to battle because they are faced with an impossible choice. Try not to hurt them."

TWENTY

MAHMUD LOOKED AROUND. HE was lying on a thin mattress on a stone floor, wearing only a shirt, his lower half covered by a bedsheet. He wasn't alone. A couple of men were standing nearby, peering at him intently. They looked familiar, but Mahmud couldn't place them just then. All his brain could focus on was the agony his body was in.

"He's awake," someone said. "Call Habib."

Mahmud tried to sit up and cried out. His testes were so tender and raw that any movement felt impossible. Lifting up the sheet covering his midsection, Mahmud saw that his scrotum was discolored and had swelled up. A wave of nausea overtook him at the sight. He turned on his side and dry heaved, which caused searing agony between his legs. He realized, after a moment, that he was weeping.

He felt a cool, gentle hand on his forehead and looked up.

A familiar, aged, lined face—older than he remembered—and those unchanging kind eyes that he had known since the day he was born, made him cry harder, as joy mixed with anguish and became something massive and terrible inside him that he could not control. He sobbed as his father held him.

After a while, the old man stroked his hair and said, "Sabr, ya amar, sabr."

Mahmud took deep breaths, trying to calm himself, to have patience and to endure like his father asked.

"I had hoped never to see you here," Habib said. "But, as they say, winds do not blow as vessels wish."

Mahmud reached out and grabbed his father's hand. "How are you? Did they hurt you too?"

"Not as badly as you. We put a bandage on your ear. You still have most of it. For your other injuries, all we can do is pray. Ice would help, if you could bear it, but we don't have any."

"And Ren? Have you seen Renata? They got her when they got me."

Habib exhaled forcefully, like a man already carrying a heavy burden being given more weight to carry, then shook his head. "Not yet, but we know she is in the women's tower and that she is safe."

"Thank God."

"Really, Mahmud, you should have forsaken me when I spoke out against your cousin. That would have been the path of wisdom. Now look what's happened."

"I couldn't, Baba. You were speaking the truth."

"I suppose it is not your fault. The blame for all this belongs to the one who taught you the values which made you stand up to a tyrant."

"That was you."

Habib patted his cheek and smiled. "Yes. Things would be better if I had raised you to be a worse person."

Despite everything, Mahmud somehow managed a little smile at that.

"At least I got to see you again before the end of my life. Better men in Mahmi Castle will not get to cool their eyes in the same way. Otherwise, my only consolation was that I had good company to die in."

"Don't say that."

"Why not?" Habib asked, his tone turning grim. "There is no escape from this place. There is nothing but desert all around. Even if we could climb the walls and get out, there would be nowhere to go. You know

105

better than to run from reality, Mahmud. It would be best if you accepted the fact that we will both likely perish within these walls. Only a fool flees from his destiny."

Mahmud went quiet for a while, then replied with a proverb. "He who tells the future lies, even if he speaks the truth."

Habib chuckled. "Very well. Hope, if you must. I just ask that you not infect me with it. I have already learned to be content with despair."

TWENTY-ONE

ATLAS WALKED ALONE ALONG the parapets of Mahmi's walls, surveying his domain. Looking down upon the one place on earth he ruled made him . . . not happy, exactly, but satisfied.

Not that he was too concerned with the exact nature of the emotion. The important thing was that it made him feel something, anything at all. That was the unicorn he had spent most of his life chasing.

Mahmi was not a grand, soaring, ornate palace. It was a fortress built to secure trade routes. It was large, sprawling, and squat, designed to garrison soldiers more than it was meant to pamper royals. A rough place made with rough stone in a rough time.

It was unsurprising that most of the original walls had survived, standing tall and strong despite the harsh conditions around them for over nine hundred years. Once, they had been manned by archers. Now, Dandarabilla snipers were stationed on them, ready to bring down intruders and escapees alike.

Those small sections of the wall that had collapsed had been recently—and badly—repaired by the Aldatani government. It was shoddy work, its gray concrete clearly distinguishable from the khaki stones the Sulayhid dynasty had used.

A travesty, Atlas thought. More enlightened civilizations would have tried to preserve this piece of their past and restored it with care and love. Instead, this place was being treated like it had no value except whatever utility could be extracted from it.

Disappointing but not unexpected. None of the half dozen ancient castles in the country were faring better, from what he'd heard. But this was not a local problem.

Neighboring Saudi Arabia was worse. According to some reports, 98 percent of historical and religious sites there had been destroyed. These included the tombs, mausoleums, and graves of Prophet Muhammad's family members and companions at the famed cemetery of Jannatul Baqi—the Garden of Heaven—which had been leveled. The remains of centuries bulldozed in days because some hard-line fanatics in positions of power decided that they understood their faith better than those who had preserved it for them.

The Garden of Heaven was now nothing more than a flat, unremarkable plot of desert sand. It still served a purpose. It was an apt metaphor for what Islamic civilization had become.

"Sir?"

Absorbed in his thoughts, Atlas didn't hear that he was being called.

Lacking a central courtyard or extensive gardens, any grandeur Mahmi had came from its four towers. One had been built for each cardinal direction, which would have been a nice touch if the square structure itself was oriented the same way.

It wasn't, however, and that meant that instead of each tower sitting at a corner, they were all offset a little. Being a believer in the theory that all beauty stems from symmetry, Atlas couldn't help but think that this was a design flaw, a mistake made by the architects of this place. He wondered if they had lost their heads for the error. They would have if he'd been in charge.

Happily, the fact that the towers were offset had no serious consequences. Their positioning did result in there being blind corners near all of their entrances, but that was of no real importance. It was just another oddity in a remarkable structure.

"Sir?"

Atlas turned around to see Chike Okoro marching toward him with the casual, dangerous grace of a trained martial artist. If she wasn't his lieutenant, he suspected she might have ended up battling in a ring. She had the physique and skill for it, and she'd spent her whole life looking for a fight, first with the American army, then in Dandarabilla.

She had been with him for many years and had seen his company's darkest day, when some would-be bandits in Syria—young men from a remote village desperate for food and supplies—had attacked a convoy containing a VIP Atlas was supposed to escort through the war zone safely.

In the fighting that had ensued, the VIP had been killed and Chike badly injured.

Atlas had rallied his forces, tracked down the attackers, launched a night raid on their village, and killed the men involved before herding their women and children into the local mosque. Then he'd set it on fire.

Dandarabilla had enjoyed excellent operational security in the region after that. None of the locals dared challenge them again.

A few members of his team had later complained about Atlas's brutality. Chike had supported him. He'd kept her close since.

She was approaching from the North Tower, where a royal family had once lived. It now held Dandarabilla's armory and quartered all guards and operatives on-site. Atlas's office and rooms had once belonged to a queen.

The East Tower held prisoners with a conscience, those Atlas thought were pure of heart. These were mostly religious clerics and leaders, along with idealists who truly believed they could make the world a better place by standing up to Nimir bin Daleel.

Opposite it, the West Tower held those Atlas deemed to have political motivations and aspirations. They were upstart princes with claims to the throne who had worked to undermine King Nimir, businessmen with wealth the Aldatani crown coveted, comedians and YouTubers who had dared to mock their sovereign for likes and views, and soldiers who had backed Habib's attempted coup in the hopes of career advancement.

There was no way to know what the true intentions of his prisoners had been, of course, but Atlas enjoyed learning about them and passing judgment nonetheless.

The South Tower was his favorite. That was where he kept all the women in his "care," but it wasn't where he had fun with them. When he wanted sex, he usually took whoever he had chosen to the Greeting Room. That way—because of the chamber's unique acoustics—his other captives, especially those in the East Tower, could hear exactly what was happening and know that they were powerless to stop it.

He'd taken several men there, too. Variety was the spice of life, after all, and fear its salt.

"Admiring the wall again?" Chike asked when she drew closer.

"It's beautiful."

"How aren't you over it yet?"

Atlas looked at her, brow furrowed. "Would you get tired of looking at the moon?"

"Yeah. I would."

He smiled. Chike was not in possession of a poetic soul. No one, as the saying went, was perfect. No one, in fact, even came close, with the possible exception of himself.

"I don't have any use for Muslims—" Atlas began.

"You use them all the time."

He glanced at the South Tower, then nodded, accepting the correction. "I have very few, limited uses for Muslims. But when they had a civilization, the art it produced was special."

"Why?"

"Because its creators had a difficult task. They weren't allowed to draw or paint living creatures, including humans. Statues were forbidden to them as, according to some, was music itself."

"So?" Chike asked.

"So they persevered. They found a way to express beauty despite the disadvantages they started with. That is admirable. And do you know how they did it?"

She shook her head.

"By focusing on patterns, by obsessing over every element of their craft. Everything they made, they tried to make flawless. They pursued excellence relentlessly. There are massive holes in Muslim artistic expression—"

"Because of all the things they weren't allowed to do."

"Exactly. Their dogma ensured that they'd never have anything like Botticelli's *Birth of Venus*, Michelangelo's *David*, or the compositions of Tchaikovsky. Efforts are being made now, by some modern Muslims, to fill these holes. The results look a lot like the concrete does on this wall, though."

"Ugly as shit?"

"Uninspired and uninspiring. However, in the work early Muslims did—if you're willing to look past what is missing in their portfolio— you'll still find great merit."

"And the fact that they had these challenges makes their art good?"

If Atlas were a different man, he would have told Chike about how much time he used to spend in front of mirrors growing up, after other children mocked his alopecia and told him that he was an ugly, hairless freak.

He had decided back then that he would be as handsome as he could be. He'd tried to achieve this by controlling every little detail of his own appearance, by perfecting his look. He had that in common with the creatives of the early Muslim world.

Like them, he had transcended the hand he'd been dealt.

Like them, there were only a few who understood and credited his greatness.

Instead of saying all that, he chuckled. "It makes it better than good. It makes it interesting."

"And this wall is art somehow?" Chike asked.

"Of course. Art is any created thing infused with a fragment of its creator's soul, whether it be a building or a history."

"No one makes history, though. That just happens."

Atlas sighed. "Wrong. That, however, is a discussion for another time. I'm sure you came out here for a reason."

Chike nodded. "Renata Bardales is in your office like you wanted."

Atlas started walking back the way Chike had come.

She fell in step beside him. "She seems like she'll be difficult to break."

"That will just make it more satisfying to witness when it happens."

"It appears that you had a rough night, Ms. Bardales," Atlas said as he strolled into his office with Chike in tow. He found Renata sitting by the cheap, plastic desk he was having to make do with.

Back home, in the States, he had a selection of hand-carved, eclectic pieces to adorn his workspace. In Mahmi Castle, far away from civilization, he had to make do with things that could be easily moved and assembled. Unfortunately, objects that were easy to transport rarely left one transported.

Renata looked up at him. Her clothes, he noted, were soaked with sweat, like she had been exercising. That was odd, but maybe she was the kind of person who enjoyed and took comfort in physical exertion. She certainly looked fit, like she took good care of herself. Otherwise, her appearance was unremarkable, except for her eyes, which were tired, swollen, and cried out.

When she didn't respond, he asked, "Was our hospitality lacking? If so, I'd be happy to make you more comfortable. In fact, that is why I have had you brought here. To talk about what I can do for you."

She glared at him.

Smirking, Atlas walked behind her, taking the long way around to his seat. He trailed his cold fingers along the nape of her neck, caressing her as he went past.

Renata jerked away from his touch.

He graced her with a smile. "Mahmud was asking about you. At least, he was before he started screaming."

A muscle in her jaw twitched.

"I do hope, by the way, that you two didn't want children. I fear I may have compromised his reproductive ability."

Renata said nothing for a while, but eventually she demanded, "What did you do to him?"

"I tried to manually separate his testicles from his body. It did not work. I did get a piece of his ear as a consolation prize, though, so there's no need to weep for me."

"Bastard."

"That's no way to speak to your god, Renata."

"God? From everything I've heard, you're just another one of Nimir's sick pets."

Atlas leaned forward and clasped his hands together. In a perfectly pleasant tone, he warned, "Disrespect me again and I'll make you watch as I fuck your man. Is that something you'd enjoy?"

She looked away.

"That's what I thought. I rule here. You'll do well to remember that. Say 'Yes, Atlas Boss.'"

"Yes," she spat out, "Atlas Boss."

"Good. Now that we understand our relative positions, we can do business."

"What do you want?"

"Nimir bin Daleel has asked me to get video confessions from your husband- and father-in-law-to-be. He wants them to denounce themselves."

"Why?"

"There are likely two reasons. Habib is the most moral, popular, and credible leader the revolutionaries in Aldatan have. If it turns out that he is compromised by greed or malevolence, well, that would be devastating to the will of any resistance Nimir faces."

Renata nodded.

"The other is that it's likely he wants to show their confessions to the world, so he looks like less of a tyrant. King Quixote desperately wants the admiration and approval of the West. This order is likely in service of his pathetic quest."

"What does this have to do with me?" Ren asked.

"I would like you to get Habib and Mahmud to cooperate. Beg. Plead. Whatever it takes. Make them play ball, as it were."

"Why would I do that?"

"Because if you don't, I will utterly destroy Mahmud. Look at me, Renata." Atlas waited until her eyes met his flat, gray gaze. "I have no mercy in me. No pity. No conscience. I will torture him until his mind snaps and his body is ruined beyond repair. Do you believe me?"

TWENTY-TWO

REN BELIEVED ATLAS BOSS.

She had been in the presence of evil before. Her early life had been shaped by cruel, merciless people. None of them had felt as soulless as Atlas did, as inhuman. It was obvious that he was perfectly capable of doing exactly what he threatened to do.

She nodded in response to his question.

She didn't add that she had no intention of making any kind of deal with him. A man with no conscience was not the kind of man who kept his promises.

Even if she helped him get what he wanted—and she wasn't sure she could—there was every possibility that he'd still hurt Mahmud. Given the glee with which he'd described his actions of last night, she thought it was likely Atlas would do exactly that. He was, simply put, a snake.

The question now was what she was going to do about it.

Here she was, barely a couple of feet from him, unbound and un-restrained.

Was she really going to let him finish giving a speech and then be led meekly back to her cell? What good would that do? What if she was never face-to-face with him like this again?

"Excellent," Atlas said. "In exchange for your cooperation, I—"

Making her decision, Renata lunged at Atlas from across the desk, grasping at his throat. His chair toppled over as they fell to the ground.

Atlas's eyes were wide for a moment as she straddled his torso, her fingers wrapping around his neck. Then, inexplicably, he started to laugh as Ren squeezed. It came out choked, raspy, and broken.

Chike sprinted in, grabbed Ren's dark hair, and tried to yank her off of him.

Renata pulled one of her hands away from Atlas and threw an elbow at Chike's jaw. The Dandarabilla woman, caught by surprise, staggered back.

Ren returned her attention to Atlas, but he was ready for her this time. He delivered a swift, vicious palm strike to her nose. Renata cried out and jerked away instinctively.

Atlas followed up with precise blows to her chin, her throat, and then her chest.

Dazed, Renata rolled off him and got to her feet, putting distance between Atlas and herself again. Chike was back on her in seconds. Ren dodged a punch that would have landed square on her face, then countered with a jab of her own that was easily blocked.

Chike stayed on the offensive, probing Renata's defenses, forcing her to move back, away from Atlas. He was standing now, but he wasn't at all concerned with the fight. He was, instead, frowning at a spot of red on the cuff of the white turtleneck he was wearing.

Ren licked her lips, tasted blood, and realized it had come from her.

She was forced to retreat again as Chike kept pushing forward. Her arms stung from the repeated blows they were absorbing. They were starting to feel heavy and difficult to move. Her katas this morning had left her fatigued. Her muscles burned in protest as she continued to push them.

The part of her mind trained to analyze tactical situations told her that it was over. Chike was exquisitely trained, which explained Atlas's confidence. Renata simply was not in her league. She was going to lose, and it was going to hurt.

The most painful thing right then, however, was the realization that her opponents were going to walk away from this almost entirely unscathed.

Ren's back hit the wall behind her as she continued to deflect Chike's relentless advance. Cornered. All that was left now was to fall.

Unbidden, the image of Mirza in Bangkok, taking damage to inflict it, sprang to her mind. He'd been willing to go down as long as he didn't go down alone. It was reckless and irrational, but damn if it didn't look satisfying.

Screaming, Renata suddenly rushed forward, copying the spear move she'd seen Mirza pull off. It wasn't something she'd ever tried before.

Her shoulder collided with Chike's sternum and exploded with pain. Her weight and momentum drove them both to the floor.

The Dandarabilla woman grunted and clutched at her chest, face twisted in a grimace.

Renata got to her knees and looked up just as one of Atlas's snakeskin boots collided with the side of her head.

TWENTY-THREE

ATLAS SHOOK HIS HEAD as he watched two of his guards drag an unconscious Renata Bardales away. That had not gone at all as expected.

He hadn't known anything about Prince Mahmud's fiancée going in, but he'd anticipated he would successfully secure her aid. Few people could bear the prospect of grievous harm befalling their loved ones. He'd had no reason to believe that Renata would be such a person. It was clear now, however, that there was more to her than met the eye.

Atlas glanced at Chike, who was standing next to him, eyes downcast, still occasionally massaging her breastbone. "Someone taught her to fight well."

"She isn't that good. I would've taken her."

He moved to stand in front of Chike and placed his hands on her neck, just like Renata had done to him.

She stopped breathing and went completely still.

He smiled. "Explain what happened."

Atlas felt her Adam's apple shift under his thumbs as she swallowed. "I . . . she caught me off guard, going from defense to offense like that. It shouldn't have. But I thought I had her so . . . I was careless. It wouldn't have mattered in the end. I would have protected you."

He began to apply a little pressure.

Chike gasped but didn't resist.

Then Atlas pulled her forward, leaned down, kissed her forehead, and let her go. "I understand, my friend. She surprised me as well."

Chike exhaled.

"Keep her in her tower and away from Mahmud until I figure out how to persuade her."

"I will. Is that something we need to do, though?" Chike asked. "If she won't do what we want, can't you just apply pressure to Mahmud or Habib directly?"

Atlas turned away to look out a window, his impossibly light, pale-gray eyes finding the wall he had been studying earlier yet again.

He saw its strength and he saw its weakness, the cheap, useless concrete repairs that defaced the ancient structure.

He caressed his throat. "Am I not entitled to have some fun? It's been ages since I've had a real challenge. Still, you make a valid point. I softened Mahmud ibn Habib yesterday. I'll keep working on him. There's more than one way to skin an Arab."

"How much more do you think he can take?"

"I do not know. But we're going to find out."

TWENTY-FOUR

"WHERE ARE YOU?" OMEN demanded as soon as Mirza answered his buzzing phone.

"You're out of breath," he noted.

"At the hotel gym. Stepping out now."

He frowned. "You're supposed to be—"

"Looking for Finn. I know. I'm taking a break. Sue me. Bey's still on it. Now, back to my question. What are you up to?"

"I told you before I left," Mirza said as he walked through a small, deserted lane. He could smell the ocean air and hear the crashing of waves. He was getting close to the location of the Midnight League. "I'm out making friends."

"Yeah? Maya just texted me. She's freaking out."

"Why?"

"She told me that you called her to say good-bye."

Mirza nodded. He'd made a habit out of calling his daughter at the start of jobs from which he might not return. It had resulted in more than one fight with his ex-wife, Caroline, who didn't think their child needed to know every time he was in mortal danger, especially given that this was not an uncommon occurrence in his line of work.

Maya herself, however, had never objected to the practice. He figured

120

she understood that having been abandoned as a child himself, Mirza didn't want her to experience the same uncertainty he had. He didn't want her to have to endure that agonizing wait or the slow, dawning, awful realization that one of her parents would never return. He wanted to be sure his kid had closure.

It was a tradition rooted in love. It wasn't meant to induce panicked calls to his colleagues.

"Teenagers," he grumbled under his breath.

"I was surprised to hear that from her because most people," Omen said, "don't think friendship is a particularly dangerous business."

"Then people are wrong."

"Funny. Come on, tell me what's happening?"

"I was just about to call you, actually," he told her. "I need your help."

"So you are in trouble, then?"

"Not yet. But I'm working on it."

Omen let out an exasperated breath.

"Listen," he went on. "I need you to get a couple of things and then come find me."

"Okay. What?" she asked.

"A gag and maybe some rope—"

"Really? Wow. I always imagined your tastes being a little more va-nilla."

"I . . . uh . . ." Mirza flailed around for an answer to that comment, cleared his throat, then decided to ignore it. "Bring a big suitcase with you too."

"Like how big?"

"Something that will fit a grown man."

"Dude. What kind of freaky shit are you into?"

Mirza sighed. "Must you?"

"Have a personality?"

"Yes. This is serious."

"You know you can count on me."

He did. "The last thing is a car. Something with all-wheel drive. You'll need to bring it onto a beach. It'd be good if it's fast. We'll be running."

"You do realize that it's nighttime, right?"

Mirza looked up at the nearly full moon, which was hanging low on the horizon in a starless sky. "So?"

"So, it's not like I can go rent something right now. And you've got all these hang-ups about theft—"

"Morals, you mean?"

"That's just another word for hang-ups," Omen informed him.

"It's a special circumstance. Do what you have to do."

"Are you—Irfan Mirza—telling me that you want me to steal something for you?"

"Yes."

"Aw. Babe. I thought you'd never ask."

"I'll text you my location. Get here as soon as you can. But don't pick me up until I've completed the mission objective."

"You still haven't told me what that is," Omen pointed out.

"We're going to kidnap Waqif ibn Khaleef."

"Cool. Who is he?"

"The Interior Minister."

There was silence on the other end of the line. Then Omen said, "So he's royalty?"

"Yes. I know where he is. He has a nighttime hobby a local imam told me about. Look, I realize this is a little extreme, but he'll know where the convoy supplying the Mahmi Castle leaves from, what route it takes, what its schedule is, all of it. We get this guy, we have a way in."

"Okay. But how are you going to get him to talk?" Omen asked.

"Fear."

"And if that doesn't work?"

Mirza shrugged. "Then I'll try pain."

"Jesus Christ."

"Have you discovered a 'hang-up' of your own?"

"No," Omen said. "It's just . . . this is a messed-up life, you know that?"

"Yes."

"You realize that I'd planned to head to a beach before . . . well, all this. Except I was going to Da Nang. To relax and maybe not commit felonies. But here we are."

"This is more fun."

"I bought a killer new bikini. You would've liked it if you'd come. I mean, you would've pretended you weren't checking me out like you always do, but you wouldn't have been able to resist."

"Wear it now if you want," he joked.

Omen chuckled. "Nah. I'll save it. I mean, we'll get time to chill out together at some point, right?"

"Inshallah."

"You know, I'm starting to think that's what Muslims say when they mean no but don't want to say it."

Mirza grinned.

She waited for a beat to see if he'd respond, but when he didn't, asked, "What will you be up to, by the way, while I'm out doing your groceries for you?"

"Looking for a homeless guy I can swap clothes with."

TWENTY-FIVE

MIRZA'S SKIN PRICKLED WITH the uncomfortable knowledge that he was wearing someone else's filthy shirt. It stank of stale sweat, had several holes in it, was terribly tight. It was short, too, and left part of his cut abs exposed. None of the homeless people around Gozel's docks had been built like him or anywhere close to his height. The tallest man Mirza had found, at six feet, was still four inches shorter than him.

Though he'd traded his Henley and given up his shoes, he had kept his own jeans and smeared mud over them. He rubbed dirt on his face and messed up his hair. Then, slouching to make himself look beaten down, he stepped onto Gozel's only beach. It was where Imam Zayd had told him the Midnight League took place.

It wasn't long before he saw two heavily armed guards in the distance, standing before an array of floodlights so bright that they made the night look like a fluorescent day. A large circle had been roped off, and around it, plastic folding chairs were arranged. Mirza counted four rows full of people.

There were two fancier chairs in the back, upholstered with leather, raised on a small platform, with an elaborate *shisha* apparatus sitting in front of them. Those were, he assumed, reserved for the Interior Minister and maybe his wife.

Because this wasn't a place for men alone. There were women there as well. Some were wearing burqas, while others were in revealing, clingy dresses.

For all of King Nimir's sins, it was undeniable that he was remaking Aldatan, transforming it into an eclectic place, a place of possibility, where people could increasingly be who they wanted. He was, paradoxically, a tyrant hell-bent upon increasing personal freedoms—the ones he liked, anyway.

Mirza knew he was catching a fleeting glimpse of a diverse society that hadn't yet been born, because whatever these women were wearing now, while they were protected by the Interior Minister's security detail, they would put their niqabs on again tomorrow. To an outside observer, Aldatan would appear to be the same place it had always been, because for now, at least, it was.

Beyond the spectators, huddled together in the distance, were the four actual combatants.

In order to join them, Mirza would have to get past the guards, who were searching everyone who entered the part of the beach they had secured. They were also confiscating everyone's phones.

That was standard operating procedure around Aldatani royalty. Mirza had experienced that firsthand last year, when Finn had briefly gotten him a job on the Minister of Culture's party yacht. The idea was to make it impossible for anyone to take pictures of the royals engaging in debauchery, because they all claimed to follow the precepts of Islam religiously.

Mirza would have to get rid of his own cell, not to mention his wallet.

He searched for a distinctive-looking rock, found one, and walked over to it. After sending his location to Omen, he buried his belongings in the sand. He hoped he'd be able to come back for them later.

When he made his way over to the guards, he tried to look as cowed and unintimidating as possible. But that didn't come naturally to him.

One of the guards wrinkled his nose as Mirza got closer, which was fair. His comrade whistled under his breath and said something in Arabic. The mercenary was able to pick up only the word *jabal*, which meant "mountain."

The first guard asked a series of rapid questions. Mirza made a sound, like he was trying to speak and was unable to, then pointed at his mouth and shook his head.

The two men exchanged glances.

Mirza held out his right hand and rubbed his index finger and his thumb together in the globally recognized sign for cash, then slowly and clumsily pretended to shadowbox.

The second guard shrugged, did a cursory search of his person, and pointed at the group of fighters beyond the collection of posh guests who were still finding their seats. Mirza nodded and ambled past.

Appraising eyes followed him as he went to take his place. He had the feeling that many of the gathered affluent would put serious money on him winning tonight. It was almost enough to make a man want to take a dive, not because it would get him anything, but out of spite.

A young boy ran up to him carrying two strips of red cloth.

The boy tried to explain what he wanted, got impatient when Mirza didn't comply, and reached out to grab Mirza's right hand. He tied one of the strips to Mirza's wrist before doing the same on the left side and then hurrying off.

The other fighters, Mirza realized as he got closer, all had similar pieces of cloth tied to their wrists, except in different colors. They were identification markers for the benefit of the audience.

Of the four men who had been rounded up to fight, three were emaciated and one . . . one was different. There was something about him that didn't feel right.

He was lean, better dressed, and better groomed than the others. Unlike them, he didn't look up to see who the newcomer was. All he did was stare at his hands and the green fabric tied to him like he was entranced.

Mirza marched over to the man and stepped into his space. This got the man's attention. Dark, haunting, menacing, bloodshot eyes came up to meet his. There was an unnatural hunger in them.

They were eyes Mirza had seen before.

They were the eyes of someone who had a taste for cruelty.

This man was dangerous.

"Madha turidu?" he asked in a rough, husky voice.

Mirza didn't understand, of course, but he had enough Arabic to introduce himself, "Ana Irfan."

The fighter sneered and shoved Mirza away. "Ana Maut."

I am Death.

"That's a good line," Mirza said. "I might steal it."

He wasn't sure "Maut" understood, but the man scoffed and looked away.

The mercenary smiled and backed off, hands raised a little. He didn't think taking Maut out in a one-on-one fight would be a problem. He'd fought and bested better men many times over.

Besides, this guy felt more like a hyena than a lion, the kind of predator who lurked in dark alleys and hunted the weak and the vulnerable. Still, he was clearly the most significant threat there.

A cheer rose from the audience behind them. Mirza turned to see a man with a massive, soft belly but scrawny arms waddle in. He was dressed in a flowing *thobe* the same shade of pearly white that the city was painted in and that Nimir bin Daleel loved. He had a woman—his wife, Mirza assumed—who was covered head to toe, close by, along with a small male entourage. They were flanked by a security detail of four armed foreign men with Belgian-made FN SCAR-Ls.

The Interior Minister, Waqif ibn Khaleef, had arrived.

Beside Mirza, Maut began to stretch, preparing himself for what was to come next.

"You've done this before?" Mirza asked.

Maut grinned in response, then his tongue darted out of his mouth to quickly wet his lips, like he was getting ready to feast.

Mirza started to take the bandages off his hands.

It was time to go to work.

TWENTY-SIX

FINN NEARLY SCREAMED WHEN he woke up. Not because he was in pain—which he was—but because for a moment he was certain he had died and was in hell. A dark, faceless figure was standing by him. From where he lay, it appeared to be floating on the ground, a black, billowing mass that some primal part of his reptilian brain interpreted as a supernatural threat.

The figure heard his strangled cry, spun around, and put a hand on his mouth. Finn started to struggle, then realized he was looking at a nun in her habit and relaxed a little. She glanced back at a door behind her. Seeing nothing, she listened, then eventually exhaled and pulled away from him.

Finn studied her. She looked to be around his own age, somewhere in her late thirties, with large, bright brown eyes that gave her the look of someone perpetually astonished. Her thin lips were drawn together so tight that they were almost white, her brow furrowed.

"Quiet. They will be close by now."

Her accent was not from Aldatan or anywhere else in the Middle East. It was very Eastern European. Albanian, perhaps.

Finn nodded to show that he'd comply, then tried to sit up. He grunted as a jolt of agony shot through his torso, reminding him he had been shot.

That hadn't happened in a long while. In fact, he couldn't even re-member the last time he'd faced live ammunition. Absorbing lead and bleeding all over everything was really more Mirza's thing. Finn preferred to work for low-risk, high-profile clients. It made for an easier life.

"How are you feeling?" the nun asked in a hushed tone.

Finn kept his voice low as well. "Unemployed."

She didn't seem to think that was funny. He consoled himself that this was just because she wasn't familiar with his circumstances.

He took a second to study his surroundings. He was in a poorly lit, tiny room with a low ceiling, resting on an uncomfortable cot. There was a window to the left across which a dark curtain had been drawn. The IV stand by his head was the most exciting thing in the place.

"I am Sister Elira," she said.

"Can you tell me what's going on?" Finn asked, choking on the end of his sentence as his dry throat seized up. He watched as she hurried to fill a cup with water.

"The police are looking for you."

This time he did sit up. His chest and left shoulder burned. There were cuts all over his forearms that had been bandaged up. There were sutured gashes on his chest and he figured there were some on his face. Even his feet were wrapped up in gauze. There are reasons why people don't usually jump through glass windows barefoot.

"Easy," the nun warned. "One of the bullets went through your back and chest. It's a miracle it didn't hit an artery or your heart. You should be dead already."

"The luck of the Irish."

"Or an act of God," she said.

Finn chuckled.

"What is funny?" the nun demanded.

"Nothing. That just sounded like something my brother would say."

"He's a wise man then."

"That's . . . not the quality he's most known for." Finn tried to move his left arm to see how much mobility he had. It wasn't much. Wincing, he asked, "What were you saying about the police?"

"That they are searching for you."

"I'm still in the slums?" Finn asked.

Sister Elira nodded. "Some refugees found you and—"

"I thought these were workers' camps."

"Many people fleeing the war in Yemen have tried to make lives for themselves here as well."

Finn grimaced. While Aldatan refused to accept refugees from that conflict, it hadn't yet built a wall like the Saudis had. This meant that those with nowhere else to go did cross the border without permission. "I've brought trouble to their door, haven't I?"

"Yes."

"I get why no one here would want to contact the authorities to hand me over. But if the police are already here, they should give me away to be rid of them."

"Maybe. Except no one has more compassion in this world than the people it has broken," the nun said. She paused, then with a small smile added, "Besides, they don't want to hurt the Order of Perpetual Mercy. We have a . . . difficult relationship with the crown. In the past, the king has threatened to shut us down. He's accused us of helping Yemenis in need of medical attention cross the border illegally."

"Is he right?"

"Not that he has been able to prove." Sister Elira took a deep breath, went to check on his IV. "If you were discovered here, however, if the police found out we'd aided you instead of handing you over to them, it'd be the end of our service in this country."

"You shouldn't have helped me then."

"You needed us. We had no choice."

"Yeah," Finn told her. "You did."

"I see that the concept of perpetual mercy eludes you."

"I suppose that's true."

"Anyway, the people of these slums will protect us. They need us. Hopefully, some of them even love us. So you are probably safe."

"Until the police search here."

"Mother Superior thinks they might not. You are in our private quarters, where men are not allowed. No one has to know we made an exception. She will ask them not to violate the sanctity of this space. It's possible they will refrain."

"That's a thin hope."

"Yes."

Finn grinned. "You're not very good at reassuring people, are you?"

Sister Elira remained completely unamused. He couldn't remember the last time he'd met someone who was this impervious to his charm, which he thought was considerable.

Finn looked around for his possessions, realized he was still in the underwear he'd had on when he'd run out of his apartment and that nothing else of his was within reach. "My phone?"

"You didn't have one with you."

"Oh. Right. I think I dropped it."

"You can use the order's, if there is someone you need to get in touch with."

Finn waved her offer away with his good hand. "I don't remember anyone's number."

"How very modern of you."

A loud but distant knocking sound echoed through the building.

"Looks like your friends are here," Sister Elira said.

"What should we do?"

"I think it is obvious," she told him. "We should pray."

———

"Pray? Now? With the police at the door looking for me?"

Sister Elira answered with a question of her own. "What better time?"

"All you religious folk are barmy, I swear. We need action, not words." At the sound of a baton hitting the front door downstairs, he threw his arms up in the air—or tried to, at least, before a severe jolt of pain in his left shoulder arrested him. Finn bit his lip to keep from yelping in pain, then moved to yank the IV out of his arm.

The nun hurried over to help him. "You'll hurt yourself."

"Ship sailed on that, I'm afraid," he said. "Tell me, Sister, did I have a gun with me when I was brought in?"

"Yes."

"Do you know where it is?"

She finished freeing him of the tubes that had been attached to him. "Yes."

"And?"

"Mother Superior put it away," Sister Elira told him. "She won't give it back to you."

"Right. Perpetual mercy and all that." With difficulty, Finn pulled himself out of bed and got unsteadily to his feet. The cuts there instantly started to scream in pain. His face twisted in anguish, but he fought through it. There was no choice.

He tried to get his mind to ignore his body's protests, urging it to come up with a solution. Down below, he heard a heavy door open. A conversation started.

The nun crossed herself.

The Special Ground Forces were here.

He decided not to waste time arguing to get his weapon back. Elira had said Mother Superior would be the one speaking to the authorities. If that's what the head nun was doing now, it was already too late to plead with her for it.

Whispering, he said, "At least hide me."

She looked around the small, spartan room. "Where?"

It was a fair point. The only real place for him to go was under the bed, which would fool the Aldatani authorities for approximately zero seconds. He couldn't stay in here, though. He pointed at the window he'd noticed before. "Where does that open?"

"Over the back alley."

"What story are we on?" he asked.

"The second."

Finn hurried over, pulled the curtain away, and looked down. It wasn't too bad a fall, though in his condition it'd be more than unpleasant. "I'll go out through here."

"You're insane."

Finn snorted. She wanted him to get on his knees and wait for a miracle, and he was the crazy one? At least this way he had a chance. "It isn't that high or that dangerous. Haven't you ever had a boy sneak into your bedroom through a window before?"

Sister Elira raised her eyebrows.

"Never mind. Listen, I'm doing this, all right? It's better than being a sitting duck. Can you stall them?"

"Stall them?" she asked uncertainly.

"Talk to them. Tell them the good news about Jesus. Anything."

"I will see what I can do."

"Thank you," Finn said.

"Go west if you're able. The police already searched there."

Finn nodded. Carefully, he opened the window and climbed up on the sill. He wobbled there a little as he crouched there but managed to steady himself.

Turning around, he used his good hand to hold the ledge tight. Then he lowered himself out one leg at a time until he was hanging from the building; this shortened the distance to the ground.

The stitches on his chest felt like they were tearing apart. His eyes blurred with tears.

He tried to breathe, to relax, to keep his body loose. He hadn't done this kind of thing in a while, but he had been trained to fall. He knew that being tense would make injuries more likely.

Sister Elira hurried over, looked down at him, shook her head, and drew the curtain.

Finn let go, pushing off the wall as best he could, planning to roll as soon as he hit the ground.

In the few seconds he was at the mercy of gravity, he couldn't help but wonder what Mirza was doing in that gorgeous five-star hotel Finn had booked for him.

TWENTY-SEVEN

MIRZA STOOD IN FRONT of the Interior Minister and his wife, lined up with the other men who were going to fight for their royal amusement. There was mayhem all around. Audience members—many of whom were foreigners—were shouting out their favorites and placing their bets.

He studied the combatants, trying to determine how to take each one out quickly while inflicting only minimal damage.

That wasn't his way. He had been taught to make sure his enemies were left broken, unable to rise again. It was a philosophy that had served him well. Overwhelming force, in his experience, was a sound strategy surprisingly often.

This night was different. This wasn't a typical fight with willing opponents.

Slowly, the crowd settled down. The people who had been recording wagers retreated. Then the young servant who had tied strips of red cloth around Mirza's wrists stepped forward carrying a large tray, and Waqif's wife rose. They walked toward the gladiators.

Mirza focused on the tray the boy was carrying. On it lay a vial with a warning label saying it contained acid, a length of rope, brass knuckles, a dagger, and a small, shining revolver so old Mirza couldn't identify it. There was one bullet next to it.

135

They were weapons—or items that could be used as weapons—but not ones that were equally lethal. He frowned. He had been expecting a straightforward hand-to-hand engagement. That was clearly not what the Midnight League was about.

In a loud, unpleasantly nasal, high-pitched voice the Minister spoke from where he was sitting. He spoke in English, probably for the benefit of his non-Arab guests. "All bets have been placed. The pens have been lifted. It is now time for the bestowal of divine favor."

Mirza glanced up at the silent night sky.

"To the virgins among you—for whom this is the first time—I say welcome to the Midnight League. If you have heard that there is something sinister about this project, know that there is not. It's no different than the mixed martial arts or wrestling federations they have in the West. Every contestant tonight was given the choice to not be here."

This was met with some light clapping from the crowd.

"It is a way to disinfect our capital from the virus of poverty and misery which continues to seep across our border." Waqif paused, then added with a smile, "A way for one of these men to improve his situation. It is work that must be done. But, as I told the king, there is no reason for us not to have fun while doing it.

"My wife has a collection of tools for the participants to use. She will flip a coin. If it is heads, the fighter who is favored to win—the big one wearing red—will select a weapon first, then the fighter with the next best odds, and so on. If it is tails, the weakest—the *miskeen* marked with yellow—will have the initial choice. Let us see who God favors."

There was absolute silence, as if the audience were holding its breath.

Mirza figured that those who had put serious money on the fight likely were. This could be a reversal of fortune for them. Whoever got to choose first would pick the revolver, even if they knew they'd only get one shot with it. Guns were great equalizers. A complete novice could take out a great martial artist at range if their aim was either lucky or true.

Anyone who had bet on Mirza would feel like their chances were suddenly a lot worse if the coin came up tails.

It didn't change much for him personally. He had known he might not live through the night. He'd figured that if he died, it'd be at the hands of one of the Minister's guards after he made his move to try to kidnap the man. This development just meant that he might be ended by someone else. He was fine with that. Dead was dead.

But the introduction of these weapons—especially the firearm—meant that the other men, who were only here under duress, might not survive.

With his dark eyes fixed on the sand in front of him, Mirza whispered a prayer. He used the words Moses had used after he'd fled Egypt having killed a man, when in Madyan as an exhausted, tired, penniless fugitive and he'd been able to help two women give water to their flock of sheep. It was an opportunity to do something right and kind, even if it was small, after having done a great wrong.

They were words recorded in the Quran that Mirza recited often and, even though they were in Arabic, he knew their meaning well by this point.

"Rabbi innee limaaa anzalta ilaiya min khairin faqeer."

My Lord, indeed I am, for whatever good you would send down to me, in need.

He watched as the Minister's wife tossed a coin in the air, where it seemed to hang for a moment before it started its descent, spinning all the way until it came to rest in her palm.

The Minister's wife looked down at the coin in her hand, paused, then declared, "Heads."

A cheer erupted from the audience.

She glided over to Mirza, looking him up and down with light-brown eyes, then reached for the dagger on the tray her servant was carrying. Slowly, she brought the blade up to the center of his collarbone. He struggled not to flinch as she dug the point in a little. Even though she was wearing a niqab, he could tell she smiled when he grunted in discomfort.

Her gaze locked with his, she dragged the weapon down his chest, slicing open his skin and his shirt. It was a stinging cut, but a surface one, slightly deeper than the kind that paper might inflict. Still it left a line of blood down to his navel, where she stopped, looking at what she'd done like a painter fascinated by her own work.

Mirza ripped off the ruined shirt and tossed it aside.

There was a murmur of appreciation from the crowd.

Waqif's spouse inclined her head a little, as if acknowledging the impressiveness of his physique, and ran a pale, cool hand over his chest. Then she turned to look at her husband and said something in Arabic. Whatever it was, it drew gasps from several people.

The Minister laughed and said, "That sounds like a fun show, but you already have many prettier, cleaner bulls to play with, don't you?"

She gave a petulant huff, turned the knife over in her hands, and offered it to Mirza, hilt first.

He shook his head. The Minister had said that if the coin toss went his way, he'd get to choose whatever he wanted. He pointed at the petite revolver on offer.

"Boring," she complained, dropping the blade back where she'd gotten it, spinning, and walking back to her seat.

Mirza loaded the gun, which felt tiny and uncomfortable in his hands, and slipped it into the waistband of his jeans at the small of his back. He had no intention of using it. He'd taken it so that none of his fellow combatants would end up with it.

As he was doing this, he saw Maut lunge for the dagger. The next fighter, who had purple cloth tied to him, took the brass knuckles. White

138

took the vial of liquid, which left Yellow with the short length of rope. The poor man looked at it as if he were going to be hanged with it.

Waqif clapped his hands for attention. "My friends, these people, these wanderers upon the earth, these beggars, these . . . these pieces of trash that winds of fortune have blown into Aldatan, are a plague upon our society. It is time for a cure. It is time for bloodletting."

Loud music suddenly blared out into the night.

Mirza looked around for the speakers. He hadn't noticed them before.

One of the guards raised his rifle and fired a volley of bullets into the ocean.

The crowd roared in approval.

The fighters scattered all over the circle they were in, hurrying to get away from Mirza.

He managed to reach out and grab one of them by the arm. It was White, the one who had picked the acid. Mirza yanked the man toward him with his right hand, while bringing up his left elbow. White ran into it and shattered his nose with a brutal crunch.

White swayed on his feet, the vial he'd chosen dropping from his hand.

Mirza moved around White, putting him in a blood choke, applying pressure on the side of his neck, compressing the arteries and veins circulating blood to his brain. He was unconscious in seven seconds.

Mirza searched in the sand for the acid White had dropped. Just as he grabbed the vial and shoved it into his jeans pocket, he heard a scream, followed by a sick gurgle. He looked up to see Yellow, throat slit open, holding on uselessly to the piece of rope he'd been left with.

Maut was standing behind him, his dagger, his hand, the front of his shirt covered in blood, giggling gleefully, kicking the homeless man who'd been all but forced into this ring.

Mirza felt a great rage building inside him, a firestorm gaining fury and speed.

He rose to his feet.

Maut licked his lips and smirked, holding his red-stained knife with the confidence of someone who had some skill with it.

Purple looked at Mirza, at Maut, at the two bodies that had fallen already, and, finally, at the brass knuckles in his hand. He began to breathe hard, eyes wide, hands shaking.

"Here," Mirza called to him, waving him over.

It was a mistake.

Purple interpreted the gesture as a challenge instead of an offer of help.

He turned around and ran.

He got maybe ten feet before one of the Minister's guards put three rounds in him.

Maut trembled with silent laughter.

Mirza closed his eyes.

Maut charged.

TWENTY-EIGHT

WHISTLING CHEERFULLY TO HERSELF, Omen pulled her AirPods out after hanging up with Mirza, popped them back in their case, and put that away in the small cross-body satchel she always carried with her. She was sweating after her workout at the hotel gym, but there were apparently going to be no showers for the wicked tonight, at least not right away. There was havoc to wreak.

That was often the case when working with Mirza, she'd found. When operating on her own, she favored precision. All her heists were carefully thought out, with plans for every contingency she could imagine. Being a professional, her father had always told her, meant being meticulous about your craft.

He was a high-profile lawyer, of course, not a thief, but the principle translated perfectly well to her chosen profession.

Omen sauntered over to the elevator and pressed the button to call it. While waiting for it to arrive, she saw a couple of hotel employees sprinting past, whispering urgently to each other.

Working with Mirza allowed her to cut loose a little.

Well, actually, it forced her to cut loose a lot. Bulls in china shops operated with more subtlety than he did, and all that chaos he seemed to thrive in . . . well, it was just fun.

It helped that he was the human equivalent of a concrete wall, so she always felt safe when he was around. Somehow it felt more likely that one of her carefully crafted schemes would get her killed than whatever tempest Mirza wanted to march into next.

An easy man to trust, she thought as she got on the elevator to leave the hotel's basement, where the gym was located.

Omen pulled out her room key and scanned it so she'd be allowed to get to the floor their rooms were on. It didn't work.

Frowning, she tried again.

Nothing.

"Great," she grumbled as the elevator doors closed and it started to rise.

Fortunately, they opened onto the hotel lobby. She was about to step out and go complain, when she noticed more worried-looking staff members huddled together, speaking in hushed tones.

An elderly gentleman carrying several shopping bags smiled at her as he got on. She responded with an absent nod, her attention focused on the front desk, where several police officers were talking to the clerk.

"Lots of excitement tonight," the old man noted. His accent was distinctly Russian. A lot of his countrymen had moved to the Middle East and Turkey recently to escape the geopolitical drama unfolding in their homeland.

"Yeah?"

"I believe someone is in trouble."

Omen shrugged. "Sucks for them."

She watched as he managed to execute the key scan without difficulty. Once they were underway again, she tried it herself for a third time.

"Strange," he noted.

"Right? It's so—"

That's when it hit her. They were the ones in trouble. She and Mirza, they were the people she'd just said it sucked to be.

She resisted the urge to bang her head against a wall.

Mirza had completely failed to account for the fact that Finn had booked their rooms for them. It was inevitable that while tracking Finn, Aldatani law enforcement would use their extensive surveillance capabilities to study his recent credit card charges. That would, of course, lead them here to see if this was where their fugitive was hiding.

Of course, Omen hadn't thought of this either, but she decided she preferred to blame Mirza for the oversight. It was, as he'd said, his mission.

This right here was why you made detailed plans, so shit like this didn't happen.

As the elevator got close to the old man's floor, she reached into her satchel and pulled out her phone, while moving slightly to obstruct the exit—not entirely, but just enough that he'd have to brush past.

Quickly browsing through her photo app, she found a selfie she had taken in the bikini she'd just mentioned to Mirza. It had been a whim. She'd thought about sending it to him and asking what he thought. A bit transparent, sure—the teasing, not the garment, obviously—but it was difficult to resist giving him a hard time because he got so easily flustered.

She had restrained herself. She could be good when she was so inclined.

When the elevator came to a stop, the gentleman tried to squeeze past her. She bumped her hand against his hard, causing her cell to drop into one of his shopping bags.

He also lost his grip on his key card, which she snatched out of midair and pocketed before he realized what had happened, his eyes searching for her device.

"Oh my god, I'm so sorry," she said, stepping out behind him as he fumbled around in his shopping bag. "That's so clumsy of me. I—" She gave an embarrassed little gasp when he finally managed to recover her phone. "Sorry. That's . . . mortifying. I took that picture to send to my boyfriend."

The man stared at her photograph, cleared his throat, and handed her cell back. "He is very lucky."

"Oh. Thanks. That's awful nice of you to say. Do you . . ." She bit her lower lip. "Do you think he'll like it?"

"I . . . well, yes, of course. Of course. How could he not?"

She flashed him her most winning smile and waved her fingers at him. "Well, have a good night."

"Ah, yes, you too."

Omen hit the call button and pretended to wait for the next elevator.

He turned left, heading down the corridor leading to his room.

She hurried, as quietly as she could, down its right side, hoping she could get to a stairwell before he turned around.

She did. Using his key card, Omen slipped inside and sprinted down the stairs.

Not the classiest of misdirections, but it was all she'd been able to think of in the moment. Her looks were an asset. Studies showed that beautiful people were trusted more, were perceived to be kinder and more honest by strangers.

Mirza's God, if he existed, had given her thieving career a major assist by making her pretty. It'd be churlish not to use the gift. She didn't want to appear ungrateful.

She made her way to the parking structure under the hotel. She didn't try to lift a car there, however. In a place like this, there'd probably be an attendant at the exit checking slips. She'd attract attention if she didn't have one.

Instead, she decided to play on the fact that she was still in her workout clothes. Putting her AirPods back in, she jogged straight out of the structure, like she was going for a late-night run.

That probably wasn't the kind of thing women in Gozel did and, indeed, the guy in the attendant's booth she waved at as she went past gave her a confused look. He didn't try to stop her, though, which was the important thing.

Once she was clear of the hotel, Omen began scanning the street, picking out her next ride.

Showrooms, after all, were for suckers.

TWENTY-NINE

AS FINN MADE HIS way through the slums, slinking from one cramped, shadowy, trash-infested alley to another, he could tell his feet were bleeding again. The bandages wrapped around them were absorbing the blood, so he wasn't leaving a trail behind. Not yet at least.

The pain was constant and intense and growing worse. All he could do was try to ignore it. The knowledge that he'd be made to hurt a lot more if the Aldatani government got its hands on him kept him going.

He'd been lucky with the fall from Sister Elira's window. Dropping and rolling had mitigated most of the damage. His left ankle was complaining a bit, but his body had other, more pressing concerns.

The "streets"—unpaved, dusty, winding trails—were deserted as he limped through them as quickly as he could. People were holed up in their huts and shanties. He could see them watching his progress from inside, silent witnesses to his predicament.

Finn heard someone speaking nearby, in rapid, sharp Arabic, and ducked behind a large pile of refuse and garbage. He suspected that the people who lived here would burn it and end up inhaling the smoke and the melting plastic soon. Then, on top of the ashes, this by-product of their lives would begin to accumulate again. It was inescapable.

He held his breath, not just because of the stench, but because he could see two officers now, heavily armored and armed, walking past.

Finn had picked up enough Arabic during his employment here to understand what they were saying.

"Filthy rats," one of them declared, wrinkling his nose.

"The king should have this cleaned up. We should civilize these people."

"Maybe," the first policeman responded without conviction, stopping a few meters away from where Finn was hiding. "Some animals can't be tamed, though."

"My son would love a picture of this," the second officer said.

"Why?"

"Social media. He could post about how terrible these conditions are and get a thousand sympathy likes."

The first officer chuckled. "Tell him to be careful. The royals might not like his likes."

Finn knew that was true. He'd heard the Minister of Culture rail against news articles in the West about the laborers here and their suffering, a problem shared by all Emirati countries. It was, in Aldatan's view, hypocrisy. The West thrived on misery and exploitation too, they just exported the worst of it far from their borders and then pretended their hands were clean, that they were superior.

There was a sudden, bright flash, which blinded Finn and caused him to flinch a little.

The officer had taken a picture after all.

A huge rat, startled, bolted from wherever it had been hiding, its claws skittering over the bandages on Finn's feet as it scurried past.

Finn shuddered but managed to keep still. He couldn't be sure, however, that he hadn't made some kind of noise in his surprise. Muscles tensing, he got ready to pounce on the officers as best he could. Given his condition, they'd take him easily, but he still intended to give them a fight.

Finally, the first policeman said, "You're crazy. Come on, let's get away from this smell."

Finn stayed where he was, waiting for their footsteps to recede.

Once they did, he made his way out from behind the mountain of trash that had hidden him. He had to get out of the slums and contact Mirza or Omen. That was how he'd be able to get to safety and, he hoped, a shower.

THIRTY

MIRZA SNAPPED HIS DARK eyes open in time to see a flash of moonlight on metal as Maut slashed at his throat. He swayed back to avoid being halalled and tried to grab Maut's arm as it whizzed by. He wasn't fast enough.

Maut withdrew, trying to circle him, a rabid dog sizing up its prey.

Mirza positioned himself so that his back was to the Minister.

Maut lunged forward, a rapid, straight strike aimed at Mirza's gut. Again, he tried to get ahold of his attacker, but the man pulled away before he could.

"Speed kills," Prince Waqif called out, laughing.

Mirza grunted. That wasn't untrue.

Maut's tongue darted out as he feinted left, then jabbed across his body and up at Mirza's right side. The mercenary snarled as the blade made contact, nicking his outer ear, but this time Maut wasn't able to pull away.

Taking hold of Maut's arm, Mirza yanked forward while stepping around the man. The move and the momentum of his own thrust propelled Maut in the Minister's direction, sending him stumbling out of the circle and onto the sand.

The crowd scrambled out of the way as Mirza followed, cracking his knuckles as he closed in slowly on Maut.

Mirza took a moment to look around, acting like he was a professional wrestler, raising his arms, and showboating for the audience. He glanced in the direction of the oddly shaped rock whose coordinates he'd sent to Omen, wondering if she'd arrived.

The quick flickering of two headlights answered his question.

Everyone else had their attention fixed on Maut, who was on his feet again.

He rushed in, snarling and swinging wildly. Mirza put up a block, his left arm stopping Maut's right, then delivered three precise jabs to Maut's face with his free hand.

Maut howled and retreated.

Mirza looked up to where the Minister and his wife were standing, less than ten feet away from Maut, and smiled.

This time, he was the one who charged, lowering a shoulder and spearing Maut's chest.

Mirza didn't specialize in knife combat, but he knew that what he'd just done wasn't advisable. Maut took advantage and tried to drive his dagger into Mirza's left arm, just below the shoulder. But he was falling back as he scored the hit, so it didn't penetrate as far as Maut would have liked.

Still, he was grinning when he got to his feet, enjoying the fact that he'd drawn blood.

They were even closer to the Interior Minister now, but Waqif hadn't retreated. His eyes were glued on the action.

There was never going to be a better time.

Mirza reached into his pocket and pulled out the vial of acid he'd picked up.

He pretended to throw it at Maut, who abandoned his defensive stance and ducked, giving Mirza the opening to run in. He got ahold of Maut's knife hand before the man could recover and forced the point of the blade in toward Maut's abdomen using just one hand.

It was a battle of sheer strength now, and they both knew Mirza would not lose.

Maut looked up at Mirza, eyes desperate and pleading, once his own weapon was aimed back at him.

"Inna lillahi wa inna ilayhi raji'un," Mirza whispered.

It was what Muslims said to console people whose loved ones had died.

To Allah we belong and to him we return.

"Finish him!" Waqif cried.

Mirza did as the Minister asked.

Using the full weight of his body, he pushed forward.

Maut tried to resist.

It was hopeless.

The dagger plunged into his stomach.

As Maut started to scream, Mirza took the vial he was holding and shoved it into the killer's open mouth. Letting go of the knife, he slammed a palm into Maut's chin. Glass shattered between Maut's teeth and the man fell back, wailing and writhing as the escaping acid burned his lips, his tongue, and part of his face away.

There were no other sounds, except for the crashing of the waves.

Everyone, including the guards, watched horrified and transfixed.

The Minister was rooted in place, pupils dilated, skin flushed, breathing hard, almost trembling with excitement as he stared at Maut's gruesome end.

Mirza moved toward Waqif, cautiously at first, and then with haste, before anyone could think to react or raise an alarm. Reaching behind his back, he pulled out the revolver he had taken. Stepping behind the royal, he put the muzzle firmly up against the prince's head.

"Put them down," Mirza said, calm in the face of the half a dozen assault rifles pointed in his direction, "or I'll put him down."

Prince Waqif, with Mirza's massive arm wrapped around his neck, managed to choke out a command: "Do as he says."

Reluctantly, one by one, the Interior Minister's expensive protectors lowered their guns and dropped them onto the sand.

"Sidearms too," Mirza ordered, still using the royal as a meat shield.

He looked around once the guards complied. No one in the audience had moved, though someone had thought to cut the music. He'd half expected the crowd to panic and run, but they had come for a bloody show. This was perhaps exactly the kind of thing they wanted to see.

It occurred to Mirza that they were all witnesses. At least their phones had been confiscated. He wasn't being recorded like he had been in Thailand.

Even so, once the authorities were done interviewing these people, Gozel wouldn't be safe for him anymore.

He took a deep breath and scanned the weapons lying on the beach, the smell of the ocean overpowered by the musk in Waqif's cologne. The guard closest to them had dropped a full-size pistol. Mirza pointed at it. "Toss that over."

The man hesitated.

Mirza increased the power of his grip around Waqif's neck.

"Now," the Interior Minister croaked. "Quickly."

"Slowly," Mirza corrected.

Making a show of his reluctance, probably for the benefit of his colleagues, the guard bent down and threw the handgun at Mirza's feet.

With his revolver aimed at the nape of Waqif's neck, Mirza had the Interior Minister retrieve the firearm. Then he reached forward, took it, and flipped the safety. He could see now that it was a variant of the CZ 75, which was widely used all over the world. It felt good, comforting even, to hold a weapon he was familiar with.

Yes, he was still massively outnumbered, but he'd gone from one bullet to sixteen. It was hard not to see that as a positive development.

Mirza tucked the small revolver he'd been using away and trained his newly acquired Czech pistol on the Interior Minister instead.

"Who are you?" Waqif demanded.

The growl of an engine turning behind them was the only answer he got. Headlights came on in the dark, and Omen pulled up beside them in a gray Jeep Gladiator Sand Runner. She had a scarf covering her hair and hiding the lower part of her face.

Mirza hadn't expected her to bring a pickup truck, but it suited him just fine. He guided his hostage back toward the bed, yanked down the tailgate, and nodded at Waqif. "Get in."

"No. Please, listen, I—"

Mirza clubbed him on the side of his head with the butt of the 9 mm, not with enough force to knock the royal out but certainly enough for it to hurt. Waqif yelped, looking stunned, like he couldn't believe someone would actually dare hit him. Maybe it was something that hadn't ever happened before.

Regardless, it got him to comply.

Mirza climbed onto the back of the truck himself, then moved into position behind Waqif again. He didn't want the guards grabbing their rifles and shooting as soon as Omen began to pull away.

Bracing himself, Mirza grabbed Waqif and slammed his gun hand on the top of the cabin.

They lurched forward a bit as Omen began to drive.

"Who are you?" Waqif asked again, his panic rising as the truck gained speed.

Mirza thought about how to answer, then said, "Ana Maut."

Yeah, he thought as he watched what color was left on the Minister's face drain away, it really was a good line.

THIRTY-ONE

THE POLICE WERE EVERYWHERE. The streets of Gozel were
bathed in red and blue.

Now in the back seat of the Gladiator with Prince Waqif, Mirza
shook his head as Omen found a deserted road, pulled over, and killed
the engine.

They had only managed to get five blocks from the beach when they
first saw cops setting up blockades in the area. Helicopters hovered in
the air with spotlights trailing along the ground, flying low, searching
for any sign of the Aldatani Interior Minister or the people who had
abducted him.

Announcements were being made on loudspeakers in Arabic. Lights
were slowly turning on in the homes around them as people started to
wake up, stirred from their sleep by the commotion.

They were caught in a net.

Parking to blend in with other vehicles would only buy them so
much time.

Omen slammed the palm of her hand on the steering wheel. "Shit."

It was, Mirza thought, an accurate assessment of their situation.
There was no way they were getting out of Gozel like they'd planned.
The speed and intensity of the government response was both surprising

and impressive. He doubted it would've been quite so good if a regular citizen had been the one taken.

Beside him, Prince Waqif, convinced that order had been restored to his universe—or soon would be—actually chuckled. In his nasal voice, he said, "You are screwed. How did you think this would end? I am royalty. You can't touch me. I am going to personally make sure that you spend the rest of your lives—"

Mirza took out his pistol, put the muzzle against Waqif's left knee, and fired three quick rounds into it. Omen yelped, surprised as the shots echoed in the vehicle, spinning around to see what had happened.

Waqif screamed, gripping the thigh above his pulverized joint. He doubled over, face contorted in agony as blood splattered onto the seat in front of him and the door at his side.

"What the fuck are you doing?" Omen demanded.

"You're right. Sorry. I shouldn't waste bullets. One would've been enough."

She threw her hands up, speechless.

Mirza reached over, grabbed Waqif's neck, and shoved the barrel of the 9 mm into the prince's mouth, silencing him mid-screech. Waqif's eyes went wide, and he tried to stay still, though his body still shook with silent sobbing.

"Here's what's going to happen. I'm going to ask you what I need to know. You'll answer. If you don't, I'll pull the trigger. I'm going to angle the shot down, away from your brain stem, so it'll take a while for you to die. You flop around like a fish out of water, in so much pain that you'll know hell before you get there. Are we clear?"

That got him a slow, cautious nod.

"Tell me about Mahmi Castle."

Waqif tried to speak but couldn't around the weapon in his mouth.

Mirza pulled it out. It was wet with saliva. The mercenary pointed it at Waqif's groin and gestured for him to speak.

"What do you—"

Mirza covered the prince's mouth with his hand and shot him again, this time in the thigh on the same side as the knee he'd wrecked.

Waqif's shriek was at least muffled this time.

"That didn't sound like the start of an answer. Let's try again. Your ministry has been sending supplies there for years. Why?"

"Pl—please, stop hurting me, okay? Please. I'll tell you. Mahmi is a place into which people disappear. The king is using it as a secret prison. It's become a legend. A fate to be feared."

Mirza nodded. "Have you ever been?"

"No. My job is just to make sure a convoy gets there every two weeks. We send water, food, petrol, all kinds of things. They need the supplies to survive."

"And where does the convoy leave from?"

"The SGF has a depot north of Gozel."

"SGF?" Omen asked.

"Special Ground Forces," Mirza answered. "It's the best police unit here. Think SWAT."

She grumbled something under her breath about how it'd be nice if they could pick a fight with someone their own size for once.

Mirza turned back to the Interior Minister. "Do you have an address for it?"

"Why would I—"

"Have you seen it? Are there any landmarks nearby?"

"It's close to where the Formula One race happens every year."

Mirza nodded. That'd have to do. "When is the next shipment to Mahmi supposed to go out?"

"In three days."

"How long does the convoy stay at the castle?"

"Around four hours," Waqif told him. "Once everything is unloaded, it heads back."

"Thank you." Mirza brought the CZ 75 up and pressed it against the Minister's forehead. "Tell Azrael I said hi."

"But—but I answered your questions. You promised you'd let me go."

"No. I didn't."

Omen frowned. "You're really going to kill him?"

"We won't be able to get out of here with him," Mirza pointed out. "Not with the police cordon. And he knows we were asking about the castle. He won't keep that to himself. It'll jeopardize the mission."

"No. Listen. I won't tell anyone. I swear. Wallahi, I won't. Please. Let me go. I have children. Small children. Have pity. Show mercy."

Mirza turned his dark eyes on the Interior Minister. "The men you forced to fight in the Midnight League had families, too."

"Those were just beggars with lives not worth living. I gave them a way out of their misery. The ones that won got money. Some of them even came back to try to earn more. I helped them in a way. I really did."

Mirza thought for a moment. Then he said, "Those are shitty last words."

He pulled the trigger.

"I can't fucking believe you put a bullet in his face," Omen said, keeping her voice low. They were hiding in a dark, narrow alley that smelled like stale piss. It was sandwiched between two apartment buildings, out of sight of the Sand Runner, which they'd left behind.

They'd tried to put as much distance between themselves and the pickup as possible, but they had to move carefully. Authorities were converging on Prince Waqif's dead body, probably alerted by locals who'd heard and called in gunshots.

"It was the most efficient way to kill him."

Omen adjusted the small cross-body satchel she was carrying, shifting its position so that she was more comfortable. He noted that she was wearing a loose, white, off-shoulder tee that revealed the strap of a light-pink sports bra underneath along with tights and running shoes. She had said she was at the gym when he'd called. He wondered why she hadn't changed.

"My issue is with the murder, Irfan, not how you did it."

"I had no choice."

"Couldn't you have found some other way to make sure he wouldn't talk?"

"Like what?"

Omen ran a hand through her hair. "I'm not sure. I just . . . don't like what happened."

"I don't like it either, but we do what's necessary."

"I know. It's just . . . shit."

"This isn't the first time you've seen me term someone," Mirza reminded her. "You've done it yourself, too."

"Yeah. In self-defense. Not in cold blood. That guy wasn't a threat to us."

"He was. He just didn't look like one."

Omen sighed. "Whatever. Are you sure it was smart to just leave him there for the cops to find?"

"Didn't have a choice there either."

"We could have blown up the car. That would've at least destroyed some of the evidence."

Mirza raised his thick, sweeping eyebrows. "How?"

She pointed at the handgun he was holding. "You could've shot the gas tank."

"That doesn't do anything."

Omen blinked. "Really?"

"I've tried it, and—"

"Of course you have."

"It causes a leak," he told her, "not an explosion."

"But in movies it just takes one bullet to—"

"That's all fake. Though I haven't tried it with incendiary rounds."

"Wow," she said. "You can't believe anything these days."

Mirza looked around their grim surroundings. "Believe this. This is real."

"I don't want this to be real."

He shrugged, then had to duck quickly when a light came on in the window across from where he was standing. He was pretty sure whoever was inside would react poorly to seeing a shirtless behemoth lurking outside their apartment.

He moved to the far end of the alley in a crouch, peering out to see if it was safe to cross the small street in front of them.

At some point, they'd have to get to and use one of the main roads, which were teeming with law enforcement. They were the only way out. Skulking from one narrow lane to another was just a stall tactic. Unless they managed to leave this part of Gozel, the Aldatanis would eventually find them.

"We need an exit," he murmured.

In a whisper, she asked, "Do we really?"

He glanced back, expecting to see the sarcasm he hadn't heard in her tone in her expression. But she wasn't looking at him. Her eyes were surveying the buildings they were hiding between. Specifically, she was studying the many windows around them.

He was about to ask her what she meant when a police car zipped past, siren blaring. Mirza shrank back into the shadows as best he could but still felt conspicuous. There were a ton of benefits to having an imposing physique in his line of work. What you gained in size, however, you lost in stealth.

That was Omen's specialty. With her slender frame and lithe body, it came to her naturally. He simply wasn't built for sneaking around.

Luckily, the cruiser blew past too quickly to notice him.

Omen's green eyes remained fixed upward. "How about we find an entrance instead?"

He waited for her to explain.

"What we really need right now is to get off the streets. Look at the windows that are still dark. Do you think people are actually sleeping through all this noise?"

"They could just be trying to ignore it."

"Yeah. Or maybe no one's home. If those places are vacant, we can use them to hide."

"We're just going to break into someone's house?"

"You just put a bullet in some guy's head. Now you've got a conscience?"

"We shouldn't bring civilians into this," he told her. "If we go in somewhere and it's not empty, if we wake someone or—"

"You know that I am a civilian too, right? And so are you."

Mirza scowled. It had just been a figure of speech, one that was so ingrained in him that he didn't even think about it anymore. He'd picked it up from the General who had trained him, Finn, Ren, and the other children at the "orphanage." "I meant bystanders. Innocents. We shouldn't involve more people. Makes it more likely things will go wrong."

"Yeah. I get it. So all we have to do is find a place we're almost sure no one is in."

"Easier said than done."

Omen pulled out her phone. "Actually, there's an app for that."

Part Three

HOUSEGUESTS

THIRTY-TWO

ADAM AZIZ—OR ADAM WITH the sad eyes, as Dina had described him—was as good as his word. Late at night, the Leopard came to the South Tower to pick her up for their . . . well, you'd have to call it a date, Ren supposed.

He was carrying a Kalashnikov Komrad. It was a handsome shotgun, though in her experience, mag-fed semiautos could be temperamental.

He hadn't come alone. There were two men with him. They were both much older than the Leopard and definitely not military. Renata knew one of them. It just took her a moment to recognize him because he had lost an alarming amount of weight in the two years since she'd seen him in person, the stoop of his shoulders had gotten more pronounced, the nails on his left hand and several of his teeth were missing. Still, he smiled broadly when he saw that she was mostly unharmed.

"Habib," Ren said, walking over to give her fiancé's father a hug. "It's good to see you."

"I cannot say the same. I wish you and Mahmud were elsewhere."

"How is he?"

Habib's smile faded instantly. "In a great deal of pain."

"Take me to him."

"That is out of my power," her father-in-law-to-be explained, gesturing to the man he'd come with. "This is Imam Ehsan bin Ghiath. You've heard of him, yes?"

Renata nodded. "Aldatan's great preacher. Mahmud wrote an article that mentions your disappearance, though it hasn't been published yet."

"It is some consolation," Imam Ehsan noted, "that I haven't yet been completely forgotten."

"Never, Sheikh," Adam said, his tone earnest.

Ren frowned at the Leopard. That was a surprising reaction from him, given what he did for a living. Before she could point that out, however, Habib went on.

"The guards have orders that you and Mahmud are not allowed to see each other. They interpreted this to mean that I couldn't visit you either. I tried to get to you earlier, but couldn't. Imam Ehsan, whom Adam here respects, helped convince Adam to let me check on you."

"Why doesn't Atlas want me seeing Mahmud?"

"We are not given reasons," Adam told her, "and we don't ask for them."

"Admirable," Habib noted, managing somehow to keep most of the sarcasm out of his voice. "Thank you, again, for bringing me here. I do have another ask of you. Give me a few minutes to have some words alone with my daughter."

"Of course," Imam Ehsan agreed, taking hold of the Leopard by his elbow and guiding him away. "We will wait outside."

Dina gave Renata a quick smile and followed behind them.

As soon as they were alone, Habib stepped closer to look at the bruise Atlas had given Ren. "Are you—"

"I'm fine," she assured him, touching her forehead gingerly. "From everything I've seen and heard, I was lucky."

Habib nodded. "That is true. Strange, but—"

"Why's it strange?"

"No other prisoner has ever entered Mahmi without getting a terrible greeting from Atlas Boss."

Ren took a moment to process this information. "Dina told me that I'm the only foreigner who has ever been here. Maybe that's it."

"It would be like my nephew," Habib agreed, "to value you more for that reason."

"So you're saying that because I'm Spanish, the king won't let Atlas hurt me?"

"He did hit you," Habib pointed out.

"Sure, but that was only after I tried to strangle him."

The old man stared at her.

Realizing an explanation was required, Ren went over what had happened in Atlas's office in detail. "It probably wasn't smart," she admitted. "But I wasn't sure I'd ever have the chance again and . . . it seemed like the thing to do."

"I . . . am not sure what to say, except that it is a pity that you were not successful."

Renata nodded.

"He will extract a price for the attempt, you know. He does not strike me as the forgiving kind."

"If I have some kind of immunity or protection—"

Habib grimaced. "Then Mahmud will pay the price."

Renata sat back down on her bunk and ran her hands through her hair. "Maybe I should've let him finish telling me what his offer was. I never learned what he was willing to give me if I could get you to confess to treason."

"I would not have given him what he wanted, even if he promised to 'put the sun in my right hand and the moon in my left.' I cannot admit to being motivated by personal gain or the desire for power. The heart of Aldatan looks to me for hope. If I break, it breaks. This I will not allow."

"No matter what the cost?" Ren asked.

"I was born to the kings of this land. The duty I owe to them, to it, to the people who are my family's responsibility . . . It sits heavier than a mountain on my heart. I cannot move it, nor will I attempt to do so."

"He might try to get to you through Mahmud, too."

"Let him strike cold steel thinking he can change it. I—"

There was a sharp knock on the door.

"I should go," Habib said. "Adam is probably growing impatient."

"What is with that Leopard?"

"What do you mean?"

"He treats the prisoners well, but he works for the people who torture them. He seems to revere Imam Ehsan, but he serves those who imprison him. What is he?"

Habib sighed. "Vile."

"He doesn't seem that bad. Dina—"

"Dina is a young woman who does not yet understand the nature of evil."

Ren frowned. "I don't know about that. She seems to have seen a lot of it."

"She hasn't seen the everyday, mundane kind, rooted not in malice but in apathy and self-interest. People like Adam tell themselves they're just doing their jobs, just marching to the tune of whatever drum is playing, so they can have a comfortable life. Along the way, they do small acts of kindness to make themselves feel better, but they ultimately care only about themselves. Without these . . . hard souls, men like Nimir and Atlas would have no power."

There was another knock, gentler this time, and Imam Ehsan opened the door to peer inside. "It's time to go, Habib."

The old man reached over and patted Renata's cheek. "Prepare yourself, my daughter, for the torment to come as best you can."

Renata watched Habib go, then lay back down. Staring up at the Mahmi's ceiling, she thought about Mahmud. Her fiancé would pay the price for her attack on Atlas. He would also be used as a pressure point against Habib. Through no fault of his own, the man she loved had become a stone with which Atlas would try to kill two birds.

No. That was unfair. Mahmud was more than a helpless victim here. He had known that something like this might happen when he'd stood against the tyrant of Aldatan. He had done so regardless. He had chosen his fate. He was as much a royal as his father.

As for Habib, Ren had always liked him. They had met a few times, and he had always been unfailingly kind and courteous. But she'd figured that he had become the leader of the rebellion against King Nimir by default, because his bloodline made him next in line for the throne.

Today for the first time, she'd seen him as more than a father figure. His strength, though quiet, was remarkable and even inspirational. His morality, his eloquence, his air of wisdom—all of it spoke to the fact that he would make a good monarch. The fact that he'd publicly stated that he did not want to rule made him noble on top of all that. It was easy to see why Nimir was afraid of him.

It struck her that she had forgotten to send Mahmud a message through Habib. Though there wasn't much to say, really, except that she loved him, which he knew, and that she wished she could see him, which he could guess.

The only solace she could offer was the hope that Mirza and Finn were still out there, that they would find them eventually, no matter how long it took. To be comforting, however, faith requires belief. Mahmud didn't know her brothers. Telling him to look forward to their coming was like telling an atheist to find hope in prayer. It would not work.

No, it was best she keep that to herself.

Renata flinched as the sound of someone screaming began to echo through the castle again. It was, she could tell, Mahmud. Atlas had started torturing him again.

THIRTY-THREE

FINN PEERED INTO A modest little home near the southern edge of Gozel. It was late at night. He'd walked for miles. His feet were bleeding in earnest now, the pain in them sharp and searing.

The tips of his ears felt like they were on fire, which was usually a sign that he had a fever. He was run-down and clammy. The urge to lie down and close his eyes was strong but not stronger than his will to live. Not yet at least.

Given these symptoms, it was obvious he wouldn't be able to keep going for long, which meant he had to act, even if it meant doing something he'd rather not.

The house was newly built, part of the encroachment of the middle class into historically poor areas. As of right now, it was the only complete one on the block, which made it relatively isolated and, by extension, perfect for Finn's purposes.

From what he could tell, there were three people inside, a woman in her early thirties and her two children, both under ten years of age. He waited for the kids to fall asleep before making his move. Best to avoid emotionally scarring them if possible.

At the front of the house, Finn made note of the fact that the door handle was on the right and the hinges appeared to be on the inside.

Taking a deep breath, he rang the bell and moved quickly to the left, flattening himself against the wall there.

There was silence, then he heard the woman heading toward the entrance to her home. He stayed perfectly still. She'd check the peephole. She wouldn't see anything. He hoped she'd open the door to see who it was.

She didn't. Given the hour, she was clearly wary, and that was smart.

He heard her call out, asking who it was. When she didn't get a response, she started to walk away.

Finn reached over and rang the bell once more.

She was back in seconds, her voice sterner, more irritated, and insistent when she spoke this time.

Again, she got no answer.

Finn hit the bell a third time.

This time, she opened up. Not a lot. Just a little. Just enough to peer out from to see what was happening.

Finn moved fast, spinning around and slamming his shoulder into the door. His wounded body hurt like the deepest depths of Satan's kingdom, but he bit his lip and powered through.

The woman cried out in surprise as the door slammed back and hit her in the face. She was too stunned to scream for a moment. Before it passed, Finn moved behind her and wrapped an arm around her neck, choking her out while covering her mouth. She struggled and tried to bite his hand, but slowly her consciousness started to fade.

"I'm so sorry," Finn whispered into her ear as her head drooped and she slumped to the ground, out for a while at least.

He closed the door behind him, then hurried in, heading to where he knew her kids were. He checked to make sure the noise hadn't woken them, then went back to the woman.

He dragged her across the floor to her bedroom. From her wardrobe there, he retrieved a sock and two hijabs. He used the scarves to tie her hands and feet. The sock he stuffed into her mouth.

On her nightstand, connected to a charger, he found her phone. It was the kind that required a fingerprint to unlock, which wasn't a problem. He looked up the number for Mirza's hotel and dialed.

The front desk clerk didn't bother trying to connect him with Mirza or Omen. She knew immediately that they weren't available. In fact, she claimed they were missing. She asked him to hold, saying that she'd transfer him to the police unit looking for them.

Finn hung up and buried his face in his hands.

He wasn't going to get himself out of the mess he was in, not in his condition. He needed to connect with Mirza. How he'd manage that, he didn't know.

Figuring he'd have better luck coming up with a solution if his pain was under control, he hobbled to the master bathroom and checked the medicine cabinet. There was nothing there.

Grumbling, he made his way over to the kitchen to see if he'd have better luck. On the way, resting on the dining table, he found a running laptop, happy pictures of the homeowner's family floating lazily on its screen.

THIRTY-FOUR

OMEN FOUND FOUR NEARBY units on Airbnb that were available starting that very day. Then she went through pictures of the properties, focusing exclusively on shots of their exteriors. She zeroed in on a building with a Kawasaki dealership next to it. When she pulled up directions to the motorcycle showroom, her phone told her it was only a couple of blocks away.

"Jackpot," she declared.

Mirza shook his head.

"What?"

"You're . . ." Mirza paused, trying to find the right adjective.

"Awesome?" she guessed.

"Wicked."

"You don't even know the half of it. Come on. It's this way."

Using back alleys, they made their way to their destination.

Once there, Omen went up to the main entrance of the apartment complex she'd found and studied the panel of doorbells, which had the unit number and name of each resident listed next to an intercom. Three were blank.

Omen chose one and hit the button for it.

For a while, nothing happened. Then the speaker crackled and a timid, sleepy voice said, "Min hadha?"

"Police," Omen declared, then winced when she realized that she hadn't spoken in Arabic.

A few seconds later, the door buzzed, and Mirza was able to push it open.

Omen moved on to the next unit that didn't list a resident next to its bell.

They waited. Nothing happened. She tried again and got the same result.

"Let's try thirty-four," Omen suggested.

The building itself wasn't very nice. The walls were grimy, the floors dirty, and the cramped elevator felt too unstable to risk. They decided to take the dimly lit stairwell, which looked like something out of a low-budget horror movie.

None of that was unexpected west of Gozel's center. Most of the beachfront was slated for reconstruction, but for now the old city persisted here.

On the way up, Mirza noted, "You forgot to bring a suitcase."

"What?"

"You were supposed to bring a large suitcase to the beach, remember?"

"Along with a rope and a gag. Yeah. I know. But my night took an unexpected turn," she informed him. "Do you really need it?"

"Not anymore."

"Why'd you even ask for one?"

"I was going to stuff Prince Waqif into it, carry him to my hotel room, and interrogate him there."

"Jesus Christ."

"What?" Mirza asked.

"Well, for one thing, there's nothing Samsonite makes that that guy would've fit into."

"Right. But I came up with the idea before I saw him."

Omen sighed. "Maybe from now on I should do the planning, Wile E. Coyote."

Outside the flat they'd targeted, Omen retrieved a bobby pin and a paper clip from her satchel and began to fashion lockpicks.

As she worked on getting the door open, Mirza said, "Finn was right."

"About what?"

"A few things. The fact that hiring you was a good idea, for one."

"Always is," she told him.

"He also said you have strengths I don't. And . . . and that I would like having you around."

She glanced over at him and smiled.

There was a click as the door surrendered to her.

Omen motioned for him to stay outside, as she crept in to make sure the apartment was clear. A few minutes later, she walked back, turned on the lights, and waved him in.

It wasn't a glamorous place, but it was significantly better than the rest of the complex. It had been remodeled and recently painted. Everything in it, from the banal decorations to the fake plants to the cheap furniture, looked like it had been bought at IKEA.

It probably had been. Mirza had been in Airbnbs everywhere from Addis to Zanzibar, and based on his experience, wherever that Swedish retailer went, monoculture infected interior spaces.

"We can rest here for a bit," Omen said. "And the shower looks nice."

Mirza blinked, not sure what that last bit of information had to do with anything. "Okay?"

"You should check it out. Maybe use it."

He remembered the homeless man he'd exchanged clothes with and how that person's body odor had nearly overwhelmed him. How he had gotten used to that stench enough to forget it existed, he'd never know.

"I'll clean up. But I don't have anything to wear."

Omen grinned. "You say that like it's a bad thing."

The bathroom was cramped but well appointed. It had a rainfall shower with excellent pressure. Unfortunately, it hadn't been designed for someone of Mirza's height, so he had to duck a little to use it. Still, he was just grateful for the opportunity to get clean.

There were two bottles of body wash. One had pictures of tropical fruit on it, the other was covered with various shapes he couldn't make sense of and was called Dark Temptation. He wasn't sure what other kind of temptation there was, but he went with it.

He turned the temperature of the water up and let it ease away, at least temporarily, the tension in his corded muscles. Gentle stinging reminded him that Maut's blade had broken the skin on his ear and cut him on the back of his left arm. He would have liked to clean the wounds out with some sort of antiseptic, but they'd clotted over already, so he let them be.

When he was done he dried his hair—a simpler affair now that it was cut relatively short—then wrapped a towel around his waist and stepped back out into the bedroom.

He found Omen sitting on the bed, browsing on her phone.

"Still no word on Finn," she advised as she got to her feet and slid past him, trailing her fingernails across his chest as she went by.

He looked over his shoulder and watched as the cloud of steam he'd left in his wake embraced her. She'd already begun to peel off her top before the door gently closed behind her.

Mirza stood still, trying not to think about how much he wanted her, how close she was, and how beautiful and how naked and how willing and how easy it would be to give in and indulge this desire he'd denied himself for a year, burying it within himself, where it roiled and sizzled and waited, like lava creeping ever closer to the surface of the earth.

After a moment, he exhaled and forced himself to march out of the single bedroom, giving Omen space and making space for himself.

Mirza focused on his breathing, chastising his heart for beating faster over nothing at all, like he was some lovestruck teenager. Life had never given him the luxury of being one before, and he was entirely too old for it now.

He went to the living room and turned on the news to drown out his own thoughts.

A young reporter was breathlessly reporting on Prince Waqif's abduction and death, struggling to keep the excitement out of his voice, trying to appear somber. This would probably be the biggest story he would ever get to break and he knew it.

According to state media, the Interior Minister had been kidnapped from a "private party" and then subsequently shot in the head. There was no mention of the Midnight League. They made it sound like the prince had been having tea in his garden with friends when some brute had snatched and executed him.

When they showed footage of the body, Mirza turned off the television.

"How does it feel to be the bad guy?"

He looked over and saw that Omen had opened the bedroom door.

Her red hair looked darker than usual because it was still damp. She was wearing the same off-shoulder white tee that she'd had on earlier, but without the sports bra underneath. She hadn't put her tights back on and was in simple black bikini-cut panties.

Mirza grunted without meaning to, then tore his dark eyes away from her.

"What?" Omen asked, all innocence as she walked over to sit next to him. She smelled like pears and roses, which he thought ought to not work as a scent, but it hit him like a hollow-point bullet shot by Eros wielding a .500 Magnum.

"You're killing me."

She pulled her bare legs up on the couch and wrapped her arms around them. "At least you're enjoying your death."

Mirza sighed.

"Come to bed," Omen said. "You don't have to sleep out here or on the floor."

They had shared hotel rooms on missions before. Their sleeping arrangements always involved a good bit of physical distance.

"I'm still married, Omen," he reminded her.

"Sure, but like barely, right?"

Mirza laughed.

"I'm serious. Aren't you just waiting for court approval?"

He nodded. In the UK, where he and Caroline had filed for divorce, the process took at least twenty-six weeks. Twenty-five had passed. In another seven days they could request a final order. "Yes, but I'm still bound by my vow."

"And Irfan Mirza always keeps his word."

"Even when it's very hard," he confirmed.

"I respect that. I mean, it's frustrating as fuck, but I do admire that about you. It's—"

"Noble?"

"Quaint. Why do you do it, though?"

Mirza raised his eyebrows. "What do you mean?"

"Why are you so obsessed with keeping promises? There has to be a reason."

Mirza rose to his feet and went to stand by the nearest window.

It wasn't the first time he'd been asked that question. He'd never answered before. He hadn't even been able to tell Caroline, so she had eventually concluded it was simply a result of him being bullheaded. Maybe, to some degree, it was.

But there was more to it. It was just a story he couldn't do justice. He didn't have the words. How do you explain what it feels like to be six, and to have just lost your mother, and to be sick with malaria, and hungry with no food in the house, and to see, in that state, your father walking to the door with a suitcase in his hand? Is it a fever dream or is it real? It must be a dream. But you call out and he turns and looks at you and you see he is crying and you ask him where he is going.

He is going to sell the suitcase, he tells you. He'll be back soon. He'll bring food and medicine. You want to believe him but something in your heart is not convinced, and you say, "Promise, Baba?" and he says, "Promise," and then he leaves and you never see him again.

So you read poetry for the rest of your life, hoping to find a way to express how you felt then, but you never do. You decide to always keep your word, though. It's the least you can do for that scared, shivering, starving little boy you once were. You make sure he's never like his father.

Finally, he turned back to look at Omen and said, "Ask me again some other time."

She sighed. "You're a difficult person to like. How did Caroline even put up with you?"

"She didn't."

"Well, okay, that's fair. But what I'm saying is . . . I don't mind waiting. I get that you're committed. It'd just be nice if . . . You know what? Never mind."

"No," he insisted. "Say what you want to say."

She ran a hand through her hair. "I know you've got this whole stoic, self-denial, 'I am man, look how strong,' ugly, sexy menace thing going on, but . . . It'd be good if you could let me in once in a while. Tell me how you feel maybe. That can't be too much to ask."

Mirza thought for a moment, then began to recite. "'My eyes meet hers and the world seems brighter. I know then that I'm thoroughly ensorcelled. But I am unable to move my lips to give voice to my heart. And she does not speak the language of my silences.'"

Omen stared at him.

Mirza cleared his throat, looked at the ground, and crossed his arms.

"There had to be a shorter way to say that."

He scowled. "I translated one of my favorite ghazals. It seemed . . . appropriate."

"It seemed appropriate to recite love poetry to a 'business acquaintance'?"

"I shouldn't have said anything."

"I'm kidding. It was . . . nice," she told him. "But maybe next time, instead of all that, you could use your own words."

"I'll see what I can do." Then Mirza frowned. "Hold on. Did you call me ugly?"

"When?"

"Seconds ago."

"Oh. Yeah. I guess I did. Obviously, I meant it in like a totally hot way."

He was about to tell her that made no sense, but the buzzing of her phone cut him off.

Omen took a peek at the caller ID. "It's Bey. We have to take this."
He nodded.

She put the call on speaker.

Bey's voice, electronically disguised as usual, came through sounding mechanical but also excited. "Omen. Is Irfan with you?"

"I am," he said.

"I called you like three times. Answer your phone, man."

"I buried it."

Bey took a second to process that, then asked, "What?"

"Don't worry about it. Tell me what you need."

"You have mail," Bey said. "Finn is trying to reach you."

THIRTY-FIVE

"IRFAN. DAMN, IT'S GOOD to speak to you, mate," Finn Thompson said, his voice heavy with relief and exhaustion. Around forty minutes had passed since he'd logged into his email account and sent out an SOS.

He'd written to Mirza first and given him a while to respond. When he hadn't heard back, he had reached out to Bey. Since the hacker had emailed him to facilitate their infiltration of the Kingdom's computer network, he had her address.

Bey had gotten back to him almost instantly and had said she'd get Mirza to call him on the cell he was "borrowing."

"Bey told me you were injured. How bad is it?"

It wasn't the warmest greeting in the world, but you couldn't exactly expect effervescence and cuddles when dealing with Mirza. "Not great. I've got two extra holes in me. Noncritical. Foot lacerations. Other stuff too, but those are the greatest hits."

"Blood loss?"

"Substantial," Finn said. "But a nun and her friends patched me up enough that I am not leaking much anymore. How're things on your end? Any progress on finding Ren?"

"Some. I'll brief you when I see you."

"That needs to be soon. I really need an extraction. Won't be able to get out of here on my own."

There was hesitation on the other end of the line. "Send me your location."

"Problem?"

"There's been some excitement. Nothing we can't handle."

"Well, get here as fast as you can. I'm afraid I've worn out my welcome with Jalila."

"Who?" Mirza asked.

Finn glanced over at the bound, now awake dark-haired woman, who was lying on the floor. She'd given up trying to struggle and shout. Instead, she was just glaring up at him, her gaze full of righteous venom. "Based on the name that I saw on some mail that was lying around, that's the nice lady at whose place I'm crashing."

"And what? You're not getting along with her?"

Finn considered the sock he'd stuffed into Jalila's mouth. "We're not exactly on speaking terms."

"Too bad. We could use a place to lie low for a few days."

"That's not going to be here. But I'll figure out somewhere we can go," Finn promised.

"Good. Call Omen's cell if your situation changes."

"Roger. And, Irfan?"

"What?"

Finn smiled as he said what he always did when signing off with Mirza. "Stay out of trouble."

Mirza snorted and hung up.

Finn tossed the phone aside and slapped his thighs a couple of times, as hard as he could. It was nearly three in the morning, and his body was begging for sleep. He was fighting it as best he could. It was a battle he was prepared to lose eventually, but not yet. He needed to stay awake and maintain control over his situation.

"Really am sorry about this," he told Jalila, whose eyes on him felt so acidic he was surprised his skin hadn't started dissolving. "It's not something I'd do if I had any choice. This is my first home invasion, actually. Considering that, I'd say I've done a cracking job."

The furrows on her brow actually deepened.

"Anyway, here's some good news. My brother is going to leg it over here, and I'll be out of your hair soon. This will be over before you know it."

Jalila tried to say something this time, but it came out hopelessly muffled because he had her gagged.

"I appreciate your understanding. Really." Finn struggled to his feet. "I'm going to get something to eat. Maybe I will make some coffee too. Just a nibble to help stay awake, you understand. Won't raid your fridge or anything."

This earned him more discontented mumbling.

"What's that? I shouldn't hold back?" Finn limped over to her, made sure she was still securely tied, and started to head toward the kitchen. "That is so nice. Your hospitality, I have to tell you, is out of this world. I feel like I have the run of the place."

THIRTY-SIX

"WHICH ONE DO YOU want to take?" Mirza asked Omen as they walked into the Airbnb's parking lot and surveyed the cars belonging to the building's other tenants.

She pointed to a nearby Land Cruiser. "How about that?"

He nodded and began studying a map of the area on her phone while she went to work on the tough, bulky SUV. Gozel's beachfront was relatively small and had only one freeway running to it. Getting on that wasn't an option. Law enforcement would have all the ramps blocked.

The nearly perfect grid of streets that had been imposed on the entire city, however, was tougher to blockade. There were too many possible exit routes for all of them to be properly covered.

Mirza looked up when he heard the Toyota's V-6 rumble to life. Omen was already in the driver's seat. He got in. It smelled like a relatively new car. He held her phone up so she could see the screen.

"It's like Pac-Man without dead ends," she observed. "The cops can't be everywhere. They'll be spread thin, with maybe two or three cars stationed at each intersection." Omen patted the Land Cruiser's steering wheel. "With this baby, we can just ram our way through one of their weak spots and keep going."

Mirza frowned.

"You don't like it? Sure seems like your kind of plan."

"The problem is that anywhere we hit them, they'll have units nearby to respond. Let's say we strike there." He pointed to a random junction. "Units at every adjacent checkpoint will swarm to us. We might get through, but the law will be right behind us."

Omen drummed her long fingers on the Toyota symbol in front of her, thinking, then nodded in agreement. "Yeah. We'd be like the Pied Piper."

"Who?"

"The Pied Piper. The guy with the magic flute from the fairy tale? The one all the rats follow out of town?"

Mirza had no idea what she was talking about, but pretended he got the reference just to keep the conversation on track. "Right."

"That sucks."

"It's not all bad," he said. "We can use this. If they're going to converge wherever there's trouble, then let's give them trouble. I'll create a diversion at a checkpoint. That'll pull all nearby officers to me and give you a clear shot out to Finn. If it doesn't work, you'll be in the same position you are now."

"You won't be, though. You'll be drawing all their attention and maybe even their fire."

Mirza shrugged.

Omen paused, trying to come up with a different plan. When she couldn't, she said, "I guess I've gotta steal you yet another car."

"Actually, I have something else in mind."

Mirza got on the Kawasaki Ninja H2 Omen had procured for him. Capable of speeds north of 180 miles per hour, it was essentially a street-legal rocket on two wheels. It'd give him a chance of evading capture by the Aldatani police, if he didn't make any mistakes riding it. A fall or collision at that kind of velocity would almost certainly be fatal.

He'd assured Omen, who was in the Land Cruiser parked next to him, that he had experience handling hyper-sport motorcycles. He had neglected to mention that he hadn't been on one in nearly a decade. Mirza was fairly sure it'd come back to him. There had to be a reason "like riding a bike" had become an idiom, after all.

He put on the reptile-green helmet he'd taken from the Kawasaki dealership. He'd also picked up an orange long-sleeve tee with the brand's River Mark symbol on the chest. It was a little tight and certainly not a color he would have chosen for himself, but there had been no other shirts around that fit his massive frame.

Mirza did have better luck finding a set of leathers there—a jacket and trousers, black with bloodred accents—along with matching gloves and boots.

When he'd first learned to ride, the principle "all the gear, all the time" had been drilled into him. The idea was simple: you always wore all the safety equipment you had. It was a directive meant to keep you alive.

Everything he had on was designed to maximize survivability. Not only did it use kangaroo leather, but also Kevlar armor, which was built in at the shoulders, elbows, knuckles, and knees.

Despite all that, whether he lived would come down to his own skill.

Well, that and the aim of the police officers who'd likely start shooting at him before the night was done.

He looked over at Omen and saw that she was chewing on her lower lip. He waved to get her attention, and when she looked over at him, gave her a thumbs-up. It was time to do or die.

THIRTY-SEVEN

OMEN WATCHED MIRZA TURN his attention to the road. Taking a deep breath, she pressed the ignition button on the Land Cruiser, bringing it to life, and waited.

They were near a blockaded intersection. Two police cars were parked nose to nose around a mile and a half away, making it obvious that no one was permitted to leave. Though all roads leading away from the beach had been closed off this way, the larger ones did have some traffic on them, even at the late hour. All of it was being rerouted toward the freeways, where she and Mirza had seen papers being checked and trunks searched before people were allowed to proceed.

Morning rush hour in this part of Gozel, which would begin in three hours or so, was going to be a bitch.

They had chosen this street for their operation because it seemed to be sleepier than most. That reduced the chance they'd endanger any "civilians," ordinary folk with delightfully ordinary lives.

Beside her, Mirza turned the Ninja's throttle and it surged forward, its exhaust snarling, spitting, popping. He picked up speed, gaining on the barricade fast. She saw an officer waving frantically for him to stop. He didn't.

Instead, Mirza pulled out his CZ 75 pistol with his left hand—his right had to remain on the throttle—and fired two bullets in the direction of the officer. He missed, which was what they'd planned. There was no reason to start executing people in uniform who were just trying to do their jobs.

The Kawasaki jumped onto a curb, going around the back of the police car to the right, before Mirza leaned into a hard left that brought his tires back into contact with the street.

Sirens came on. One of the officers radioed for backup while scrambling to give chase.

Mirza was past the barrier and gaining speed.

Omen lost sight of him.

She closed her eyes and, for the first time in forever, said a quick prayer, though she wasn't sure to whom or what. But if there was some divine being out there, watching, listening, and helping, maybe her hopeful gesture would count for something.

Then she shook her head.

Mirza was rubbing off on her, and not in a fun way.

She watched as patrol cars from all directions flowed into the intersection Mirza had passed, lights flashing, signaling that they were on the hunt.

Omen kept the Land Cruiser exactly where it was, waiting for the police response to end. When the coast seemed clear, she pulled out and drove over the same street Irfan had just gone down. It seemed like there was no one left to try to stop her.

THIRTY-EIGHT

MIRZA RACED THROUGH THE streets of the capital, leaning forward on the Ninja and staying low, keeping his head behind the Kawasaki's windscreen. The speedometer was at 160 miles per hour and climbing.

The desert wind was an adversary at these speeds. The faster he went, the harder it pushed back at him. It whipped around him furiously, trying to drown out all other sounds, but it didn't succeed. The Kawasaki growling under him was too loud, as was the legion of sirens behind him.

The cops chasing Mirza were in upgraded Dodge Chargers. He counted six of them. They seemed plenty fast enough to match the Ninja's pace. He risked a quick look over his shoulder. They were doing better than just keeping up. They were closing.

The dealership Omen had helped him break into stocked only street-legal versions of the Ninja. The track variant of the bike would've given him a lot more top-end speed. The roads were perfect for it, too: smooth, new, flat, and—because of the hour and the police cordon—empty.

But he had to make do with the model he had. At least this wasn't Dubai and law enforcement didn't have a fleet of Lamborghinis and Bugattis to send after him.

One of the Chargers got close, nipping at his back wheel.

Mirza pulled the Ninja to the left and slowed enough to bring his back tire in line with the cop's front one. Then he grabbed his pistol and took aim at the officer driving.

The officer's eyes went wide. He ducked and hit his brakes.

Mirza changed his target, aimed at the wheel closest to him, and fired.

The cop lost control, skidded, clipped a hydrant, flipped, spinning as water exploded up from the ground, and crashed into the storefront display of an antique shop.

Mirza returned to his riding stance as metal shrieked and glass shattered behind him.

Getting lower and shifting his weight as far forward as possible, he urged the bike to push harder.

170. 175. 180.

The farther he got from the beach, the taller the buildings around him became. He kept heading toward downtown.

A spotlight hit from above. Mirza didn't have to look up to know they'd rerouted a chopper to trail him. He'd known they had air support. It was only a matter of time before they called it in. That was why he was going into the concrete jungle. The gleaming silver skyscrapers there would give him cover.

184 mph.

The Ninja screamed at him, the tachometer needle in the red, vibrating in place with nowhere to go.

Up ahead, he saw more flashing lights. Three more cop cars were waiting for him.

Surprising, given how many had been dispatched to the beachfront. Some portion of the force must have been held back, and these men were part of that reserve.

Two officers with ballistic shields hurried forward, carrying something between them. He recognized that it was a stinger—a strip of spikes to put down on the road, designed to puncture the tires of an escaping suspect.

Mirza's options were limited.

Hitting the strong front brakes hard at this speed would send him flying over the handlebars. The wheels of the Ninja could take a lot of force, but they couldn't take it suddenly, not without consequences. He wouldn't survive those.

Riding a motorbike puts you on intimate terms with Newton real quick. It gives you an instinctive feel for the physics involved, and Mirza's instincts, rusty as they were, told him that trying to stop would be a mistake.

He kept going but eased up on the throttle, buying his mind a little more time to find a way out.

It took him a second to solve the puzzle.

He started to shoot at the officers laying the trap for him, forcing them to stop.

They dropped the spike strip and ducked behind their shields.

One of them stood straight and tall and returned fire. The other, however, crouched down, his shield tilting over his body and nearly hitting the hood of the car behind him. It was poor form. It was also, to Mirza's eyes, a ramp.

Shifting his body weight, he steered the bike straight at the cowering man.

The officer screamed in alarm first, and then in utter anguish as six hundred pounds of Kawasaki's machine and two hundred and fifty pounds of Mirza's muscle slammed into the shield he was holding at high velocity, pulverizing the bones in his arm and shoulder, splintering them as he was pinned against his own car.

Mirza didn't know if the officer survived.

There was no time to care.

He was flying, the Ninja arcing up through the air as the remaining policeman shot at it. For a second, Mirza felt weightless. Then gravity yanked the motorcycle back toward earth. The Kawasaki's back wheel landed hard on the trunk of one of the patrol cars before hitting pavement, and Mirza was on solid ground again.

The Chargers chasing him screeched to a halt, stymied by their own tactics and the half-deployed tire shredder. They'd have to go around the block and then try to catch up with Mirza. It was an opportunity to escape.

Except the light from their helicopter was still on him, tracking him as he tore through the chaotic night.

THIRTY-NINE

"WHAT PRECISELY IS HAPPENING to our friend here?" Atlas Boss asked the four prisoners kneeling before him, his tone professorial. Anyone who was just listening, who could not see Mahmud dangling from the ceiling of the Greeting Room suspended by his legs, would have easily believed the Dandarabilla leader was giving an academic lecture of sorts. "Anyone?"

None of Atlas's "students" replied. The fact that they were bound and gagged made this less than surprising.

His pale-gray gaze came to rest on Renata, who was the only high-value captive in the bunch. "Ms. Bardales? Do you have any idea what your fiancé is going through?"

She glowered at him.

"No? Allow me to educate you. When a person is placed in this inverted position, gravity pulls blood down into their head. As you can see, Mahmud's face is now a beautiful shade of red as a result."

Atlas glanced at the entrance to the chamber, then at his watch. "I do hope for his sake that Chike brings his father along relatively soon. Poor Mahmud is already in a good deal of distress. The intraocular pressure he is experiencing will continue to get worse. He'll become dizzier and more disoriented. He might start having trouble breathing. Who knows, he could even have a stroke."

Ren's protest was unintelligible and useless.

"Don't worry. Chike is usually very punctual. It is unlikely that your beau will die tonight, however much he might wish it. Ah. There she is with Aldatan's great revolutionary. How are you, Habib?"

Mahmud's father, disheveled after being dragged out of bed in the middle of the night, froze when he saw the state of his son. When he noticed Renata and the other prisoners, he looked confused. "What is this? Cut my son down this instant."

Atlas gestured to the guards standing by, and one of them hurried forward to hand him a shotgun. Another tossed a vicious-looking whip at Habib's feet. "Pick that up, Your Highness."

"What are you doing?" Habib demanded.

"I need you and your son to confess to being traitors to Aldatan, to being foreign agents. Now, I have spent quite a bit of time convincing Mahmud here to cooperate, as I'm sure Mahmi's walls have told you, but he absolutely refuses. So, I am forced to try this new brand of . . . argumentation."

"And this is the best you could come up with? Hanging him upside down?"

"Oh. No, there is more. But I won't be hurting your son tonight. Not anymore. You will. Like I said, pick up that whip. Use it on Mahmud."

Habib snorted. "You are insane."

Atlas shook his head. "That is not a nice thing to say. I thought you were a liberal, all for freedom, democracy, and the American—I'm sorry, the Aldatani way." He turned his attention to the prisoner kneeling closest to him. She was a woman of around thirty, with curly dark hair. "You'll offend Zara with your ableist language. She's a liberal too. Have you heard of her?"

"No."

"Really? That is quite sad. Here she is in prison, thinking she has earned the praise and admiration of people like you. But you don't even know who she is." Atlas reached down and stroked Zara's cheek. The woman flinched under his caress. "Should I tell you about her?"

"Let my father go," Mahmud croaked, the strain in his voice evident. "Please."

Ignoring the plea, Atlas walked behind Zara and placed the barrel of his shotgun at the base of her skull, aiming so that if he shot her, the splatter would hit Habib. "Zara is a long-term guest. No one talks about her now, but for a while, she was mentioned in many foreign newspapers. She was arrested for protesting against women being forced to wear the niqab."

"The king overturned that policy," Habib pointed out.

"You are right. He did. But defiance cannot be forgiven, so Zara is still here, a victor who has lost everything. Well, except for her life. She'll lose that shortly, unless you pick up that whip and hit your son with it."

"You're sick. This is a bluff. You won't just—"

Atlas pulled the trigger.

There was a deafening sound and Zara's head exploded as a 12-gauge round ripped through her. Her blood and brains sprayed all over Habib, who asked Atlas to stop but too late. He stood there, eyes wide, mouth open, covered in gore, the very picture of shock.

Renata, who was on her knees a few feet away, let out a muffled scream.

Atlas stepped over to the next prisoner, who was whimpering. A pool of liquid was gathering between his legs. He'd soiled himself. Making a face, Atlas leveled the shotgun at the man's head. "This is Nasir. Say hello to Prince Habib, Nasir, your would-be liberator from the crown."

The man complied, though the gag in his mouth made him incomprehensible.

Atlas patted the prisoner's head. "Good dog. Now, let's see if Habib will pick up that whip and teach his son a lesson for being such a stubborn boy."

"Please," Habib begged. "Do not do this. The king would never go this far. If he knew what you were—"

"Here, I am your king," Atlas said softly.

Then he pulled the trigger again.

Nasir, nearly headless, toppled over to the ground.

"Sorry. I forgot to introduce him, didn't I? Nasir was arrested when he was in college. He was trying to create a student group to advocate for the abolishment of the monarchy in Aldatan. He had the same cause as you, though obviously his profile was much lower. He did get some coverage in a German newspaper through one of his friends who lives in Dresden. He was briefly a hero. But he's ended up looking like a smashed watermelon, and no one will ever know or even think to ask what became of him."

Atlas moved on to the next prisoner.

"Stop!" Mahmud yelled.

"Your father can stop me," Atlas told him. "If he would just pick up the whip."

"Do it, Baba," Mahmud called. "Do it."

"Look at that," Dandarabilla's leader said. "True nobility. Come on. Obey your child."

With trembling hands, Habib reached down and picked up the weapon he'd been given. Then, walking over, he struck Mahmud with it as gently as he could.

Atlas shot the next prisoner.

Renata, who was next in line, closed her eyes.

"No. Why? I did what you—"

"I could tell your heart wasn't in it. Do it properly or don't do it at all. What was it your Prophet said? Everything a believer does, he should do it in the most excellent way possible. Or maybe it was the most beautiful way possible. Something like that. Now. Do as the Messenger of God commanded."

"I can't," Habib whispered. "Don't make me."

"Then confess and tell the world that you were wrong about Nimir bin Daleel. Agree to kiss his ring. Bend the knee, as people say these days, and all your troubles will vanish."

"Never," Mahmud called out.

Atlas sighed and turned his weapon on Renata. "Very well. Now this one—"

"Baba. Not Ren. Baba, save Renata. You must. Please. He'll kill her like he killed the others. She's family, Baba. Do what you're told."

Habib swallowed, tightened his grip on the whip, and struck his son hard across the back.

Mahmud cried out.

Atlas laughed.

"Did you have to do this in the middle of the night?" Chike Okoro asked Atlas as he walked out of the Greeting Room. He nodded, then handed her the silver Mossberg 590A1 he was carrying. She immediately engaged the safety at the top of the shotgun, which was something Atlas never did.

He didn't care about the rules of weapon handling, but she couldn't help herself. Proper procedures had been ingrained in her during her military service. Atlas's opinion that the safety mechanism ruined the "romance" of firearms, whatever that meant, couldn't change what had become an unbreakable habit.

This "romance" was the reason why he had a revolver in his office—a Taurus Raging Bull—instead of a pistol. He had gotten her one, too, and insisted that she use it. It was a "purer" experience, apparently.

Chike had learned long ago not to argue with Atlas when he started talking about beauty or art or any other such nonsense. It was easier to just nod along and do what he said.

"Of course. The late hour added to the drama of the experience. You, however, missed your cue."

"What?"

"You were late bringing Habib to me," he said. "Explain."

"Sorry. I got distracted. The Leopards were talking about a security event in Gozel. I stopped to listen in."

Atlas frowned. "What happened?"

"Someone kidnapped and killed the Interior Minister."

"Waqif's dead?"

Chike blinked. "You knew him?"

"Only in passing. He likes . . . liked seeing his wife with other men, and she was intrigued by my hairlessness."

"I don't know what to say to that," she admitted after a beat.

"I suppose it doesn't matter, so long as our supply convoy is not affected."

"It shouldn't be."

"Good," he declared. "If there's nothing else, I am going to get some sleep. You're not wrong. It is an ungodly hour."

"Actually," Chike said, falling in step next to him as he started to walk away, "I was wondering what your plan was now."

He waited for her to elaborate.

"Torture hasn't worked on Mahmud or Habib. Maybe you should talk to the king about trying it with someone else? A religious leader like Imam Ehsan might be as good a choice. It'd get attention."

"Muslims do seem to get hard for famous scholars," Atlas conceded. "But I'm not sure if I would get the prize I want if I cannot give Nimir exactly what he has demanded."

"What prize?" Chike asked.

"You will see when I prevail, which I will. No. I am not yet ready to move on from our little trinity yet. Tell me, have you ever kept an Arabian horse?"

"No, of course not."

"They can be willful and difficult to control," he told her. "But if you know what you are doing, eventually you do break them. It's very satisfying when that happens, and I do so enjoy being satisfied. Don't you?"

FORTY

REN TRIED TO GET her hands to stop shaking as the Leopard, Adam Aziz, escorted her back to the South Tower. Atlas Boss had come to get her himself, claiming that he was going to give her something she wanted: a chance to see Mahmud. Though she hadn't believed him at first, it had turned out to be true.

Like all the devil's gifts, however, this one was also laced with poison. Yes, she had seen her fiancé, but she had also been forced to watch Habib rip the skin off of Mahmud's body with a whip. If this was punishment for her attack on him, it was exquisitely planned.

"That was . . . unkind," Adam said.

Ren scoffed and met the man's eyes. Dina was right. They were indeed sad. "It was more than that, don't you think?"

He shrugged. "The princes don't have to suffer. They're choosing to do so."

"Really?"

"None of this is necessary," Adam told her, his tone almost mournful. "All these prisoners, they're fools, really. They make their own lives miserable. No one forces them to speak out against the king. Life is good for—"

"People like you?" Renata guessed.

"Most people in Aldatan are like me. They know that if they follow the law and do what they are told, it's unlikely anything bad will happen to them." He paused to see what she would say. When she didn't speak, he added, "The two princes, the military men, and the rebels who follow them, all they talk about is freedom. Freedom of speech, of expression, of religion, of self-determination . . . whatever that means. It's all garbage."

"You don't want to be free?"

"I want to be happy," the Leopard declared. "And, actually, I am free, freer at least than Mahmud and Habib. I have my wife, my home, my car. What do they have? Jail cells."

"I don't understand you," Renata admitted. "Dina says you are good to her, to all the captives, that you don't take advantage of them. If you're okay with Nimir's evil and Atlas's, then why not be like them yourself?"

"As a Muslim, I am responsible for my own actions, not theirs. I don't have to believe what my rulers believe. I don't have to support it. If I think they're doing something wrong and I feel bad about it, that is jihad enough."

"You work for them."

"I work to feed myself and my family. I joined the army because I needed money, and then I was assigned here. I killed people when I was in uniform because I was told to do so, and I kill people now when I'm asked. I was a hero for obeying before. How can I be a villain for obeying now?"

Ren just shook her head.

Close to the tower, Adam slowed a little. "Should I come for you tonight?"

"No."

"I'm not sure Dina explained. I don't . . . I'm not like some of the other guards or Dandarabilla men or Leopards. I won't hurt you. I'm a decent person. This is just a lonely place, you know? I miss having company. When I take girls with me, it's just to talk. That's all. It keeps them safe."

"I don't need your protection."

Adam shrugged again. "Maybe not now, but a day will soon come when Atlas will let his men loose on you. You will wish then that you had made more friends."

FORTY-ONE

OMEN DROVE CAREFULLY THROUGH Gozel, following the speed limit exactly, making sure to obey every single rule of the road.

She wanted to speed up, to go faster, but a police cruiser had spotted her six blocks from the intersection Mirza had cleared. Five blocks and several turns later, it was still behind her.

Her green eyes darted to the sky briefly, keeping track of the police helicopter closest to downtown. It was likely the one that had sight of Mirza. As long as she knew where it was, she had some idea where he was.

But Omen had her own problems just then.

She checked her rearview mirror. The cruiser was still tailing her. Why hadn't the cop pulled her over yet? She rubbed her forehead with one hand, trying to make sense of the officer's behavior, when blue and red lights started flashing behind her.

"Fuck," she grumbled.

She'd figured this would happen.

Police all over the world were similar though not the same. Dealing with the authorities in Amsterdam, for example, was a lot better than having to deal with them in Karachi. Personal experience had taught her that much.

They had things in common, though, which was to be expected. After all, they were a self-selected group. They chose to go into this line of work. They were people of action. Once you caught their attention, once they started hounding you, they would eventually confront you. It was in their nature.

Omen slowed and guided the Land Cruiser to the side of the road without hesitation.

Because she'd anticipated what the officer would do, she'd had the time to think about how she'd react. With her left hand, she lowered her driver's-side window. With her right, keeping her movements as subtle as possible, she pulled her satchel toward her. The small revolver Mirza had been given at the Midnight League was in there.

Omen knew it only had one bullet in it. She'd have to make it count if it came to that.

She watched the policeman approach in her wing mirror. Young, skinny, and bearded, he walked with the easy swagger of someone used to having power over other people.

Omen gave him her most winning smile as he came up beside her door and leaned in to speak to her. His breath smelled of sharp peppermint, like he'd only just finished with a stick of gum. A tag on his uniform told her he was Lieutenant Bilal Hadi.

"As-salamu alaykum," she said.

His eyes traveled with frank, bold interest from her face to her one bare shoulder and down to what he could see of the rest of her body. He nodded, as if in approval of her appearance, then asked in heavily accented English, "That's a greeting for Muslims. You don't look like one of us."

A story Mirza had told her about how his favorite poet, Ghalib, had once handled a similar inquiry popped into her mind for some reason. She decided to use it. It was charming, and charm had gotten her out of more than one traffic stop in her life.

"I'm half Muslim," she told him.

"What do you mean?"

"I drink wine," she said, "but I don't eat pork."

Hadi stared at her for a moment. Then he laughed.

With concern in her voice, she posed a question of her own. "So what's going on?"

He didn't answer. "What's your name?"

"Grace."

"Show me your papers, Grace."

"Papers?" Omen repeated like she didn't understand. It was the standard "license and registration" line you got in America, of course. She just didn't want to comply. She couldn't. Biting her lip, she asked, "I'm sorry. Did I do something wrong?"

"You are not supposed to be here. This is a restricted area."

"A restricted area?" She injected a bit of alarm and indignation into her tone. "What do you mean? It's just a regular street. I didn't see—"

He held up a hand, gesturing for her to remain calm. "It is not your fault. We had officers posted here to warn people away, to direct them to our checkpoints by the freeways, but they left to chase after a killer."

"A killer? Oh my God. That's crazy. Is there a manhunt? Is that what the helicopters are about?"

"Yes, we—"

"You know," Omen babbled on purpose, "when I told my family and friends I was going to visit the Middle East, they all said it wasn't safe. I looked at the stats and told them they were wrong. And I told them that I couldn't really be a traveling YouTuber if I was afraid to go anywhere, you know? But there's a manhunt on my first day here? My folks are going to flip."

"You're on YouTube?"

She blinked, surprised by how impressed he sounded, like it wasn't something just anyone with a camera could do. She hadn't told him that she was successful on the platform, but he seemed to have assumed that. "Yeah."

"What is your channel called?"

"Oh," Omen stalled trying to think of a name. "You wouldn't know it. I don't have that many subscribers yet."

He shrugged. "No problem. Now you will have one more. What is it?"

"A Graceful World."

"That's very clever. I'll remember it."

It was awful, actually, but she had noticed long ago that men were quick to give her compliments even if she hadn't done anything to deserve them. It was like they were under the impression that flattering a woman would make her believe they were interesting or something. It usually made her cringe. She was, however, ecstatic that it was happening now.

If Lieutenant Hadi persisted in asking her for documentation, bad things would happen. When she failed to produce it, would he try to arrest her? Probably. There was no way she was going with him, though. She'd have to either take the officer down or put him down.

She could fight, but she wasn't Mirza. It wasn't clear to her that she'd win a physical altercation with Hadi. He seemed fit. If he turned out to be anything more than competent in hand-to-hand combat, she'd need the advantage of a weapon, and the only weapon she had was a lethal one.

Trying not to let on how dry her mouth felt, Omen forced herself to sound sweeter and flirtier than she ever did. "Do you want to be in a video?"

"Me?"

"Sure. I can record you giving me a warning and letting me go." She adjusted the strap of her sports bra unnecessarily. "That is what you are going to do, right? I mean, you said yourself it's not my fault I'm here. Still, it's an opportunity. I'll get to show everyone this cool policeman I met—"

Hadi shook his head. "That is not a good idea."

"Aww," Omen pouted, and hated herself for it a little. It was, she tried to remember, for a good cause. She was either saving this guy's life or her own, not to mention Finn's, who had sounded like he was in bad shape. "Are you sure?"

"It would not be appropriate," he said. "Not tonight. A serious crime took place. It would not look good if—"

"Of course. That makes perfect sense. I'm so sorry. I was being silly. It's just . . . well, I've got YouTube on my brain is all."

He gave her a tolerant smile. "It's fine. But I agree with you. You did not do anything wrong."

"Then why were you following me? Why'd you pull me over?"

"I was running your plates and our system is a little slow tonight." He paused, gave her an unreadable look, then corrected his prior statement. "Well, they're not your plates, are they?"

She bit back a curse. She tried to think of possible stories she could spin. If she wasn't going to be able to come up with something convincing, it'd be best to go on the offensive now, first, before he was expecting it.

That's what Mirza would want her to do, but just because they were working together didn't mean she had to adopt his methods.

"This car," Hadi went on, "is registered to a man called Rayan Abbas. How do you know him?"

"I . . . uh . . . I mean, I don't know him, really, he's . . . my Airbnb host."

"Your Airbnb host?" the lieutenant repeated slowly, his brow furrowed. "And he just gave you his car to drive?"

"No. Of course not. It's . . . it's a long story, Officer."

He crossed his arms against his chest, as if to say he had all the time in the world.

"The thing is," Omen explained, "I didn't come here just to see Gozel.

I mean, it's a beautiful city, don't get me wrong, but I want to see other parts of the country, too. I want to go out into the desert. There are already plenty of YouTubers who've shown the capital. The world doesn't need my take on it."

"What does this have to do with—"

"I booked Rayan's Airbnb because he promised to be my guide. He said he'd show me around Aldatan." She dropped her gaze and tried to make herself blush, then remembered that wasn't something she could do on command. "Between you and me, it turns out he wanted to show me more than just Aldatan, if you know what I mean."

This earned her a small, knowing smirk from the policeman.

"Rayan didn't like it when I made it clear nothing was going to happen between us. And he totally flaked on me. Can you believe that? Something about how work stuff has come up and he can't find the time. I threatened to give him a bad review, but he said that I could still go out to the desert myself, that it isn't dangerous. As a peace offering, he let me take one of his cars. So . . . well, here I am. All this was before I knew people were out here getting murdered, obviously."

"Where are you going?" Hadi asked.

"Sorry?"

"It's late at night. Where are you going right now?"

Omen only knew of one site in Aldatan that someone might go to see that was within driving distance of Gozel. "It's early in the morning, actually, and I'm headed to Mahmi Castle."

She wasn't sure what Hadi had been expecting her to say, but he clearly hadn't been ready for that. "Why?"

"I skimmed a book about Aldatan's history—you know, to add value to my content—and saw it mentioned. It sounds cool. I figured I can get there early and be back before—"

Hadi shook his head. "You're wasting your time, Grace."

"Does it suck? Have you been?"

"I meant to but never did. Now I can't. Mahmi is closed to the public. The government has made it illegal to go there."

Omen gave him an expression of what she hoped was utter astonishment. "Really?"

"I read in the paper that its walls are collapsing and it isn't safe, so the Ministry of Culture has sealed it off until they can restore it. You are chasing . . . what is the phrase? A wild cock."

The smugness with which he said the last bit told her that he knew exactly what the idiom was and that he thought he was incredibly clever for having changed it.

She sighed. Men will be boys.

"Goose. And . . . well, that sucks. My day's ruined, I guess."

"There are other fortresses built at around the same period that you could visit. Nayhan or Al Batinah are a bit bigger and a little closer. People also go to Arman Keep and the citadel of—"

"You guys built a lot of palaces, huh?"

"We have had many kings and they've all had their strongholds. I think there are eight or nine in the country. Mahmi is one of the larger ones, but losing it temporarily is not a big issue."

"All right, then," Omen said. "Thanks. I'll check them out."

"What about your living situation? Will you go back to this same Airbnb with this Rayan Abbas person?"

She nodded.

Hadi clicked his tongue. "What if he tries something inappropriate with you? It doesn't sound like he has good intentions."

"Oh, he seems harmless. I'm sure he wouldn't—"

"He sounds like a creep. He lured you here just to take advantage of you. Did he know what you looked like before you booked with him?"

"Well, yeah. I mean, I told him about my channel, so—"

"That explains it. I do not think you should trust this person. You white women, you are not careful enough. These short-term rentals are not always safe for a lady by herself. One of my friends caught a case where it went badly. Did you know that Airbnb has a crisis management team to deal with assaults that happen to people using their service?"

Omen didn't have to pretend surprise this time. "You're kidding."

"I am not. It used to be run by a man who was once high up at the CIA. They hire serious people and pay around fifty million dollars every year to victims to make them go away."

"Jeez. I had no idea."

"So, I would feel better," he went on, "if you gave me your phone number. That way I can call and check on you. Just to make sure you are safe."

Brightly, she said, "That would be awesome. Thank you so much, Officer."

"My friends call me Bilal."

She smiled. "Mine call me Gracie."

"Stay away from downtown," he advised her, after she'd given him her digits. "You do not want to be out there tonight."

Omen looked back over her shoulder to see if she could spot the helicopter that was tracking Mirza. "Yeah," she whispered, "it doesn't look good."

FORTY-TWO

MIRZA COULDN'T SHAKE THE spotlight.

The helicopter overhead kept it shining on him as he blazed through Gozel, pushing the Ninja to go as fast as it could. The fact that he'd managed to evade the police's ground forces would mean nothing if he couldn't elude the bird tailing him.

He was in the financial hub, among the highest skyscrapers in the city, where banks and insurance companies and multinational conglomerates had their offices. If he kept going, he'd tear through the heart of downtown into the suburbs and then the desert, where he'd find nowhere to hide.

If he was going to escape, he had to do it now.

Without warning, Mirza hit the bike's front brakes as hard as he dared. The back wheel of the Ninja lifted off the road, like a horse bucking, and Mirza felt like he was going to be thrown off.

With his heart beating hard, he eased off a bit and let the Kawasaki roll on one wheel. It stabilized and then slammed back onto the ground. Mirza killed his headlight and looked up. The helicopter had overshot him. It was spinning around, turning back in his direction.

He rotated the throttle again and took the bike left up the street closest to him, before pulling another left and then a hard right.

The police searchlight was moving around rapidly now, trying to relocate him and hitting the many massive buildings Aldatani royalty loved so much. They didn't have a line of sight on him.

Mirza guided the Ninja into a narrow alley, waited, then rushed across the street, finding the next gap between tall structures he could hide in.

Darting from one shadow to another using this method, he put some distance between himself and the police chopper still circling above.

When he was half a mile away, he looked back.

Two more birds were in the air now, but none of them had a fix on his location. A cacophony of waiting sirens rang through the night. The ground forces he'd evaded had rejoined the fray, though he couldn't see them, just like they couldn't see him.

As he yanked off his helmet, he noticed his hands were trembling a little. He regarded them curiously, like they weren't a part of him, holding one up to stare at the tiny, involuntary movements it was making.

That had been a close call, not just because of the police, but because of how he'd almost lost control of his bike. That could have killed him. He hadn't been in the saddle for a while and he hadn't tried to pull off an endo—or front wheelie—in even longer. The Ninja was not the kind of bike you wanted to try that on, not at that speed, especially not if you were a rider who has rust on him.

Mirza felt about as calm as could be expected under the circumstances. The conscious parts of him, his mind and soul, knew he had survived worse. It was his body, which had for large parts of his forty years been an indomitable lethal weapon, that was telling him it'd had enough.

He shook his head. He'd think about this later. Just then he had more pressing concerns. He made a fist, then released it, before reaching for Omen's phone. She had insisted that he keep it with him in case he needed it. He entered her passcode, which she claimed he could remember because it spelled out the most useful word in the English language—3825—and dialed out to Finn.

"Irfan. Are you here?"

"Omen will be there soon. She'll be worried about me. Let her know I'm alive."

Finn chuckled.

"What?" Mirza asked.

"It's just that other men call people they love to let them know they'll be late from work, not that they survived it."

"I've never said I loved you."

Finn started to laugh, then groaned, "Damn. That hurts."

Mirza smiled. "I have to go."

"All right. Stay out of trouble, Irfan."

The mercenary pushed his hair back in anticipation of putting on his helmet once again and hitting the road. "You know what's scary? That actually sounds like something I might want to do."

FORTY-THREE

TWO DAYS LATER, WHEN Atlas strode into his office, Chike was waiting for him. She had placed some kind of contraption on his desk. At first glance it looked like a large, partially squashed electronic insect. Upon closer examination, he noticed a few intact rotors, designed to allow the machine to hover and fly. There was a camera attached to it as well. A damaged surveillance drone.

"One of our snipers brought it down," Chike said, "and it crashed into the wall. It was circling the castle."

Atlas's eyes narrowed as he examined the machine. It seemed almost benign lying there, no more dangerous than a child's toy, and yet he knew it represented a potentially serious security breach.

Massaging his temples with the index and ring fingers of both his hands, he asked, "Who was operating it?"

"The range on that model is around three miles. So—"

"You don't know," Atlas guessed.

Chike looked down. "That's right, sir."

He stared at the drone until his vision grew unfocused. Out of the corner of his eye, he saw Chike step back in anticipation of an outburst. Atlas tried to calm himself. He was aware that he'd been more irritable than usual over the last few days. He was unused to having his will thwarted, but Mahmud, Habib, and Renata had still not broken for him, despite continued torture.

It was a matter of time. Under enough sustained pressure, they would eventually crumble. It was inevitable, and it wasn't like King Nimir had imposed a deadline by which their confessions had to be obtained.

Gritting his teeth, he tried to draw upon what meager patience he had left. He had named himself Atlas Boss to let the world know he would not be resisted or defied. He would have his way, especially in places where he ruled. Being denied the submission he required, especially with a prize like Aldatan's Yemen operations within his grasp, was aggravating in the extreme.

"Sir?" Chike prompted tentatively.

Returning his attention to the problem at hand, Atlas took a deep breath. "What do we know about this device?"

"It's new and expensive—"

"How expensive?" Atlas asked.

"Around eight hundred dollars. It's not specialized. You can buy it anywhere. It has Wi-Fi and data capabilities, but obviously there is no signal out here. It didn't manage to send any pictures out."

The purpose for which Mahmi was being used, therefore, was still undiscovered. That was fortunate. "The question remains," he noted, "why it was out here in the first place."

"I think it was a tourist," Chike said.

"Why?"

"The name on the SD card. Whoever formatted it called it 'Gracie's Travel Vlog.'"

Atlas put his hands on his hips. "Are you telling me that Aldatan's premier black site prison was nearly compromised by a damn YouTuber?"

"No," Chike assured him. "I am telling you it was not compromised.

We don't have anything to worry about. Well, except for the fact that this Gracie might come looking for her equipment."

"You know what to do if she shows up."

"Of course, sir."

"Remind the men. No one who approaches Mahmi should be allowed to live."

FORTY-FOUR

MIRZA NODDED TO SISTER Elira when he walked into her "clinic" that morning to check on Finn. The Order of Perpetual Mercy had refused to take Finn in when he'd shown up at their door again—this time with his friends—for want of a place to go. Their presence posed too great a risk to the slum and its inhabitants. The nuns did not want to put their charges in further danger.

But they also couldn't make themselves turn someone in Finn's condition away, so after some deliberation, their Mother Superior had proposed a solution. They'd assign Elira to care for the Irishman and treat him at one of their other facilities.

That was how Mirza found himself in what was essentially a ghost town two hours southeast of Gozel.

In the eighty years since the copper mine that supported the settlement had been depleted, the residents had trickled away, searching for better lives elsewhere.

There were still people around, but none of them were local. They were refugees from Yemen, Sudan, and Ethiopia who came here to rest for a while before continuing on their journey.

They recognized Elira and were happy to see her. Finn explained that in addition to providing aid to the refugees, the Aldatani government suspected the order was facilitating their journey across the border. Based on the conversations Mirza overheard, it seemed like the Al-datanis were right.

Finn was being kept in a modest, largely intact brick structure. It had been cleaned and already had some medical supplies in it. A sporadic stream of injured or sick people kept Elira occupied when she wasn't tending to Finn.

The nun bowed her head to acknowledge Mirza and seemed to at least consider smiling before deciding against it. "I was just thinking about you."

Mirza raised his eyebrows.

Elira walked over to a bag she had brought with her and pulled a gun out from it. She held the weapon gingerly, far away from her, as if it were something disgusting. "You are leaving tonight, yes? Take this with you. I don't want it here."

Mirza took the piece. It was a SIG P226-XFIVE with a stainless-steel finish, a green fiber-optic front beam, and wood grips.

"This belongs to Finn, doesn't it? He buys German and he'll spend money on pretty things."

"Is it very expensive?" the nun asked.

"With the fancy tree bark, it probably cost him twenty-five hundred dollars or more."

"Is that a lot for a gun?"

"The plain version of this is a third of that and serves basically the same function."

"Death should cost more, I think."

"You're probably right," Mirza agreed.

"Try not to use it."

Instead of responding to that, he asked, "How's your patient?"

"Certainly not well enough to go on your little misadventure with you. Go on in and see for yourself. Omen is already with him. You do not want to miss your war council."

"You sound like you don't approve of what we're doing, Sister."

"I am sympathetic to your goals."

Mirza tucked the pistol she'd given him behind his back. "But you don't like our methods?"

"Do you like your methods, Irfan?"

"I enjoy them," he said.

"That's not the same thing, is it?"

He inclined his head to concede the point.

"I find your morality very interesting."

"Not Finn's? Or Omen's?"

"They are not people of faith. You are. I have seen you pray here with men and women who share your religion. Yet you fight and fornicate like everyone else—"

"Better than everyone else," he corrected. Then added, "The fighting part, I mean. The second thing . . . I'm not sure what impression you got. Omen and I aren't—"

"But you will, once your divorce is final." She seemed amused by his surprise. "At least, that is Finn's theory. Even I can tell he is probably not wrong."

Mirza cleared his throat, then offered a shrug.

"I just don't see how your life squares with your Islam."

"It doesn't," Mirza admitted.

"And as a fellow worshipper—though at a different altar—I find that fascinating. But please forgive me. It's not my business. There is no diversion here except for talk and, well, you know what they say about idle hands."

"It's fine," Mirza said, stepping past her. At the door to Finn's room, however, he turned back and said, "Hafez wrote: 'A secret whisper came to me, from the Tavern's corner, "Drink! He forgives." God's grace is bigger than my sin.'"

Elira sniffed. "Or so he hoped."

Mirza chuckled. "Yes. So I hope as well."

FORTY-FIVE

"THERE YOU ARE," FINN called from his bed when he saw Mirza. "We were just talking about you."

Mirza closed the door behind him. "Looks like that's become a habit of yours."

"What?"

"Your nun has formed some opinions about me."

Finn burrowed himself a little deeper under his covers, which caused his IV to snag on them. He freed it with an irritated sigh. "A man has to keep himself entertained somehow. Unlike the two of you, I'm not out there doing recon or preparing for this mission. Have some sympathy for the devil."

"We were discussing," Omen explained, "how you shouldn't assault Mahmi Castle alone."

"It's a death sentence," Finn agreed.

Mirza pulled over a rickety chair, put it next to Omen, and sat on it gingerly. It creaked horribly in protest, but it held. "It's a dangerous mission no matter how many people go. If someone has to die, I'd prefer to be the only one."

"Let me come with you," Omen said.

"You're not a soldier."

"Which doesn't mean I can't take care of myself. Tell him, Finn."

"He doesn't have to tell me," Mirza interjected. "I know you."

"Then you know exactly how pissed I'm going to be if you leave me behind."

Mirza glanced at Finn, who shook his head. "Don't look at me. You're the one mental enough to get involved with a redhead."

"This is my mission too," Omen reminded them.

Mirza leaned forward in his chair and ran both his hands through his hair. "Fine."

"And don't forget—" she started to go on, then stopped. "Wait. Really?"

Mirza grunted by way of confirmation.

"Wow. Um . . . good then. Glad that's decided."

"What's next?" Mirza asked.

Omen and Finn exchanged a glance.

"We kind of figured convincing you would take most of the morning, mate."

Omen got to her feet. "I'll get the gear I've collected so we can talk specifics."

They watched her walk away, then Finn said, "I'm surprised you caved, to be honest."

"It's like you said. Her skills and mine don't overlap a lot. I'm better when she's around."

"Look at the lone wolf forming a pack."

Mirza scowled. "That's not what this is."

"You know, now that I'm out of work, we could team up, since that's your new thing. It'd be a craic. We'd need a company name, though."

Mirza shook his head.

"How about 'the Merc Bros'? No. That leaves out your hot little matchstick, doesn't it? Wouldn't want to hurt her feelings. How about—"

"Why are you enjoying this so much?"

Finn grinned. "I'm happy for you. It's good to see you with a woman. It'll improve you."

"What about Caroline?"

"It's good to see you with a warm-blooded woman," the Irishman said, amending his statement. "It was never going to work, you and her. Caro was fine, but she wanted a different you. Irfan Mirza sitting by a fireplace sipping tea with his pinky up, exchanging pleasantries with her snooty friends? It was like trying to fit a claymore into a kitchen drawer. I'm not talking about the land mine, mind you. I mean the big-ass sword. You are a nodachi, brother. An absolute zweihander."

"You never said anything."

"I figured she was a really good lay and you were tying the knot because of your gammy religion. The smart ones are wild sometimes. Always a fun surprise when that happens."

"Finn?"

"Yes, sir."

Mirza smiled. "How high are you?"

"I'm a cherub in heaven, my friend. I'm in no pain right now. None. When was the last time you felt that way?"

"Can't remember."

"Right? Not even before the orphanage. These pills Elira has are killer. You should get the recipe for them. Try 'em out. Don't you deserve to feel like I do right now?"

"No," Mirza said. "I don't think I do."

FORTY-SIX

MIRZA MET OMEN OUTSIDE of Finn's room and steered her away, leading her to what had once been a kitchen. It was empty now, shorn of appliances, with nothing of note except stacks of bottled water and canned food the Order of Perpetual Mercy had provided. It was best to finalize their plan without Finn, given his current condition.

They sat cross-legged on the floor, around a tactical backpack she'd brought along, and went to work.

They went over, in broad strokes, the steps they intended to take. A convoy was leaving from Gozel and heading to Mahmi Castle tomorrow morning. Based on the information they'd gotten from Aldatan's late Interior Minister, Omen had been able to scout the Special Ground Forces depot from which it would originate. They were going to break in and hide among the supplies being transported to King Nimir's black site.

Once inside Mahmi, they'd have limited time to find Renata and Mahmud and make their escape.

Mirza estimated they'd have four hours. The supply trucks they were hoping to sneak in on were also their best way out of the fortress, and according to the late Prince Waqif, they took that long to unload. All of them needed to be back on the convoy before it left.

Omen disagreed, pointing out that it was extremely unlikely the unloading operation would proceed as normal once they disrupted it. Either the convoy would be sent back loaded, which seemed unlikely, or the unloading would be delayed while she and Mirza were hunted down.

She reasoned they'd have six hours. Given the distance between the castle and the capital, it would take at least that long—if not slightly longer—for any help to arrive from Gozel. As long as they got out before the prison was reinforced, they'd be golden.

Either way, the whole thing was easier said than done.

It was Omen's briefing in that she had the most to say. She had been out in Gozel, buying equipment and scouting their target locations. Mirza hadn't been able to help much. Too many people had seen him fight in the Midnight League for the police not to have a good description of him. He was recognizable, and it wasn't logical to risk his freedom by having him run around town.

Omen, on the other hand, had been able to move around freely by using a niqab.

One of their main problems was a severe lack of intelligence about the strength and nature of the forces stationed at Mahmi by King Nimir. Omen had sent up a drone to try to solve this issue, but it had been shot down. They were essentially going in blind.

Everything they had been able to learn about the castle was historical in nature, and even that information was sparse. Mahmi hadn't been the center of Aldatani life since 1517, when the Ottomans had conquered this territory and moved the center of government to the port city of Gozel.

In the last half century, as the trade route it had been built to protect became obsolete, Mahmi—without moving, obviously—had gone from being situated in an important part of the world to being in the middle of nowhere.

The last interesting thing to happen there, until the reign of Nimir bin Daleel, was in the midsixties. Aldatan's king then seemed to have developed a fondness for the place. He'd go there with his inner circle at the end of Ramadan for a religious retreat. Specifically, the Muslim practice of *itikaf*, which Mirza had never undertaken himself. It was self-imposed isolation, a withdrawal from all worldly affairs to focus on meditation, worship, and prayer. It was a state many entered in the last ten days of the holy month.

That king had spent some money on the castle, making parts of it habitable for himself and his court. When the moon ending Ramadan was spotted, he'd hold a private celebration there before returning to Gozel for Eid. Those who reported on these annual events made special mention of the fireworks and the food.

Unfortunately for Mahmi, he passed five years after taking the throne, and no one else in his family was as into Islam or history or camping in medieval fortifications as he had been. The traditions he'd tried to establish had died with him.

The most strategically relevant fact about Mahmi was the presence of secret passages within its walls, so Mirza wasn't surprised when Omen brought them up.

"I spent most of my time trying to figure out how to get access to them," he admitted. "I found nothing useful."

He related a legend he'd come across that claimed that one of Mahmi's conquerors had been convinced his enemies would use these passages to assassinate him. He became obsessed with finding them but never could. It was said that he went mad looking for them.

"Well," Omen said, "let's not do that."

"Right. The only other thing we need to be aware of is its offset towers."

"Yeah. They should be at the corners, right? It looks weird. Someone screwed up."

Mirza shook his head. "No. I think they did that on purpose."

"Why?"

"To create blind corners. It adds defensive depth to have those near every tower's entrance. Defenders can use them to ambush attackers during an invasion."

"Doesn't look pretty though."

Mirza shrugged. "Who cares? What matters is that it's a double-edged sword. Blind corners give attackers an advantage, too, if they know to use them. We just need to be aware they exist. Now, do you want to talk about the equipment?"

She nodded and reached for the backpack. From it, she handed him a satellite phone and a Bluetooth headset. "The phone will last eight hours on a single charge with continuous use and for a few days in standby mode. Here's an extra battery pack in case you blow through the juice somehow."

"We won't be there for that long."

"Right. But it's better to have something and not need it than to need it and not have it. Okay, here's the fun part."

She'd gotten Mirza clothes too. She hadn't been able to find desert camo, so she'd decided he would wear a wolf-gray, full-sleeve compression shirt under a khaki, half-zip pullover with a collar that, when closed, would cover his entire neck. She'd gotten him cargo pants in the same color, along with a matching *shemagh*—a cotton scarf that could be wrapped around his head and face, leaving only his black eyes exposed.

"My outfit's pretty much the same."

"Weapons?" Mirza asked.

Omen pulled out two combat knives with Neoprene and Velcro straps for him to wrap around his thighs.

"For wet work. Nice."

She made a face. "Whatever floats your boat, I guess. I also got you a shoulder holster for that pistol you executed Prince Waqif with."

Mirza eyed it skeptically. "That's not military grade. What is that? Pleather?"

"I got it from a cosplay shop."

"Do I want to know what that is?"

She grinned. "I'll show you sometime. You might like it."

Mirza took out the SIG P226 Elira had given him and thrust it into the holster. It was a little loose, but it surprisingly didn't feel like it was going to fall apart.

"Ooh. New toy? Shiny."

"Finn's," he explained.

"Makes sense. Much too good-looking for you."

"Between the CZ and this, we've got twenty-five rounds."

"Better make them count," she said.

"Thanks for doing the shopping."

"You haven't even seen the pièce de résistance." Omen produced a watch and gave it to him.

Mirza frowned as he took it. "What is this? It has more than one button. I don't like that."

"That is a Garmin tactix Delta Solar Edition," she explained.

"In English?"

"It's a time-telling thingamajig that the sun makes tick."

"What's the point of it? It feels fancy. And expensive."

"This is one of the best tactical watches on the market and it's not all that easy to find."

Mirza looked unimpressed.

"It's got a ton of high-tech features that are—"

"All of that sounds terrible."

Omen threw her head back. "Dude, just put it on, okay? I'll teach you how to get to the screen that lets you know what your exact coordinates are. That's important. If this whole operation goes south and you're in the desert somewhere, at least you'll be able to tell Finn where to find you."

"And where are you in this scenario?" he demanded.

Her smile was small and strained for once. "We might get separated.

Or you might be the only one to make it out. Like I said. Better to have it and not need it—"

He leaned forward, tipped her chin up, forcing her green eyes to meet his dark ones. "That's not going to happen. There's no possible world in which I leave there without you. Know that."

"What if I'm dead, Irfan?"

"There is no possible world," he repeated.

Slowly, she nodded. Then, in her usual, playful tone, she asked, "Is it weird that I'm super turned on right now?"

Mirza chuckled.

"You know, maybe you should call Caroline and ask for a hall pass. You might die before you get to fuck me. If that happens, you'll regret it for the rest of your life."

He raised his eyebrows.

"You know what I mean. I'm just saying, this code of honor of yours, it comes with a cost."

"Trust me, I know," he said. "Is that everything?"

"All that's left is knickknacks."

These consisted of gloves, a leather belt with a clip for the SAT phone, a compact backpack, a length of rope, three canteens full of water, a pair of binoculars, an assortment of energy bars and dried fruit, a small flashlight, a first-aid kit, a compass, a set of lockpicks fashioned out of bobby pins, and a small bottle of prescription-strength ibuprofen, thanks to the Order of Perpetual Mercy. The last thing in the pack was a packet of Imodium.

"Why do we need that?"

"We're going to be stuck together in a confined space on some truck for quite a while. It'd be nice if neither one of us had to take a major bathroom break."

"Smart. So, earlier you said your outfit was almost exactly like mine. You got yourself all this equipment too?"

"Yeah. I mean, except for the holster. I thought we only had one gun."

"And I thought," he said, "that we only just agreed that you were coming on this mission."

"You only just agreed," Omen pointed out. "Which I wanted you to because otherwise you'd be a grump the whole time, but I was always going to go. Never needed your permission. I don't take orders from you. Not a soldier, remember?"

"You make that impossible to forget, jaan."

"I could pretend to be one, though, if you're into that. And just like that, we're back on cosplay . . . Wait, did you just call me John?"

He laughed. "No. I said 'jaan.'"

"What does that mean?"

Mirza scratched the back of his head. "It's something people call each other."

"That doesn't actually answer my question."

He glanced away. "I guess the translation would be something like 'my life.'"

"Wow. That's a pretty intimate thing to say to a business acquaintance."

Mirza scowled. "Are you ever going to let that go?"

"Nah. I don't think I will."

FORTY-SEVEN

"WE'RE HERE," OMEN ANNOUNCED as she pulled an old Suzuki Jimny to a stop a block away from the Special Ground Forces depot they were targeting. The boxy, off-road-capable SUV from the early nineties was the fourth car she had boosted in the last two days in an effort to rotate the vehicles she was driving around. Getting arrested in a country where people in her profession still had their hands amputated just for doing their jobs was not on her bucket list.

"Finally," Finn grumbled from the back seat.

"You're a lot less chipper than you were this morning."

"It's a side effect of being sober."

"I'll medicate you," Elira, who was sitting next to him, promised, "once this . . . caper has concluded. Just try not to start bleeding again. I'm tired of stitching you up."

Mirza opened the passenger-side door and stepped out, his attention already fixed on their objective.

They were around thirty miles north of Gozel. There wasn't much here except for two racetracks, one built for an annual F1 event, the other for contests between camels. Late at night, everything was quiet.

The depot was a flat, rectangular building surrounded by floodlights and patrolling guards. It had been built to store and protect the weapons, ammunition, and protective gear used by Gozel's elite police unit. Under King Nimir, it had been shoehorned into shipping supplies to his infamous black site.

It was surrounded by an easily scalable chain-link fence, beyond which a large convoy of trucks had been parked. Already loaded, they were positioned at the edge of the property, out of the way of the SGF's own vehicles.

Omen had brought them to the back of the facility, and as Mirza drew closer, he spotted four security cameras attached to the rear wall of the depot. One of the cameras was stationary, focused on the single door on this side of the building. The other three were panning across the entire area, but they obviously couldn't see through the trucks. As long as Mirza, Omen, and Finn stayed behind those, their approach wouldn't be detected by electronic surveillance.

He counted three patrols of three men each circling the building at all times. They'd pick up on any sounds Mirza's team made while jumping the fence, opening a truck's trailer, and slipping inside. Even Omen couldn't pull all that off in absolute silence.

That was why she'd suggested they bring Elira along to act as a distraction.

He heard several of the Suzuki's doors close. Turning around, he saw Omen speaking to Elira, giving her instructions. Finn, carrying Mirza's tactical backpack, was limping toward him.

"You all right?" Mirza asked when his old friend drew closer.

Finn managed a smile. "Grand. I've just been giving out so Elira will hand me the good stuff when we get back. Here. Carry your own crap."

"Thanks."

Finn mumbled a response and looked past Mirza at the depot. "Sorry I'm not coming with you. Can't believe it's stoppage time and I can't even be on the pitch." He paused for a moment, then added, "That was the part when you were supposed to say something comforting to make me feel better."

Mirza saw Omen heading toward them, clapped a hand on Finn's shoulder, and asked her, "Ready?"

The Jimny sputtered to life as Elira, now in the driver's seat, turned the ignition.

Omen nodded. "That's our cue. If anyone's got any last-minute wisdom to drop or any inspirational shit to say like in the movies, now's the time."

They looked at one another for a moment.

Mirza was the one who eventually spoke. "Let's go to work."

Mirza led them toward the depot's fence, walking carefully, keeping low, stepping with his toes first, breathing steadily, and making sure that he never left the blind spot the convoy trucks had created for the cameras.

They waited in silence.

A minute later, they could see Elira driving the Suzuki up to the road that ran parallel to the facility. She stopped there.

Mirza began to move. Omen and Finn were right behind him.

There was a sound like a gunshot.

Two of the guard trios closest to Elira ran to investigate.

One patrol group, whose route had taken them to the front of the depot, remained unaccounted for. But there was no help for that. Mirza grabbed ahold of the fence and swung himself over without much difficulty. It rattled a little, but another apparent gunshot echoed all around them and no one noticed.

Omen managed to follow almost silently. Finn had to stifle a cry of pain, but he managed.

They heard what seemed like a weapon going off a third time.

Elira was playing her part perfectly. She'd turned off the Suzuki's engine to make it look like the vehicle had stalled. Then she'd started the engine again and hit the gas hard as she could, causing the aged SUV to backfire.

After that, all she had to do was rinse and repeat until the guards came to check on her. She waved at them enthusiastically before rolling her window down. Her radio was blasting some loud, obnoxious song.

It occurred to Mirza that it might have been best if the nun were wearing something other than her habit. It was too late to worry about that, though. The guards would just have to buy that Sister Elira was into heavy metal.

The music drowned out any noise they made as they hurried over to the trucks. Mirza got to them first but stepped aside to let Omen pass when he saw the cargo containers already had padlocks on them.

She dropped her backpack, crouched down, searching for her improvised lockpicks.

Mirza glanced over his shoulder to make sure the guards were still occupied when Elira's radio stopped. She'd be talking to the guards now, explaining that she had gotten lost and was now having car trouble. No one had raised the alarm so far. Hopefully, they were finding her credible.

He relaxed a little when he saw Omen had her tools and was about to start working on a lock. They still had no visual on the third patrol. It could be anywhere.

A confrontation here would be fatal, not necessarily to them but to the mission. If the Aldatanis realized that the convoy was being targeted, they'd modify their security protocols to make it impossible to use as a Trojan horse to get into Mahmi.

They'd be back to square one.

It took Omen seconds to get the lock to give.

She began to open the trailer's door. There was the squeal of metal sliding against metal. Finn winced.

Mirza heard footsteps approaching. Quickly, he reached out and grabbed Omen's arm. She turned to a statue in response, not moving at all, controlling even her breathing.

Next to him, Finn gave the smallest of nods. He'd picked up on it too. Someone was heading in their direction.

An approaching guard called out in Arabic.

Mirza felt Omen tense.

Had they been discovered?

One of the men helping Elira shouted back a response. Mirza figured that the new arrival was looking for a status update. The three guards who were roaming across the front of the depot must have noticed that no one was following them, so they'd stopped their route and sent a scout out to investigate. Made sense.

The three of them waited until they were sure he was gone.

Then Omen carefully finished pulling the truck's trailer open. The thing was nearly full of cardboard boxes, but there was enough room for her and Mirza to squeeze in.

Reaching into her backpack again, she pulled out her flashlight, climbed up, and beckoned Mirza to do the same.

He looked at Finn, inclined his head a little, and hoisted himself up.

Finn closed the door behind them, engaged the bolt, then put the padlock back in place.

"Mission accomplished," Omen whispered.

Mirza shook his head. That wasn't remotely true. This had been the easy part.

The first thing Mirza and Omen did in the trailer was take off their boots. The floor was made of metal and was, therefore, prone to being loud. Then he moved a few cardboard boxes around, creating space for them to sit.

It was cramped and would have been uncomfortable with anyone else. With Omen . . . He took a deep breath as she padded over to him. The smell of vanilla and lavender, a scent he'd come to associate with her, flooded his senses. The primal part of his brain—which seemed to make up a large portion of it—lit up in response.

He reminded himself that they'd soon be in mortal danger, that he needed to focus on the mission at hand, and that calmed him down somewhat.

"This is cozy," she noted.

He tried not to look at her lips or her eyes or her neck or her . . . well, everything really. Instead, he turned away, took off his pullover, and folded it into a pillow.

"Get comfortable," he suggested. "It's going to get hot in here."

"Promises, promises," Omen joked but mimicked his movements. While their outerwear was the same, she wasn't wearing a long-sleeve compression shirt underneath like he was. Instead, she had on a black tank top.

Soon, they were sitting side by side, leaning against the trailer, and she turned off her flashlight.

He listened to her breathing and tried not to focus on her presence next to him. Unfortunately, his other thoughts were grim. He had been serious when he'd warned her that the temperature around them would rise.

A locked trailer was a pretty good approximation of a closed box. As the night wore on, the air around them would get humid and stale. They'd sweat a lot. It'd be a struggle to stay hydrated despite the multiple canteens they were carrying.

When the sun rose, the heat inside would rise with it. A few years ago,

Mirza had been hired by the parents of a young man who'd disappeared. It wasn't a kidnapping. The teenager had voluntarily left Baluchistan and entered Iran with a caravan of immigrants and refugees. Their goal was to get to Turkey in search of a better future.

The kid's parents hadn't wanted him to be brought back. They just wanted to know he was alive. Mirza had tracked him down. At least, he'd tracked the boy's body down. It was in a container much like this one, along with twenty or so other corpses. They had successfully managed to get themselves smuggled into Istanbul but had suffocated on the way.

He still remembered the stench of urine and refuse and mortality from when he'd helped unload those dead, desperate people. Their situation had been uncomfortably like the one he was in now.

"You okay?" Omen asked softly.

"Sure."

"You're very quiet."

"Always am," he said.

"Yeah, but since I'm usually talking, I pretend it's because you're a good listener."

He snorted, then began fiddling with the ridiculously complicated gadget Omen had made him strap to his wrist. It wasn't a watch. Being a watch was something it did in its spare time. He knew he'd never bother to look into half the things it could do.

He wasn't sure what button he pressed, but it began to display what he initially thought was a battery reading, showing how little life the machine had left. That was weird, because he'd charged it before they had left.

It took him a moment to register that it was, in fact, talking about him. The graph he was looking at was supposed to be a representation of his own fading energy reserves. According to it, Mirza was almost depleted.

As Omen wrapped one of her arms around his and put her head on his shoulder, it occurred to him that it might also be an accurate representation of how much time he had left in the world. It was possible that the sand in his particular hourglass was about to run out.

"I forgot to call Maya," Mirza realized, "to let her know I might not make it back."

Omen sighed. "How many times is she going to have to hear you say good-bye, Irfan? It makes her anxious. Teenagers don't want to get status updates telling them one of their parents might be dying in some godforsaken part of the world."

"She knows what I do is dangerous."

"Yeah, but we all let ourselves forget the awfulness of life so we can muddle through it. She's fifteen. Give her a break."

He was silent for a while.

"Sorry," Omen whispered. "Maybe shouldn't have said anything. It's just . . . she's told me she hates it. You should know that."

"She never told me."

"Remember when I came to Istanbul, but you had to leave for that job in Mardin for a few days?"

Mirza nodded.

"I got to know Maya a little on that trip. I was with her when you called to let her know you might not come back. I saw what it puts her through."

He bowed his head.

"I know you think it's best, but—"

"I never got . . . My father . . . I'm not really sure what happened to him," Mirza explained. "He probably abandoned me, but I have always wondered if maybe there was some other reason he didn't come back. I hate not knowing. I don't want my kid to have to live with that."

Omen intertwined her delicate fingers with his thick, rough ones. "Remember this morning, when you said there was no possible world in which you'd leave me behind at Mahmi?"

"Yes."

"Do you think there is a world in which Maya would believe, even for a second, that you'd abandon her?"

"No," Mirza answered. "I don't think so."

"Then maybe there's no reason to continue being cruel to be kind."

"Huh."

"What?" she asked.

"Calling Maya before missions . . . It's become a tradition of sorts. What am I supposed to do now when I think I'm going to die?"

"Don't," Omen advised, not altogether helpfully.

Mirza leaned over, kissed her forehead, and smiled in the darkness.

FORTY-EIGHT

FOUR HOURS AND FORTY minutes after the truck started moving the next morning, Mirza and Omen began to prepare for the fight to come.

They were sweating through their clothes. The hot air was thick with diesel fumes and difficult to breathe. Omen's skin was flushed. The few strands of her red hair that had escaped her ponytail clung to her forehead and temples. Her wit had evaporated. They'd spent the ride mostly in silence.

Breakfast was two protein bars they'd brought along. The chocolate in them was chalky and tasted more like an amalgam of unidentifiable chemicals than anything else. They drank a little water and conserved the rest.

Mirza stretched, put his pullover back on, redid the laces on his boots, then checked to make sure both Finn's SIG and his own CZ were ready to fire by pulling their slides back until he saw the brass of their rounds in their chambers.

Omen, who was getting ready herself, asked, "You gonna share?"

Mirza held the CZ out to her. "Don't shoot until you have no choice."

"Are you hoping to limit casualties? 'Cause I don't think that's going to happen."

"I want to limit wasted bullets. We only have so many. That one has five."

She nodded.

He slipped a Bluetooth headset on, clipped his SAT phone to the belt around his waist, and then retrieved his flashlight.

They'd been using Omen's so far. It was no longer enough by itself. He wanted their eyes to be as used to brightness as possible in these conditions. They couldn't afford to be blinded by the sun when the door was opened for them. Every second would be vital.

"I'll go out first," he said. "Stay inside and cover me."

"Got it."

The truck began to slow, then came to a stop.

They set the timers on their watches to six hours.

Yanking on his gloves, Mirza donned his *shemagh*, wrapping it around his head and covering his mouth and nose with it. He stowed his flashlight and drew the combat knives Omen had gotten him, holding one in each hand in a reverse grip with the edge in.

When it came to knife combat, he was always at a speed disadvantage.

The way he was holding them made that problem worse. It also reduced his reach because the blade was pointing away from his opponents.

But it helped him lean into his strengths.

He was fine giving up some reach. He was taller than most people he fought, so at worst this became a wash.

What he gained was even more power than he already had, which meant he could push the blades deeper. It made him more lethal. One of his trainers had called it caveman-style fighting because it depended on heavy, hammer-like blows that lacked grace but were brutal and effective.

Some fighters preferred to have the cutting edge facing out instead. Having it facing toward his forearm instead meant that Mirza lost the ability to slash. But he preferred his method for one simple reason. It was, in his experience, easier to yank your knives out from a human body if you held them this way.

He heard someone undoing the padlock.

He didn't glance back to see if Omen was ready. He trusted she was.

Whoever was on the outside was talking to someone, saying something in Arabic.

Mirza coiled and tensed, ready to lunge.

The door opened.

Light poured into the trailer.

Mirza exploded out of it, arms extended and turned so the insides of his wrists were pointing up at the sky. He brought his hands together in a pincer-like movement. The knife in his right hand plunged into the left side of the startled prison guard's neck. The left-hand knife did the same to the guard's right side.

The blades met inside the man's throat, and then Mirza jerked them back toward himself. They tore through his trachea and larynx, his jugular and carotid arteries, and his vagus nerve. A shower of red exploded outward, drenching Mirza, after which the guard just stood there for a second, dead on his feet, blood gurgling out of him in waves as his heart kept pumping away uselessly, not realizing the soul it was trying to keep alive was already departed.

One.

Mirza didn't wait to see the man fall.

There were two more guards within his immediate reach. They shouted and cried out in alarm but were still rooted to their spots by shock and fear.

Mirza turned toward the one on the right and drove the knife in his left hand into the man's stomach, then his diaphragm, then his heart. Three rapid backhand strikes were all it took.

Two.

The third guard, who was behind Mirza, recovered from his surprise and charged forward. Mirza spun around, right hand coming up backward, knife up and out. He wasn't able to generate his usual amount of force because of the angle, but the blade caught the guard in the soft flesh between his chin and neck. The knife sliced through into the man's tongue and up through the roof of his mouth.

Three.

Mirza surveyed his surroundings. He was in open ground, surrounded by high walls. There were snipers on them, but they hadn't had time to react yet. They weren't an immediate threat, but they were an imminent one.

Next to where he was standing, four other trailers were being unloaded by a couple of men each. Six were on his left, two on the right.

Once they realized what was happening, they charged him.

Mirza sheathed his knives and pulled Finn's SIG from his holster as he turned to face the larger group, the one to his left. The beautiful pistol's stainless-steel barrel gleamed as he brought it around, holding the weapon with both hands. The sight caused his targets to freeze. They'd been running toward him thinking they were going after someone armed only with blades.

A gun was a different proposition entirely. It caused them to hesitate. That was fatal.

Four shots rang out as Omen opened up on the guards Mirza had turned his back on.

Mirza started shooting almost simultaneously. The SIG was smooth, precise, and rapid-firing. He got off eight rounds. Two missed. One went through a liver, three through chests, and another through a man's eye. The final one was a head shot.

He pivoted, faced right, ready to keep firing, but found no live targets.

Omen jumped down to join him, gun drawn.

"We need cover," Mirza said.

"Leopards!" someone on the wall screamed. The rallying cry seemed to echo through the compound.

Mirza looked up to see a thickset, powerfully built, short soldier bringing a mini-gun off the castle's external defenses and aiming it down into the courtyard where he and Omen were standing. The snipers he'd spotted earlier were getting into position as well.

"Move!" Omen yelled.

They ran, ducking behind the truck they'd hidden in just as the sand they'd been standing on was absolutely pummeled by the fearsome weapon.

There was no way they were going to be able to stand up against that thing.

It'd shred them to pieces.

The only thing they could do in the face of that kind of firepower was retreat.

Part Four

THE PRICE OF
HEAVEN

FORTY-NINE

DINA MALIK WAS BEING dragged out of Atlas's office when Chike got there. The former actress had a few tears running down her face, but she wasn't weeping. Ignoring the venomous look she got from the prisoner, Chike hurried inside.

Atlas was standing by his desk, shirtless, his pale, smooth back to her, when she entered. The outline of his vertebrae was visible, and she saw his shoulder blades move under his skin as he zipped up his pants.

"We have a problem."

"She doesn't beg like she used to," Atlas said, ignoring the urgency in Chike's voice entirely. "I suppose it's true what they say. The magic never lasts. But she's become close to Renata Bardales, apparently, and . . . well, the friend of my enemy is my enemy."

"Sir, I—"

"Yes, yes. There is a situation. I thought I heard shots. Was there an escape attempt? Did a fight break out among our men?"

Chike shook her head. "We have intruders."

Atlas's eyes narrowed as he reached for his white turtleneck. "Give me details. Now."

"I don't have any. Tareq—he's one of the guards on the wall—came to get me as soon as it happened. He says they snuck in with the convoy from Gozel."

"How many people are we talking about?"

"Two."

Atlas seemed to relax, not a great deal but a little. "Tell me they're dead."

She shook her head.

Atlas, his face twisted with sudden fury, strode past her, heading for the courtyard at Mahmi's entrance. His mind darted from one thought to another as he considered and rejected possibilities as to who these infiltrators could be.

Chike hurried after him. "We will catch them. They've got nowhere to go."

"Do you really think operatives capable of penetrating this facility would do so without a plan for exfil?"

"No, sir. But we—"

Atlas cut off her words with a sharp, chopping motion of his hand. They marched in silence for a while as he simmered. Finally, he asked, "Are you still sure about the drone?"

Chike frowned. "I don't understand what—"

"You told me that the drone we shot down yesterday could not have given away the true nature of Mahmi. Do you stand by that assessment?"

"I do. Are you saying you think it was sent by these same people?"

"If it wasn't, it would represent a monumental . . ." He trailed off as they stepped outside.

A pile of bodies greeted them.

Atlas stopped walking and counted the dead.

Eleven.

"Shit," Chike whispered beside him.

Atlas looked around, trying to find something or someone who could help make sense of the scene. His gray eyes, wide and bulging now, fixed on Yahya the Mini-gun. The Leopard had gotten that name not just because of his weapon of choice but because at five feet three inches he barely cleared the height requirement for the Aldatani army. What he lacked in vertical dimensions, he made up for in bulk. He was cool under pressure and not prone to exaggeration. Atlas knew he'd get an accurate account from him.

"Two intruders did this?"

Mini-gun took a deep drag from the cigar he never seemed to be without, blew out a cloud of smoke, then said, "Yeah."

When word of this got out, Dandarabilla's reputation would be severely damaged.

Nimir bin Daleel would lose his mind when he learned that his legendary black site had been compromised. He'd likely renege on his promise to give Atlas exclusive operational control over the Kingdom's activities in Yemen.

Decades upon decades of work ruined in moments.

"Two men?" Atlas demanded, the pitch of his voice high and disbelieving. "Just two men? And you couldn't stop them?"

"Pretty sure one was a woman," Mini-gun said, his voice matter-of-fact. "And . . . well, they were very good."

"Who were they?"

"I don't know. They had keffiyehs on."

"What are those?" Atlas asked, trying to remember where he'd heard the term before.

Mini-gun, who had his cigar between his fingers now, waved it around as he explained. "It's the scarf thing Arabs wear to protect themselves from the sun and the sand. Call it a shemagh if you want. It was khaki and black and was wrapped around their heads and faces. They could be anyone."

Atlas huffed out a deep breath, trying to expel his growing frustration.

"The man was big," Mini-gun added, clearly hoping to be helpful.

"Could make it onto the roster of the WWE big. Looked like he was built like Triple H."

The leader of Dandarabilla threw his hands up in the air and turned to Chike for a translation. "What in the never-ending fuck is he talking about?"

"A professional wrestler."

It was, in other words, a completely unhelpful reference for Atlas. He sighed. "Just find them."

Chike nodded. "Should I use just the Leopards?"

Atlas considered the deployment of his forces. There were five Leopards on-site and three Dandarabilla operatives, in addition to himself and Chike. These were the best troops he had. Next were . . .

"How many SGF officers came with the convoy?"

A man in uniform stepped forward and bowed his head. "Sir. There were nine of us in total. Three are gone. But we have to get back to our station and report—"

"No one leaves," Atlas snapped. "Lock the facility down. Disable all vehicles. I want all SAT phones in my office in five minutes. No one is to have any communication with the outside world, not until these intruders are caught."

"But—"

"This will be over in an hour. You can follow my orders and be part of my team for that duration," Atlas told the leader of Gozel's elite police unit, "or you can stay here indefinitely as a prisoner."

The cop held up his hands and stepped back, retreating.

Atlas returned to his deliberations. They made him feel in control, reminding him that this was just an aberration. Mahmi was still his domain. He would bring order to it like God did to the universe.

He usually had a contingent of thirty guards. He counted six among the dead, so with the addition of the SGF men, he was still almost at full strength.

"Chike."

"Sir?"

"Station two Leopards at the entrance to the North Tower and two Dandarabilla men outside the armory there. Our last operative will guard my door, along with you."

She nodded.

"Assemble three teams of five to comb the castle. Each team should have four guards with a Leopard to lead them. Assign one to Mini-gun."

"Our task?" Mini-gun asked.

"Search and destroy."

"Can do."

"I want two guards at the main gate," Atlas continued, "and two at the base of each tower as usual. Restrict all prisoner movement. All common areas are to be shut down. The remainder of our forces, along with the SGF, will defend the wall."

"Yes, sir."

Raising his voice to address anyone within earshot, Atlas announced, "Two infiltrators against all of us. In relative terms, we are practically an army. We cannot lose now that they no longer have the element of surprise. So let's make this fun, shall we? I will give whoever kills them a prize of ten thousand dollars. Happy hunting, gentlemen."

"You want their heads as a trophy?" Mini-gun asked.

"Let's not be cliché." Atlas took one last look at the collection of carcasses before him. They had been men not so long ago. "Do what you want with the woman, but I'd like to see this man's balls. Bring me those. They must be massive."

FIFTY

"THAT WOMAN WHO IS always with Atlas came to get Mahmud last night," Habib told Ren as she went through her katas. They were alone in the deserted, highest level of the South Tower, where Ren had continued to practice. She had taken to her old drills like a fish to water. She didn't feel any stronger than she'd been in Bangkok. Not enough time had passed for that. But her movements were less hesitant. She had gained back a little of her fluidity, and with it a bit of her confidence.

"Chike," Renata supplied.

"Yes. Adam says she's locked Mahmud in the Greeting Room with a knife. He won't be given any food or water unless he starts cutting himself. Only when he's made himself bleed to Atlas's satisfaction will they let him out."

Ren glanced in the direction of the stairs leading down. Adam with the sad eyes would be standing at their base, waiting to take Habib back. She remained the only prisoner restricted to her assigned tower and the prohibition against her seeing Mahmud also stood. The only reason Habib could be here with her now was because of the Leopard's largess.

About her fiancé, she said, "This won't break him."

"No," the old prince agreed. "But it will hurt him. I do not know how much more he can take."

248

"What about you?"

Habib snorted. "What about me? So far, Atlas has just gone after my son. I wish he would start torturing me directly. That would be easier to bear."

"He knows that," Renata said. "So, for now, Mahmud will have to endure."

"Until when? I will not give Nimir what he wants. Neither will Mahmud. We have said so over and over again. This can only end one way. He should just kill us and—"

Renata held up a hand to silence him, straightened, and listened hard. "Hear that?"

Habib frowned. "Thunder?"

"No. Gunfire."

"What do you think is happening?"

Ren smiled.

"What?" Habib demanded.

"I think maybe," she said, "my family is here."

FIFTY-ONE

"I DON'T GET WHAT is happening right now," Bey grumbled on the other end of the line.

Finn Thompson sat up in bed as Sister Elira strode into his room carrying a tray with his lunch on it. Putting Bey on speakerphone, he set his cell aside, ready for his meal. "I'm convalescing and have nothing to do. I figured you'd be free too, given that your part in this mission is over."

"Wrong," the hacker said. "I've got other clients."

"Well, sure, that makes sense. Still, you can't tell me you aren't wondering about how things are going with Omen and Irfan. We can chat about our anxieties."

"Okay, but why are we talking?"

Finn frowned. "What do you mean?"

"We can chat online. Why'd you call me?"

Finn shook his head. Young people.

Elira chuckled as she put a bowl of tomato soup, freshly rehydrated from a can, and a few saltine crackers in front of him.

The truth was that he had an ulterior motive in reaching out to Bey. His hobby was collecting people. Not just because they could be useful to him, but because often he could be useful to them, if only by connecting them to his other contacts. His network was his greatest strength, and he nurtured it with the zeal of a constant gardener.

When it came to technical know-how, his garden was a little sparse. That hadn't mattered in the past. For years now, he had relied on the Aldatani government whenever he'd needed nerd services. Now that he was suddenly a freelancer again, it was possible he'd require a keyboard sorcerer of his own.

"This way I can add Irfan in when he calls. Should be soon. The convoy should have gotten to Mahmi twenty minutes ago."

"I really hope Omen doesn't get hurt," Bey said.

"And Irfan?"

"He's a tank. He absorbs damage. That's what he's for."

"I guess that's true," Finn agreed. "He is human, though, even if he doesn't always act like it. One day he's going to get hurt so bad that he won't be able to get up again. It's inevitable. When that happens . . . well, you can't ever plow a field by turning it over in your mind."

"What?"

"He means," Sister Elira explained, "that it is useless to worry."

"Then why not just say that? And who are you?"

Before Finn could respond, his phone began to ring.

"Thank God," he muttered as he reached for it. "We're on a conference call. Tell us you're okay, brother."

"I need a dry cleaner," Mirza told them, his voice low.

"What?" Bey asked.

"He's covered in blood," Finn explained. "It's not his." To Irfan, he said, "You've used that 'joke' before, mate. It's old and tired. Retire it."

Mirza grunted.

"What's the craic?" Finn asked.

"Still doing some belated recon. We've counted thirty hostiles so far, but there should be more."

"That is . . . really bad," Elira muttered.

"That's some party. Have you danced with anyone yet?"

"We've put ten—maybe eleven—on the floor."

"Sounds like a rager," Finn said. "Sorry I'm missing out."

"Is this English?" Sister Elira asked.

Instead of answering her, Finn kept speaking to Mirza. "Seems like you're having fun. Here I was worried you were stuck with a bag of balls."

"We do have one problem. The castle is larger than I thought it'd be. Finding Ren and Mahmud will take some time."

"You two going to split up to cover more ground?"

"I'm not crazy about that idea," Mirza said. "Especially because we might be here longer than we thought."

Elira frowned. "What do you mean? You said you would come back when the convoy returned in a few hours."

"That was the plan. But we saw men taking spark plugs out of the trucks and the Jeeps the police drove in. As of right now, we've got no way out of the desert."

"I'll come get you," Finn volunteered. "Just get to a safe place and send me your coordinates when you're ready for pickup."

"That's an incomplete solution," Bey noted.

Finn cocked his head to one side. "What do you mean?"

"All of you are going to need to find some way out of Aldatan. No way you're getting past exit control at the airport. Their system will flag you for sure."

They went quiet for a second, then Finn admitted, "I hadn't thought that far ahead, to be honest."

"I believe," Sister Elira spoke up, "I might be able to help."

Finn raised his eyebrows. "Real help? Or prayer help? Because we only want one of those."

"Speak for yourself," Mirza said.

"The refugees around here are from south of the border. They were transported into Aldatan by . . . importers with a very flexible attitude toward the law. I don't see why they wouldn't be able to take you in the opposite direction."

"We're going to escape into Yemen." Finn shook his head. "There's a sentence I bet nobody has uttered for at least a hundred years."

"That just means," Mirza said, "no one will see us coming."

FIFTY-TWO

MIRZA HUNG UP WITHOUT sharing their third, most pressing problem with Finn. It wasn't something he could help them with. They would have to find a solution to it on their own, and they'd have to find it fast.

They were running out of ammo. There were only thirteen rounds left.

They'd need a lot more before this was over, and the only way to acquire it was to take some off of any guards they could kill.

Mirza had heard people say you had to spend money to make money.

Today, he was going to have to spend bullets to get bullets.

That would have been a simpler task before the defenses of Mahmi Castle had organized. They'd still had surprise on their side then. After running from the soldier with the mini-gun, however, he and Omen had been forced to take time to orient themselves to this place, to get some idea of its layout. Charging around a field of engagement with no idea where you were going was usually a good way to get killed.

They'd used their time well, but so had the enemy. From a distance, Mirza had gotten a glimpse of a slender man, bald and dressed completely in white giving orders.

Atlas Boss, he assumed.

Atlas's strategy seemed to be to make sure that none of his men were left alone to be picked off easily. Plus, he had teams of five roving through Mahmi to try to track Mirza and Omen down.

The entrances of the four towers seemed like easy targets, with only two sentries in front of each one. However, without any clue as to the total strength of the enemy, it was impossible to know if there were reinforcements hidden inside the structures and, if so, what their numbers were. If he and Omen attacked one, and a legion of guards poured out to defend it, it'd mean their end.

Worse, with echoes built into the very walls of the castle, as soon as shots were fired, the report would give their adversaries a rough idea of their location. Stealth was not a viable strategy here.

"Let's hit the South Tower," Omen suggested. "That's where at least some of the women are. Renata might be there too."

That was true. They'd seen female prisoners being herded in there as the facility was locked down. It seemed like under normal circumstances the captives were given significant freedom to roam around.

There was no reason to keep them under lock and key. Anyone attempting to escape would be seen from the walls and killed. Even if they somehow managed to get past the snipers, they'd be on foot, facing the prospect of crossing six hundred miles of desert with no supplies, difficult terrain like deep sand and steep hills, sunstroke, snakes, scorpions, wolves, caracals, and hyenas.

Nimir bin Daleel had chosen his black site well.

"It could be a trap," he countered.

"We've got to roll the dice. If they're hiding a bunch of dudes in there to ambush us, we'll just have to deal with them. Waiting isn't going to change anything about our situation, is it?"

"And Finn calls me a fecking chancer."

Omen started to smile, but then her expression soured. "Wait a minute. He's right. You are a fucking chancer."

"Fecking," he corrected.

"What's the difference?"

He shrugged. "I think it's somehow supposed to be less rude."

"Well, feck you then, sir," she practically hissed as she leveled a finger at him. He could tell she was struggling to keep her volume down. "Because I just figured something out. If you were here by yourself, you'd have already gone in guns blazing and damn the torpedoes. That's how you work. You're hesitating because of me. Aren't you?"

"I'm trying not to be reckless," he conceded.

"But that's your whole brand."

He didn't really know how to argue with that. It was the truth.

"Listen. There is no one I'd rather have here with me than Irfan Mirza. So I'd appreciate it if you would stop being a cautious, thinking, rational person and go back to being him, please."

He grunted in response.

"That's more like it. So, we're going at the South Tower?"

Mirza drew his pistol and took a deep breath. "Sure. Let's go get Ren."

Mirza moved to a position behind a wall from which he could see two men guarding the entrance. His focus was entirely on them when he heard a sharp intake of breath from Omen.

By the time he spun around, she already had her weapon trained on a potential threat that had appeared behind them. Fortunately, her target discrimination was excellent. If she hadn't realized in a fraction of a second that it was a prisoner, not a guard, who had surprised them, she would've pulled the trigger.

The woman who'd walked into the corridor gasped, covered her mouth with both hands, and somehow managed not to scream. Mirza held up his free hand to his lips, covered though they were by his *she-magh*, indicating that she should be quiet.

He wasn't sure she'd be able to comply. Her eyes had popped open and were filling with tears, her breathing was rapid and shallow, like she was about to lose control of her senses.

With her gun still trained on the woman, Omen rushed forward and pinned her against the nearest wall. Instead of resisting, the prisoner went limp.

Omen put the muzzle of her CZ under the woman's chin and whispered, "We're not here to hurt you. Calm down and this won't get ugly. Nod if you get what I'm saying."

The prisoner bobbed her head down swiftly.

"Great. We're not bad guys. We're here to get some people out. There's no reason to be scared."

Mirza lowered his weapon a little and gestured for Omen to do the same. "Is there somewhere we can go and talk? Somewhere without guards?"

Hesitation, followed by an affirmative.

"Good. We could use some information."

The woman led them away from the South Tower, down the way she'd come, and into a relatively small room. It was full of junk. Mirza saw old tables and chairs, massive, rusting steel pots, and vintage decorative string lights with incandescent bulbs.

He also spotted two crates of cylindrical fireworks, a box of plastic fuse connector clips, and a long spool of fuse line. Next to it were dusty piles of discarded traditional Aldatani clothes. They looked like they'd once been festive.

By the time Mirza noticed a couple of curved swords and a steel shield lying in a corner, he'd figured out what he was looking at. This was a storage room for party supplies. Everything here likely dated back to the Aldatani monarch he'd read about, the one from the sixties who used to come to Mahmi Castle during the last ten nights of Ramadan for a spiritual retreat.

Before leaving, he used to celebrate the successful completion of the holy month with a feast. This was what was left of the materials used for it. The presence of the weapons seemed odd, until he remembered that many Arab countries had a sword dance. The Aldatani variant, apparently, incorporated bucklers into it.

While he was looking around, Omen had started questioning the prisoner, who said her name was Dina Malik.

Dina explained that she'd discovered this space three years ago, shortly after she'd first been sent to Mahmi, and had been using it to pull herself together after Atlas Boss was, as she put it, "done with her."

She'd been here when the prison had been locked down, which was why she hadn't been confined to the South Tower like the other women.

"We're here to rescue Renata Bardales," Omen said. "Do you know her?"

A small, bitter smile briefly touched Dina's lips.

"What is it?"

"Nothing. Ren is a good person. I'm glad. It's just . . . all these Arab lives and all these Arab years wasted in this place and no one comes to help. They pick up one Westerner, and all of a sudden the world learns mercy."

"It's not like that," Omen assured her. "That's Irfan. He's . . . well, he doesn't like to say it, but he's her brother."

Dina looked at him, perplexed.

"Don't worry about it," Mirza advised.

"Who is with you?" Dina demanded.

The question caught him by surprise. He wasn't sure how to answer it. Finally, he said, "God."

She stared at Mirza like he was some kind of strange sea creature she hadn't known existed. "No. I mean here, in person, who did you come with? Where's your team? Your army?"

"I am an army," he said.

At the same time Omen explained, "We're alone."

"Alone? That's suicide."

Mirza shrugged. "We're not dead yet."

"Why is that?" Dina asked. "How is it possible?

"He's a mercenary. Very punchy, stabby, and all that. I'm . . . a specialist in procuring highly desirable items for discerning and affluent clients."

"What?"

"Don't worry about it," Mirza said again as he walked over to examine the tiny cache of armaments left there.

Kneeling down, he picked up a *saif* and ran a thumb along the edge lightly. It was disgustingly dull. He tossed it aside, causing it to clatter on the stone floor.

Dina winced. "Careful, please. The walls have ears here."

He inclined his head to acknowledge her warning, then reached for the round shield he'd seen earlier. It was a replica, not a medieval original. It was made of metal and had decent weight to it. The strap behind it was broken, meaning it couldn't be worn. Not that Mirza was going to carry it into battle.

It wasn't meant for actual combat, so it was probable that low-grade steel had been used. Even if that weren't the case, given the fact that it wasn't very thick, it probably wouldn't stand up to anything but the smallest-caliber weaponry. Finally, it wouldn't cover much of him. The glory days of the buckler were well past it.

That didn't mean it couldn't be useful, though.

He decided to take it.

". . . would really help," Omen was saying. Mirza realized he had stopped paying attention to their conversation and tuned back in.

"What do you want to know?"

"Like, can you tell us how many guards there are? Roughly, I mean. Where are they usually stationed? Are there any in the towers? That kind of thing."

"I'll help you with whatever you need. But you have to take us with you when you leave."

Omen looked over at Mirza.

"Us?" he asked.

"The women who are here."

"How many are there?"

"Thirty-five. No, thirty-four."

He met Omen's gaze. Slowly, he shook his head.

"Counting everyone, it's a hundred and ten maybe, and all the prisoners deserve to get out. But the women . . . The way they treat us here, the way they use us, they . . ." Dina's voice started to shake, her dark eyes began tearing up. "Please. We're breaking. Help us."

Omen bit her lower lip and looked away.

"We'll take just you," Mirza offered.

"You . . . you want me to leave the others behind? You really are a mercenary."

Omen shook her head. "That's not fair. This is just about numbers. We have to get Ren and Mahmud, evade security, and figure a way out without getting caught. We can't do that with thirty-three more people."

Dina covered her face with her hands, sank to her knees, and began to weep.

"Fuck," Omen said softly.

"There's nothing wrong with being a survivor," Mirza pointed out.

"You don't understand," she managed to say between sobs. "This is actual hell. You're asking me to be okay with leaving people I know, people I care about, in hell."

It struck Mirza then, for the first time, that this was the true price of heaven. Entering it required that good people—kind, loving, empathetic, forgiving, virtuous people—become callous enough to be blissful, while other human beings—flawed souls they knew and perhaps even loved—were burning in an eternal fire from which there would be no relief.

The very virtues needed to enter the Garden, if you truly possessed them, would keep you from enjoying it.

Even so, he didn't think he had a heart strong enough to hesitate at the threshold of salvation like Dina Malik was doing then. He was witnessing a remarkable thing.

Oblivious to his thoughts, Dina went on crying, the sorrow she had held on to for hundreds of days seeking release. "My God. We even have our own devil. He'll just keep on hurting them, and I won't even be around to help."

Omen sat next to Dina, wrapped her arms around the woman, and tried to offer some comfort.

Mirza crouched in front of them and asked, "Tell me more about the devil."

FIFTY-THREE

OMEN AND MIRZA WATCHED Dina walk past the guards stationed at the entrance to the South Tower and disappear inside. They now knew that Mahmi was held by a relatively small force, somewhere between forty to fifty guards and soldiers. It was part of their routine to enter the towers and check on the prisoners, but they weren't permanently placed there. At least, not under normal circumstances. How they were deployed now remained a mystery.

It was one that Dina was going to solve for them. Once inside the tower, she'd check to see if there were additional defenders inside it. If it was clear, she'd return to the door within ten minutes and ask the sentries there a pretend question. Otherwise, she'd stay inside and hunker down for the upcoming fight.

Omen checked her watch, noted the time, then asked, "You think our gear is going to be safe in that storage room?"

They had hidden it as well as they could, and according to Dina, that space was never used. Given all that—not to mention how empty most of Mahmi was—they'd have to be extraordinarily unlucky to lose their supplies. The risk was certainly acceptable given the benefits of not being encumbered during combat.

"Probably."

A long, unusual silence stretched between them.

He knew Omen would break it. Eventually, she did. "We can't let it get to us. What Dina said, I mean. The suffering of these women, these prisoners, all of them. We came for Ren and Mahmud."

"They are our clients," he agreed.

"So stop thinking about going after Atlas Boss."

"I'm not thinking about it."

Omen turned to face him. "Really?"

"Much," he added.

Mirza had known about Dandarabilla before. While it wasn't as well known as DynCorp, the Wagner Group, Academi, or Aegis Defence, it was still a significant player in his industry, renowned for providing efficient and sometimes ruthless solutions to security and military concerns.

He'd heard tell of Atlas Boss, too, but knew little about the man. Dark rumors swirled around the founder of Dandarabilla, but Mirza understood the fog of war. It was dense and looking through it was nearly impossible, especially at a distance. You couldn't see the true nature of any individual surrounded by it.

Now that he had heard Dina's testimony, however, he knew that the terrible whispers about Atlas did not do him justice. Like the creature he had named his company after, Atlas was a merciless viper, a beast in the truest sense of the word.

It was tempting to put him down when he was this close.

"It's not our job to fix the world," Omen pointed out.

"Are you trying to convince me?" he asked. "Or yourself?"

She looked away again. "Bit of both."

"I might come back for him."

Omen stared at Mirza. "What?"

"It wouldn't be fair to Renata or her prince to endanger them any more than necessary. Our duty is to extract them. Changing the mission wouldn't be right by you either. You didn't sign up for a war. When you're all safe, though"—he cracked his knuckles—"I might go hunting."

She remembered the conversation they'd had before this had all begun and asked, "Trying to do some good in the world by beating people up?"

"That's the only way it's fun."

Omen was about to respond when they saw the door to the South Tower open. Dina tried to step out, but one of the guards stopped her. They spoke briefly, then she retreated.

"That's our cue," he said.

Mirza and Omen exchanged weapons, with her taking Finn's SIG and Mirza getting the CZ, which had only one bullet left.

Omen scowled at the buckler he'd brought along. It was resting against a wall, waiting for her to pick it up. "I don't like this plan."

"It'll work," he assured her.

"I'll be shooting in your direction. I could end up killing you."

"True."

"That's not helpful," she snapped. "Say something useful."

He thought about it for a moment, then grinned. "Hit what you're aiming for."

"I hate you."

"Give me two minutes before—"

"Making like Captain America. Got it."

He started to walk away, then paused and looked back. "They're carrying MAC-10s. You know what that means, right?"

"Yeah. They're gonna blow their loads real fast."

Not exactly how he would have phrased it, but she was right. "And they'll miss high, so get low."

"Got it." She gave him a tight smile. "See you on the other side."

FIFTY-FOUR

THE ENTRANCE TO THE South Tower was located in a long, wide corridor. Since the tower was offset, it was significantly closer to Omen, hidden behind a corner on the right, than to Mirza, who had circled along the left side of the passage. This placed the two guards between them.

Once she was ready, she grabbed the round shield Mirza had picked up and rolled it straight down the corridor, toward the guards. Mirza had asked her to throw it at them, but he'd either underestimated the weight of the buckler or overestimated her strength.

It hadn't traveled far from her before it started to wobble. Then it collapsed on the floor with the loud clang of steel hitting rock.

The tower's sentries reacted immediately. They drew their MAC-10s, aimed them at the shield, and shouted warnings to each other in Arabic. Though Omen was still hidden from their view, they reasonably concluded that old-timey armaments weren't spontaneously appearing in front of them, that someone had to have given it the momentum that brought it into their view.

They called out what Omen assumed were demands for surrender as they approached her location with a great deal of caution.

Tightening her grip on the SIG, she came out of cover for a second, got two shots off before ducking back around the corner.

The response was instant and powerful.

Both SMGs unleashed an absolute storm of bullets, chipping away at the stone walls and leaving clouds of dust in the air. These guns could shoot at the rate of a thousand rounds per minute, but their accuracy was poor.

As Mirza had anticipated, their spray of lead kept rising higher and higher as the infamous kick of the weapons pulled their muzzles up.

Dropping to her knees, Omen spun out of cover again as she fired off a few more rounds. One of them tore through a guard's knee, causing his leg to give way. He was too preoccupied with screaming and stumbling to realize that Mirza had come up behind him.

Sweeping the man's good leg away, Mirza caused him to fall forward, driving his face into the ground with all the force he could muster. A wretched crunch reported the fracturing of his nose and facial bones.

Pulling the now unconscious guard's head back with both hands, Mirza twisted hard. A telltale crack from the spine announced that he'd just created a corpse, and he let go.

The second of the tower's sentries, who had been focused on unleashing another volley in Omen's direction, realized what had happened to his comrade after his clip was spent. He turned slowly to face Mirza, who was crouching down next to the dead man, grinning.

Omen stepped out and put her pistol up against the base of the guard's occipital bone. Without being asked, the guard raised his arms up in the air. He said something neither one of the attackers understood.

"Think he's surrendering?"

"Pretty sure," Mirza replied.

"How do you say," Omen asked, "'thanks, but no thanks' in Arabic?"

Then she pressed the trigger and blew the guard's mind.

———

As Mirza started to walk toward the tower's entrance, Omen reached for the MAC-10s lying by the terminated guards.

"I can't believe I might have to use this garbage," she muttered.

He smiled.

A submachine gun was a great choice for the kind of close-quarters fighting a place like Mahmi Castle required. It was the ideal tool for clearing a room. There were, however, much better, easier-to-control options on the market than these ones.

Almost all the MAC-10s Mirza had seen, he'd seen in movies. Hollywood had fallen in love with the look of the weapon when it had come out, and it had sizzled on-screen. That popularity had never translated to the real world because of the firearm's many shortcomings.

He was sure the Leopards and the Dandarabilla operatives on-site would have better stuff.

Mirza pushed the tower door open and stepped inside.

Ren was there waiting for him, her expression caught between relief, joy, concern, hope, and validation. Hurrying up to Mirza, she pulled him into a hug. Quietly, triumphantly even, she said, "I knew you'd come."

"Who are your friends?" he asked.

Around thirty women had gathered behind Ren, Dina among them, and as soon as he acknowledged their existence, a flood of questions came pouring out of them. Dina stepped in front of Mirza to fend them off.

"Calm down. Calm down. He only speaks English. Stop for a second."

She kept repeating herself—even though she was wrong about what languages Mirza was able to speak—until most of them fell silent. He didn't correct her. It didn't matter just then.

One person still asked, "Who are you?"

Mirza waited for Renata to answer. When she didn't, he had to figure out what to say, how to explain the complicated threads that bound Finn and Ren and those who had survived the General's orphanage together. In the end, he just said, "I'm Ren's brother."

"And who's that?" Renata asked as Omen entered the tower behind them.

"Omen Ferris," she said, introducing herself before Mirza could. "Irfan and I are business acquaintances."

He sighed.

"Okay then." Renata turned her attention back to Mirza. "What's next?"

"Everyone here stays inside. Given the noise we just made, we'll have hostiles to deal with soon."

Omen offered one of the MAC-10s she'd recovered to Ren. "I'm guessing you've got a talent for guns."

"It runs in the family," Renata replied.

Before she could accept it, however, Mirza took it while asking, "Do you know where Mahmud is?"

"I think so."

"Good. After we clear the incoming force, we'll go find him and get you both out of here."

"What's your exit strategy?"

"Don't ask," Omen said. "He doesn't have one."

"That's not true."

"What is it, then?" Ren demanded.

"I'm going to try violence."

"Footsteps!" Dina shouted. "They're coming."

Mirza strode toward the door. As he passed Omen, he reached over and took the SIG she'd tucked away at the small of her back and transferred it to his own.

"Omen," he ordered, "with me. Ren, close the door behind us and fall back into the tower."

"No," Renata growled. "No me voy a esconder!"

He frowned, turning back. "What?"

"She's not gonna hide," Omen translated.

Ren marched forward, snatched Omen's MAC-10, and pushed past both her rescuers.

"I like her. In fact, I'm feeling positively disarmed."

"Stay here," Mirza said. "Please. Keep these people safe."

"Okay." Omen relented, then added, "But only because you asked nicely and I have no ammo."

He spun around and hurried back outside.

The enemy wasn't trying to be covert. They were marching in from the right, where Omen had struck the guards from. He saw Ren standing with her back against the wall, exploiting the corners leading to the South Tower just like he and Omen had done, except from the opposite side.

When the patrol closed in, they'd march right past her. If they didn't notice her in time, she'd decimate them.

A MAC-10 could be accurate up to fifty yards. Ren was going to be much closer than that.

He jogged over to join her, readying his own SMG.

Together, they waited in silence.

As the patrol closed in, they spotted the bodies of the guards Mirza and Omen had dispatched. Two of them rushed forward to investigate, entering the corridor before their peripheral vision could warn them there were ambushers waiting.

Mirza and Ren attacked.

He aimed the MAC-10 and swept it right to left after he depressed the trigger, fighting the kick, trying to hold the weapon steady. A barrage of metal burst through the two men, leaving them riddled with bullets.

Mirza dropped the spent submachine gun, popped out of cover, and was bringing his SIG around when two men tackled him. The pistol skittered away out of Mirza's reach.

He pushed them away and rolled to his feet.

A fighter dressed like the men who'd come to Bangkok was squaring off against Ren. Mirza knew she could not take him. She'd tried to stave off the Leopards before but hadn't been able to do so. She would need his help.

Before that, however, he'd have to dispatch the two guards who'd brought him down and who were rising to face him again.

FIFTY-FIVE

REN WATCHED AS MIRZA got up before the guards who'd caused him to fall could. He didn't seem to realize that a third assailant armed with a shotgun, trailing behind the others, was taking aim at his center mass. His display of agility would be fatal.

Ren lunged forward, grabbed the barrel with both her hands, and forced the muzzle up just as the third attacker fired. A 12-gauge slug smashed into the castle's ceiling.

It was a gas-powered shotgun, which expelled the spent casing and loaded the next round by itself. The casing pinged on the ground as Ren threw a right uppercut that connected with the gunman's jaw.

Just before her punch landed, she realized who she was facing. Adam Aziz with the sad eyes and his semiautomatic Komrad shotgun. He was carrying it with a nylon sling that ran diagonally across his body, from the left side of his neck to his right hip.

His head jerked back when she hit him, but he kept both hands on the Komrad, trying to bring the muzzle down to bear on Ren. If he put a round in her at this range, it would mean her end.

He was stronger than she was, but she strained against him with all her might.

Slowly, inexorably, he began to overpower her and bring his weapon into position. Ren gritted her teeth and screamed, spit flying, trying to summon every ounce of power in her frame. It was not going to be enough.

She needed to hit him again, to even the odds somehow, but she couldn't stop wrestling for control of the shotgun.

With a roar, Ren jerked her neck back and slammed the top of her head against Adam's nose.

Sharp pain exploded in her skull, but she felt the Leopard's grip on his shotgun go a little slack.

Steeling herself, Ren repeated the move.

The force of her blow staggered Adam, cut his bottom lip open, and made the side of his mouth and the corners of his nose bleed.

Ren followed up with yet another headbutt, dizzy and disoriented herself now.

Adam fell, landing on his right shoulder.

The left side of his neck, where the nylon sling was, was exposed.

Ren let go of the Komrad, got on top of him, and took hold of the strap in both hands. She crisscrossed it as best she could and began choking Adam with it.

Adam sputtered, struggled, and gasped for breath. He tried bucking Ren off, and when that didn't work, he pawed at his throat, eyes bulging.

He was turning purple. He'd lose consciousness any second.

Renata was sure she had won.

Then there was a flash of metal in the Leopard's right hand, which came flying back toward her left side.

Agony tore through Ren's leg.

Her grasp on the sling broke.

Adam took in a deep, gulping breath of air, pulled the sling's strap over his head, and freed himself.

Ren looked down.

There was a knife stuck in her left thigh.

She'd been so focused on the shotgun that she hadn't seen the sheathed blade on his hip.

Grimacing, she yanked it out as Adam crawled to secure the Komrad again. A steady stream of blood poured out of her wound.

Ignoring it, Renata thrust the knife into the Leopard's side, piercing his kidney.

He screamed and reached back to retrieve the blade.

Ren pulled it out for him.

Then stabbed him again.

Rolling off him, she lay beside him as he writhed on his back.

She didn't notice his fingers still trying to reach his Komrad.

FIFTY-SIX

MIRZA DROVE ONE OF his massive boots into the midsection of the guard closest to him. The man clutched his abdomen and bent at the waist, doubled over by the sheer force of the kick.

Mirza clapped both his hands on the man's ears hard, causing him to wail in pain. While holding his head in place, Mirza drove a knee into his face, sending him sprawling back.

The second guard attacked and landed a solid punch on Mirza's flank.

Snarling, Mirza turned to face him, then launched a strike of his own with his left hand. It was slower than usual, and his adversary had plenty of time to sway back, out of the way.

This distracted him from the fact that Mirza's right hand was drawing a combat knife.

Driving the blade deep into the man's side, Mirza yanked it all the way across the man's torso, slicing his guts open entirely.

Eyes wide with shock and pain, the second guard stood where he was for a while, holding his torso as if he was trying to keep his intestines from spilling out. Blood started dribbling from his lips.

Mirza grabbed his quarry's neck and turned him around, so that he was facing in the opposite direction. A moment later, red vomit exploded from the man's mouth. Then he went down, collapsing into his own sick.

Mirza went over to the first guard, who was still on the ground, and stomped viciously on his chest. He howled in response. Mirza kept at it past when he heard the grotesque sound of breaking ribs, past when the man fainted, past when his trunk caved in on itself, pulverized.

He glanced over to where Renata had been fighting the Leopard.

They were both down, but the Leopard was reaching for a shotgun that was just barely out of reach.

Mirza marched over, picked it up, and leveled it at the exquisitely trained soldier Renata had downed.

"No. Please no. Please . . . just . . . Shit. Shit. Listen. I'm not like the others. I'm not . . . I'm good to the prisoners. Ask her. You'll see."

Mirza looked over at Ren. Her face was red and bruised. Her nose looked crooked, likely fractured. She was struggling to stand, an open wound in her left thigh.

He held out a hand. She took it and pulled herself up, wincing as she did so.

"You know him?" Mirza asked.

"Adam Aziz," she said. "He was always . . . decent."

"See? Look, I'm not a bad guy. This is just a job. I've got a wife at home, a kid on the way. I need the money is all. Let me go. I'll even join you if you want. This isn't personal. All I do is follow orders."

"What do you think?" Mirza asked Ren.

She stared at Adam for a while, then shook her head and started to limp back toward the South Tower. "Show him the mercy he deserves."

"Thank you. Thank you. I was just trying to feed my family. A man has to eat, you know?"

Mirza aimed the shotgun at the Leopard's mouth.

"Eat this," he said, before he pressed the trigger.

———

Mirza slung the Komrad over his shoulder and searched Adam for anything he could use. He found a five-round magazine for the shotgun and a two-way radio. Then he retrieved the SIG he'd dropped and went to check on Ren.

Omen was with her, examining the knife wound Renata had suffered. "How bad is it?"

"This?" Ren asked, gesturing at her thigh. "This is nothing."

Omen shook her head. "What the fuck did they do to you people at that orphanage to make you like this?"

Ren's only reply was a brief smile.

"To answer your question," Omen told Mirza, "it's deep, but I don't think it hit anything major. Let's move her to the storage room. We can avoid any guards and our first-aid stuff is there."

Mirza shook his head. "There's too much blood. It'd be better if we didn't leave a trail for them to follow."

"Right. Can't have them Hanseling and Greteling their way to us."

"I'll go get the kit," he volunteered.

"Can you go?" Renata asked Omen. "I want to talk to Irfan for a second."

"Yeah. Not a problem. Be back in a sec."

When they were alone, the two "siblings" regarded each other for a moment.

"I see you're just as affectionate and demonstrative as ever," Ren said.

Mirza grunted, then made an observation of his own. "You fought well."

"Thanks."

"But it's usually best not to get stabbed if you can help it."

Renata chuckled. "I'll make a note."

"You're done now, understand? If you can't move freely, you're a liability. Omen and I will go get Mahmud."

Ren glared at him.

Mirza crossed his arms against his chest. "There are two kinds of people who come to me for help. Those who listen and those who're dead. Make your choice."

It took a while, but eventually Ren waved a hand and said, "You're right."

"I know. Now tell me where he is."

"They brought all the prisoners back in, so he's probably in the East Tower. That's where he was being held. Either that or he's still in what they call the Greeting Room."

"Where's that?"

"Just past the East Tower. It's a large hall that's the heart of the place, sends echoes everywhere. Impossible to miss."

Mirza glanced at his watch. "We have just under five hours before reinforcements show. Let's hit it and quit it."

"I'm pretty sure that doesn't mean what you think it means."

He shrugged.

"Finn didn't come?" Ren asked.

Mirza brought her up to speed on Finn's condition.

"Damn it. I'm sorry I dragged you two into this mess."

"If I weren't in trouble here, I'd be in trouble somewhere else. And as for Finn, he's been on the royal road for a while. Getting off of it might do him good."

"Did you wonder why I wanted your help? Specifically yours, I mean."

"I'm very good at what I do."

"It wasn't just about your ability. It was your character."

He blinked. "What do you mean?"

"Remember when we were kids?"

"I try not to."

"Same," Ren said. "Look, I don't know what it was like for you early recruits, but by the time I got there, there was a hierarchy at the orphanage. The strong hurt the weak for no reason. They just tried to make us break, you know? Only one person ever bothered to stop them. Not the General, not the instructors. You."

"I just stepped in a few times. Finn did the same."

"He followed your lead. Without you we would've been even more miserable than we were."

"Why are you telling me this now?"

"To remind you that you have a built-in moral compass."

Omen cleared her throat behind them. "Sorry to interrupt, but"—she held up the medical supplies she'd returned with—"maybe you two can catch up after I keep you from bleeding out."

Ren raised her eyebrows at Mirza. "She's very dramatic."

"No one's perfect."

Omen walked over and handed him what she was carrying. "I should wash my hands."

"Ask any of the ladies here," Ren said, "and they'll show you where you can do that."

Mirza, meanwhile, popped open the kit.

Omen had selected a good one. It was meant to deal with proper trauma, not the kind crammed full of standard Band-Aids, which were pretty much only useful when your kids scraped their knees and were whining about it.

This thing was designed for use in the field and included a splint, a tourniquet, and, more helpful in this case, an Israeli bandage. There were PVC gloves as well, though those were flimsy and much too small for his hands. He was pretty sure they would tear if he tried to put them on.

The world was built for ordinary people.

"Like I was saying," Ren went on, "you've always known right from wrong, and you—"

"Why does it feel like you're trying to sell me something?"

"I am, actually," she admitted. "Aldatan needs to be liberated, a cause for which the people in this prison are vital. We can't just leave them behind. Mahmud won't agree to it. Nether will Habib and, honestly, after seeing what those two have been through, after seeing what everyone here suffers, I won't either."

Mirza scowled. "I came here to get you to safety. You're saying you don't want it?"

"Of course I do. But this is bigger than that. You're here because God wants Samson in this horrid temple. This is an evil place. You need to bring it down."

Omen, who'd overheard as she was walking back, pointed out, "You do know that Samson and everyone around him dies in that story, right?"

"I'm not afraid. Neither is Mahmud. What about you, Irfan?"

"I don't understand what you want me to do. I can't blow up Mahmi Castle. I don't have the ordnance I'd need."

"Atlas rules here. We kill him, we kill his soldiers, and we free everyone. The fires of rebellion Nimir bin Daleel has snuffed out? We can rekindle them all. I mean, I'm the client, right? Can't I change the mission objectives?"

Mirza looked at Omen.

She came up to him and grabbed the sterile gloves. "You'd do it if I weren't here, wouldn't you?"

"Probably."

"How come you don't have any regard for your own life?"

"Ali ibn Talib said, 'What is meant for you will never miss you, what misses you was never meant for you.' If that's true, I might as well be fearless."

"Okay," Omen countered. "I can get with that. But if that's what you believe, why don't you apply the same standard to me? Why get cautious when I'm on the field?"

"It's easier to wager a rock," he explained, "than an emerald."

Her lips started to form a response before she realized her brain didn't have one. She just looked up at him, her green eyes shining.

"Still bleeding here," Renata reminded them.

"Right." Omen took some antiseptic pads and the bandage she needed out of the kit and hurried over. "Sorry. Personally, I think starting a war with Dandarabilla in order to break this prison, given the odds we're facing, is like . . . galactically stupid. We should do it."

"So what do you say, Irfan?" Renata asked.

He took a deep breath. "All right. Let's go cut the head off a snake."

FIFTY-SEVEN

MIRZA CALLED FINN TO let him know about the change in plans. If they were going to get over a hundred people out of Mahmi and then Aldatan, they'd need transportation for them. His brother and Elira would have to figure out how to procure it.

After hanging up, Mirza grabbed the two-way radio he'd taken from the Leopard Renata had downed, pressed the talk button, and said, "Atlas Trash. Come in, Altas Trash."

The response came almost immediately. "Identify yourself."

"Ana Maut."

"That's Arabic for . . ." Atlas trailed off as he struggled to translate the phrase. "'I am death,' correct? Is that supposed to be a joke?"

"No. I'm really going to put you in the ground."

"You're an assassin, then?"

Mirza shrugged. "Not usually, but I'm doing a favor for a friend."

"And who would that be?"

"How about I tell you when we're face-to-face?"

"You want a meeting? I'm in the North Tower. Come see me now. Or, better yet, tell me where you are and I will come visit you."

Mirza, who was in Mahmi's kitchen, smiled. Atlas had made a tactical error. He had allocated all his resources to tracking down the intruders in his domain and guarding his prisoners. He hadn't, however, thought to defend the supplies that made life at Mahmi possible, like food.

This was not a fatal mistake yet, not in these circumstances. There were literal truckloads of the stuff outside. Even if Mirza stole or destroyed everything edible in the kitchen, Atlas's men wouldn't starve.

Those trucks, however, would have to be unloaded in short order. Desert heat didn't get along much with perishables. Those needed cold storage, and all the refrigeration available was in this one place, between the South and West Towers.

Soon, Atlas would need this space Mirza now controlled.

The kitchen was a large room but not a grand one. The ceiling was lower than anywhere else in the castle, where it was vaulted, high, and arched. A lot of the equipment—from modern coolers to much older stone ovens—was crammed in without any regard for aesthetics. That was understandable. No one considered important was expected to set foot in there, not in medieval times and not now. It was functional, and that was all it was ever meant to be.

It did have two access points, which were vital to Mirza's gambit.

There was a door that led into the kitchen and another one that led from the kitchen to the outside, no doubt to allow servants and cooks to enter and leave the premises without disturbing Mahmi's royal inhabitants.

"I asked you," Atlas repeated with brittle restraint, "where you are."

Mirza took a bite from a cold apple he'd pilfered. "What's the rush? Let's play a little first."

"I am a busy man. I don't have time for games."

Mirza knocked a couple of pans together. "That's not really my problem."

"I know you've stolen my women from the South Tower. Ask them about the kinds of things I've done to them, just so you know what your future holds."

The mercenary took another chunk out of his fruit and mumbled a response.

"You shouldn't talk with your mouth full," Atlas chided before he cut off the connection.

Mirza glanced at his watch, then calmly finished his snack. This was the tricky part of his plan.

Well, it was one of the many tricky parts of his plan.

He was betting that Atlas, having been given more than enough clues to figure out Mirza's location, would now realize the folly of not securing the kitchen and dispatch a team to do so.

Mirza estimated how long it would take for Atlas's response to arrive. It wasn't something he could know with any certainty, but Mirza had spent over two decades in this line of work. His guess was, if nothing else, educated.

Once he was finished with his apple, he walked over to a portable gas stove, obviously a recent addition to the appliances in the castle, and turned it on. He took a matchbox lying nearby, but he didn't light a fire.

Instead, he walked away. He passed four backup propane tanks arrayed against a wall; he turned their nozzles open to let the gas stored inside escape.

He went over to the door leading in from the castle proper and set his apple core down in front of it.

Then he hurried across the room to crouch behind cartons of canned foods—tuna, olives, tomatoes—that he'd stacked together near the back exit. They weren't meant to protect him from bullets, just to hide his location. He took out a single match and got ready to strike it.

At his feet lay a fuse line. Next to it was a MAC-10 with a fresh magazine.

The line ran on the ground all the way around the kitchen. Mirza had taken it, along with all the fireworks he'd found, from the storage room Dina had shown him. He had placed them everywhere in the space as if they were explosives. Using the plastic connectors some royal pyrotechnics guy had left behind, he could light them all with one flame.

According to Finn, who'd looked up what happened if you tried to light really old fireworks, it was possible to set them off successfully even if they were over half a century old. There were videos of people doing so online, apparently, because of course there were.

It was inadvisable in the extreme. The chemicals and components of fireworks broke down over time, which meant that they became prone to failure, making them dangerous to use.

So far as Mirza understood, this breakdown was caused by the fireworks being exposed to the elements, especially moisture and sunlight. He hoped that being stored in a medieval castle in the middle of a desert had kept these ones more or less operational.

Anyway, dangerous was kind of exactly what he was going for.

He glanced at his watch.

Atlas's team was running behind.

Mirza frowned.

The squad led by the Leopard carrying the mini-gun should have barged in already. He'd made sure that patrol was closest to him before he'd contacted Atlas. The massive firearm that small man carried around was a huge threat. He had no real answer for the weapon, so he had to take down the man wielding it.

More and more propane was leaking into the air.

Where were they?

Were they even coming?

Had Atlas failed to guess where Mirza was? Had he sniffed a trap and decided not to take the bait?

Mirza licked his lips.

He clenched and unclenched his fist.

For once in his life, he allowed his mind to dwell on all the bruises he'd suffered recently and the pain he was in. That was a much more pleasant thing to think about than the fiery, pointless death that awaited him if this failed.

How long could he afford to wait for Atlas's men to arrive?

At what point would this ambush become a suicide?

"Come on. Come on," he whispered, hoping that his hunters would come find him.

Finally, he heard footsteps approaching. There was no time for relief. He tensed and got ready to run.

The kitchen door finally opened, hit his apple core, and sent it skittering away. Mirza struck the match he was holding. Someone yelled "Clear!" and Mirza heard the sounds of an assault team shuffling into the room.

He lit the fuse, knowing that as soon as he did so, he'd have maybe ten seconds to escape before the first of the explosions started.

"Do you smell—" one of the guards began to say when Mirza grabbed the MAC-10.

He jumped up and opened fire.

It was a wild, uncontrolled burst, not meant to hit anyone but to cover his exit.

Mirza could practically see the seconds tick away in his mind's eye.

His targets scrambled for cover.

He had been expecting Mini-gun's squad.

He'd been expecting five men.

But there were ten. Atlas had sent two Leopards and the guards under their command after him. That's what had caused the delay.

Now they were preparing to fire back.

His shoulder collided with the exit door and he fell through.

Atlas's men moved forward to follow.

The first firework went up.

Mirza crashed onto the ground outside and rolled away.

Then a second firework went off.

Then a third, fourth, and fifth.

Suddenly the kitchen was full of whistles and bright, cheerful, colorful explosions and the screams of men being burned and catching fire.

Five large explosions followed as the propane tanks ignited one by one.

Mirza covered his face as the glass in the kitchen windows blew outward and dark smoke billowed into the air.

Lying prone in the sand, he looked up at the North Tower and smiled.

FIFTY-EIGHT

"ARE YOU SURE ABOUT this?" Renata asked Omen as they prepared to attack the East Tower. "We're going with a straight-up frontal assault?"

"Not what I'd usually do," Omen said, "but Irfan said he'd provide a distraction."

"So this is his idea?"

Omen grinned at Ren. "Walking up to two armed guards and trying to shoot them in the face? Yeah. Of course it's his idea."

"How is he still alive?"

"He'd probably say God loves him," Omen guessed. "I think it's more likely that God just likes being entertained, and Irfan is fun."

Ren chuckled.

"Not in a 'holy crap, what an awesome party' way, but in a 'Jesus Christ, did you see what ridiculous shit that guy just pulled off' kind of way. Like an Evel Knievel who kills people."

"Did he at least tell you what this distraction of his was going to be?"

"Nope. He just said it was going to be huge, which is the kind of thing men promise all the time, so a girl learns to be skeptical, but in this case, I believe him."

Renata raised her eyebrows.

"I make jokes when I'm nervous," Omen explained. "And also when I'm not nervous."

"Great," Ren muttered under her breath, peering out of their hiding spot to study the two men standing at the base of the East Tower. Once again, they were hiding behind one of Mahmi's built-in blind corners at some distance from their targets.

Omen had walked her through how she and Mirza had taken the South Tower by encircling its defenders. That wouldn't be necessary this time. Mirza had promised that the guards would look to the left, meaning that they could approach from the right side without being seen and get off clean shots.

When this would happen, of course, he hadn't—

A series of explosions rocked Mahmi. The deafening sounds echoed through the entire structure.

Ren watched as the two sentries turned away from their position to try to see what was happening out of a nearby window.

Beside her, Omen began to move, firearm at the ready. Her strides were deliberate, quick, and confident, but not loud enough to attract the guards' attention over the explosions reverberating around them.

Renata limped behind her.

They were well within the effective range of their MAC-10s before one of the guards heard them and started to turn around.

Ren pulled her trigger.

Omen did the same.

The corridor was clear in seconds.

There were two remaining dangers. The first being the possibility of reinforcements from within the tower. The second that one of Atlas's roving search-and-destroy parties, led by another Leopard, might come to track them down.

Omen gathered weapons from the fallen guards and watched for the latter, while Ren moved to check if the East Tower was now clear.

She was only a few feet away when slowly, tentatively, the door started to open. She froze in place, ready to start shooting again, then saw Imam Ehsan's face and relaxed a little.

"Who is inside?"

Seeing her, the elderly preacher threw the doors open, and several prisoners walked out. She found Habib among them.

"Where's Mahmud?" Ren asked.

"Not here."

"Shit. Omen?"

The other woman glanced at her over her shoulder. "I heard. I'm sorry. What do you want to do?"

Ren sighed. "I want to march over to Atlas's torture room right now. But it's probably smart to wait for Irfan."

"Yup."

"What was that explosion? Did you guys bring grenades?"

Omen shook her head. "No. Whatever he used, I'm sure it was stupid and dangerous."

"What makes you say that?"

"Irfan would've told us what he was going to do otherwise. I'm guessing the reason he didn't is because he didn't want to argue about it."

That seemed like sound reasoning to Ren. "I hope he's okay."

Omen sighed. "Yeah. Fecking chancer."

"What?"

"Never mind. Let's secure these people and wait for our fearless leader to return."

FIFTY-NINE

ATLAS SHOOK HIS HEAD as he watched a massive plume of soot, ash, and embers rise from the far side of Mahmi Castle. He was in his office with Chike and the Special Ground Forces captain who had led the supply convoy here.

"There's no way anyone survived that," the policeman murmured under his breath.

Atlas suspected he was right.

"We've lost three Leopards," Chike said quietly. "Assuming both teams were taken out, that's a total of twenty-eight men—"

"I know how to count," Atlas snapped, his voice rising in intensity and pitch with each word until he was almost shrieking at the end. "Your doing so is not helpful. Give me a solution. Who is this man who contacted me? Why is he here? How is he not dead?"

Silence followed.

Tentatively, Chike said, "It doesn't matter. We need help. We have to tell the king—"

"No!" Atlas screamed, slapping his hand against a wall. "Unacceptable. We are Dandarabilla. We are excellence. We can't be beat by . . . whoever this is. I will not allow it."

"The lady is right," the SGF officer chimed in. "You've lost control.

I've held off on reporting this long enough. The SGF can fix this mess. We'll come in force, take over, and—"

"This is my palace. No one is going to take it away from me. Not you or your SGF or your king. I will get this under control and then—only then—will we agree upon a story we can tell everyone else. Something that—"

"That doesn't make you look as toothless as you are?" the cop demanded. "No. I'm going to take my SAT phone from your desk and I'm going to call this in. Enough is enough."

"Don't test me," Atlas warned.

"Everyone, just calm down," Chike said.

The policeman moved toward his phone.

Atlas tried to grab him by the arm, but he pushed Atlas off.

Atlas stumbled back. Regaining his balance, he ran across the room to retrieve his Raging Bull revolver. He didn't disengage the safety, Chike noted. He didn't have to. It was always off.

A small part of her wondered when he'd notice that she had engaged the safety of his Mossberg shotgun when he'd given it to her earlier. That had been a mistake. She was sure he'd be irritated when he found out.

Most of her thoughts, however, were about ways to de-escalate this situation.

"Sir," Chike cautioned, "don't—"

"How dare you? I am a member of the Special Grou—"

Atlas fired.

The police officer's brain became mist and filled the air.

His body fell to the ground.

"Shit," Chike muttered.

Atlas put his revolver away and turned to face her. "Have I made my point? We will manage this incident ourselves. Tell me you agree with me."

"I . . . agree with you, sir."

"Good." Atlas straightened up to his full height, tugged at the hem of his white turtleneck, then examined it for stains from the SGF officer's demise. "I like it when we are on the same page."

"How are we going to explain what happened to him?"

Atlas shrugged. "Obviously, these mysterious infiltrators got in here in great numbers and killed this fine representative of the law. It was very unfortunate."

"Great numbers?"

"Of course. This kind of damage could never be done by just two people. That'd be impossible to explain to the king. No. We had multiple intruders, probably trained by the CIA or Mossad or India's RAW. Someone interested in causing instability in the region. Spread the word so that all our men know the scale of the problem we're actually dealing with."

Chike gaped at him. "You want to spread disinformation? In our own ranks?"

"What harm does it do?" Atlas countered. "If anything, the prospect of dealing with large numbers of such highly trained operatives will make them more careful. It is a win-win. It will even make him"—he gestured toward the cop he'd put down—"look like a hero, one who went down fighting against impossible odds."

"And how long before the next ranking member of his squad wants to report back? This doesn't buy you much time."

"I don't need time. I need results. Get them for me."

Chike hesitated. "What are you saying? That you want me to go after these intruders myself?"

"You are the best we have. Well, second best. I am sure you can handle it. However, if you're afraid, take the two Dandarabilla men protecting the armory with you. There is no one alive that three of our operatives can't take down."

She looked back out to where the smoke from the latest blast was still rising. "Just this morning I would've believed you." With that, she turned to go.

"Chike?" Atlas called.

She didn't turn around. "Sir?"

"If you die, that would be . . . it would be very inconvenient for me. You would be difficult to replace. Do keep that in mind."

SIXTY

RENATA FOLLOWED MIRZA THROUGH the deserted halls of Mahmi Castle. With all three Leopard-led search teams eliminated, large swaths of it seemed safe to move around in. Still, it was a hostile environment, so they traversed it slowly and with care.

Despite their recent wins, Atlas Boss had plenty of men on the castle wall. He could call them in at any time. He might have already done so, in fact. They had no way of knowing.

Based on what Mirza had told her about his interactions with Atlas, it was obvious that her brother wanted their enemy angry and off-balance. Pushing Atlas's buttons, making this personal for him, was meant to get him to act irrationally.

It made sense. Emotional opponents made unforced errors, and those could help you prevail when you were outmanned and outgunned.

It was a double-edged strategy, though. If it worked, it'd also make Atlas less predictable. The less rationally he acted, the more difficult his tactics would be to anticipate.

Not that they had the luxury of playing defense. There were only two and a half hours left before reinforcements from Gozel would start showing up. Anything they did, they'd have to do fast.

They were closing in on the Greeting Room now, which meant that she was close to Mahmud. She could practically feel his arms around her. Just a few more feet without incident and she'd know for sure he was safe.

Habib had wanted to come along to see his son, but Mirza had refused, which was cold but also wise. If they did come under attack, the aged prince would be a liability.

Ren was a little surprised Mirza had let her come along. Maybe he'd figured—correctly—that he wouldn't be able to get her to stay behind.

She wondered if the snail's pace he was setting was a courtesy to her wounded leg.

It didn't matter now. They were there.

He gestured for her to open the door to Atlas's favorite torture space. Mirza was more than tall enough to keep his shotgun ready to fire over her shoulder if need be. If that did happen, it'd be bad news for Ren's hearing, but that would only be a concern if she survived captivity.

Mahmud was alone, huddled up in a corner. Ren saw his bloodied, slender form, the tearstains on his face, his exhausted, worn appearance, and gasped. Abandoning caution, she was running to him before he'd even registered who had opened the door.

"Ren?" Mahmud asked, his voice disbelieving, as she gathered him up into an embrace. It was like he couldn't believe she was real, even though she was touching him. "Ren? How?" His confused gaze drifted to Mirza and then to the Komrad in Mirza's hands. "Who are you?"

Renata pulled back and studied her fiancé, checking for wounds. They were everywhere. He'd been whipped and beaten and tormented without mercy. She gently touched the side of his face where Atlas had bitten part of his ear off. A now dirty bandage hid the extent of the damage from her.

"Are you okay?" she asked. "Can you walk? We need to get out of here."

"Out?" Mahmud repeated.

"Yeah. Irfan came to get us."

Mahmud looked at her brother again, this time with a mixture of surprise and respect. "Irfan Mirza?"

He got a grunt for a response.

"Come on." Renata wiped her eyes as she stood. "Let's go."

"Wait," Mirza said. "Not yet."

SIXTY-ONE

MIRZA KNELT AND PICKED up a knife off the ground. It looked like it had been tossed aside. "What's this?"

"I heard Atlas's lieutenant left him with it," Ren explained. "He'd be let out if he cut himself and bled enough to satisfy Atlas."

"I threw it away," Mahmud added.

Mirza studied the weapon. It seemed better weighted than the ones Omen had gotten him, so he took one of those knives out from its sheath at his thigh and replaced it with this blade.

"I'll make sure," he assured Mahmud, "that she gets it back."

Mahmud gave Ren a confused look.

Renata shrugged.

Mirza then made his way up to the wall Mahmud was leaning on. He knocked on it and listened. Stepping back, he reversed his grip on his shotgun and slammed the stock against the sandstone. The clang of metal hitting rock seemed hollow to his ear, but he couldn't be sure.

He walked a few paces down and tried again. The noise seemed to reverberate all around him.

"This room is famous for how far sound travels from it," Renata reminded him. "You're telling every guard in Mahmi exactly where we are."

"Why, though?" Mirza asked.

297

"What do you mean?"

"Why do echoes go so far from this one spot? It has to be because there is a large passage right behind this wall. Maybe more than one, like a junction."

"Makes sense," Ren said. "But what difference does that make?"

Mirza shrugged. "It's a good place to make a way in."

"How?"

"By applying force."

"So . . . what, exactly? Are you going to punch it?"

Mirza thought about the bruises on his hands, which his gloves were currently covering. "No, I'm not twenty anymore. I think"—he held up the Komrad—"I'll let the Russians do it."

"Wait," Mahmud said, catching up now. "You can't. Mahmi is thousands of years old. It's a national treasure."

"It's a prison. And prisons are meant to be broken."

"They're literally not," Ren pointed out.

Mirza gestured for them to get back. "Grab some distance."

"He's really going to shoot it?" Mahmud asked as Renata helped him to his feet. "Is that going to work?"

It was Mirza who answered. "Twelve-gauge slugs will put some hurt on sandstone at close range."

"Hold on," Ren said. "Let's think about this for a sec—"

Her words were drowned out by the loud *bang* of the Komrad firing. She covered her ears.

The round smashed into the rock, sending chunks of it flying up into the air along with a cloud of dust.

Mirza kept his aim steady and pressed the trigger again.

The shot landed next to, not on top of, where the first one had hit. The result was the same.

A third round tore through the damage caused by the prior shots, breaking through the wall.

Mirza walked up to examine what he'd accomplished while he loaded a fresh magazine into the Komrad. He'd managed to create a small hole, though he couldn't see anything through it. The other side was pitch-black.

The wall was relatively thin. The architects who built it hadn't expected someone with a semiautomatic shotgun to blast it.

"I can't believe that worked," Ren muttered.

Mirza shrugged. "Physics. You have to respect it."

"And what about history?" Mahmud demanded.

"That only matters if you're around to read it," Mirza said. "Look, this thing is not much more than a facade. It'll come down if we hit it hard enough."

"What are you going to hit it with?" Ren asked. "As I was about to point out, you don't have the ammo to tear through the wall enough for anyone to get through."

This was true. The submachine guns and pistols they had weren't going to be able to help, and he only had five shells for the Komrad left.

"We need—"

The walkie-talkie on his belt crackled with static, after which Atlas's voice came through. "What are you doing to my castle?"

Mirza pressed the talk button and said, "You heard the noise, huh?"

"Everyone heard it. That does not answer my question. What are—"

"I'm remodeling. This whole place looks dated. But there's good news. Well, it's good for me. It's going to suck for you."

"What?" Atlas snapped.

"I discovered something. Did you know that the walls inside this fortress of yours are hollow?"

Silence.

"That's right," Mirza crowed. "I know about the secret passages, and I've gotten access to them. I can go anywhere undetected. Think about that when you're trying to sleep tonight."

"You are lying," Atlas accused.

"Okay. I'm a liar. Have sweet dreams. There is no monster under your bed."

Mirza handed the walkie-talkie over to Ren, hoisted up the Komrad again, and put two more slugs into the wall before them, just a few inches from each other and near the destruction he'd already caused. This drowned Atlas out for a moment.

A solid blow from the stock of his shotgun, he was sure, would clear away a little more stone. Nowhere near enough of an opening for him—or anyone else—to squeeze through, but it was a start.

Atlas, meanwhile, was screaming, insisting that he be acknowledged.

Mirza took the communication device back from Ren and spoke into it. "What?"

Atlas took a deep breath on the other end. "Maybe it's time for a civilized discussion."

"Not really my style."

"You are still facing incredible odds. You have been fortunate. That is undeniable, but you don't want to be the guy who stays too long at the casino and loses all his winnings."

"I don't gamble," Mirza said.

"Why? You are not a cautious man. Is it because you are a practicing Muslim? If so, what was it your Prophet said? Something about how if your enemies incline toward peace, then you should also incline toward it."

"God said that."

Atlas chuckled. "You're free to believe what you want. Let's say your Allah did say it. Won't you pay heed?"

"What's your offer?"

Ren started to protest, but Mirza held up his hand for her to wait. *You can't trust him,* she mouthed silently.

Mirza nodded.

"I am unable to make one," Atlas said. "I don't know why you came here. Why don't you tell me and we will see if we can reach an agreement."

"My client wants you dead."

"Well," Atlas said, "as you can imagine, that is a bit of a nonstarter for me."

"Sure."

"What would it take for this client of yours to change their mind?"

Mirza looked at Renata, who shook her head.

Then he glanced at Mahmud, who did the same.

"From what I can tell? They won't. Seems they really don't like you."

"I see. You are choosing certain death over a reasonable compromise, then?"

"Now, that," Mirza said, "is my style."

"You have no idea what is coming for you, Maut."

A feral grin spread across Mirza's face. "Bring it."

SIXTY-TWO

ATLAS SWITCHED FREQUENCIES ON his radio so that he was on the channel only Dandarabilla shared. "Chike. Come in."

The woman who was his right hand responded within a few seconds, as she always did. "Sir?"

"The intruder claims he's in the walls."

"What do you mean in the . . . Shit. Really?"

Atlas ran a hand over his face. "There is no way of knowing for sure. I haven't been able to find a way in. Given the sounds we've heard, however, it seems like he may have just made himself one."

"Smart."

"Sacrilegious," Atlas snapped, thinking back to his reverie earlier about how Muslims did not respect their own historical sites. Whoever had broken into his castle clearly had the same barbaric attitude toward the past as the rest of his coreligionists. Anyone could just blast their way into the corridors, but that was the behavior of a Neanderthal.

"Sir? Are you still—"

"I'm here. Look, Chike, this means I need more security. I cannot have these people just appearing in my office."

"You've searched for passage access points there before," Chike reminded him. "You weren't able to find any. I'm sure your office and rooms are safe."

Atlas looked at the walls around him. He was used to them. They felt familiar. It was terrible to think they might hold a secret that'd be the end of him. "Just because I could not find one," he pointed out, "doesn't mean it does not exist."

"That's true."

"I'm reassigning our two operatives who were guarding the armory. They're going to be responsible for my personal safety. I want them up here right now."

He could hear the confusion in Chike's voice. "You told me to take them to hunt the intruder down."

"Now I am telling you different."

"Are we aborting that mission?"

"Negative. I still want this Maut character eliminated. Get it done."

"Should I take the Leopards guarding the front of the North Tower with me?"

"No," Atlas said. "This could be a bluff. The intruder may be planning a frontal assault. I need those men where they are."

"But—"

"You need numbers. I understand. Take two men off the wall."

"It isn't just about numbers," Chike argued. "I'm going to need skill to take this guy down. We need to send our best."

"I am. I'm sending you."

"I just . . . I have a bad feeling about this, Atlas."

She had never, so far as he could remember, used his first name before. It gave him pause. Was he sending Chike to her death by dispatching mere regular guards with her? No. She'd manage fine. "I believe in you."

He heard her exhale, then, like the good soldier she was, she said, "Yes, sir."

"I mean it. You will take him down. I realize that this man's results have been exceptional so far. However, think about how he has done most of his damage. He used surprise. Then a trap which—"

"Which?" Chike prompted.

"Which I fell into. Still, if you think about it, there's no evidence that he's some incredible fighter."

"We don't know what happened at the South Tower," she pointed out.

"You can't judge him based on the results of one engagement. Don't let him get in your head. He is nothing special. He's just lucky, and you know what Shakespeare said about luck."

She knew he'd tell her, so she remained silent.

"'O fortune, fortune! all men call thee fickle.' All men. Our intruder and his colleague will run out of luck. Everyone does. It is simply a matter of time."

Atlas could hear the seconds tick by as Chike evaluated the task before her.

Finally, she said, "You're right. I got this."

"Good," he said. "And, Chike?"

"Yeah?"

"Just in case he really is unusually dangerous, take a sniper with you. Everyone, no matter how skilled, is equally weak to a bullet fired from a distance. Remember that you don't need to beat him. You just need to kill him."

SIXTY-THREE

IN THE STORAGE ROOM where Dina Malik had first spoken to Mirza and Omen, the mood was . . . not happy, certainly, but determined. The prisoners present spoke in hushed tones about what they would do when they escaped. Despite the peril they were in, they were smiling because they were giving voice to hope for the first time in ages.

Mirza had wanted to have everyone they'd freed in one place, so that he'd be better able to protect them. The bigger a room in Mahmi was, however, the farther echoes from it seemed to travel.

The silence of nearly a hundred people being impossible to guarantee, Renata had suggested scattering small groups of them all over the castle. The only people actually in danger, she reasoned, were those prisoners in Mirza's or Omen's vicinity. Atlas had no more reason to kill his captives now than he'd had before.

"I don't understand," Omen admitted, "why you told this Atlas guy you already had access to the passages behind the walls. What does that do for us?"

"It makes him uncertain. He has to worry about where I am at all times. I'm trying to mess with him."

"Makes sense. It is surprising, though, because . . . well, you never lie."

"The Prophet said, 'War is deception.' I'll take any advantage I can get."

"How about you take the advantage of a little break?"

He glanced at his watch. A little under two hours until reinforcements from Gozel could arrive. "No time. We've got to press on."

Omen sighed. "Okay, well, we've got three targets left. The North Tower, the West Tower, and the forces on the outside wall. Where do you want to hit them?"

"What do you think?" he asked.

"Let's go for the West Tower. I heard some half dozen military officers who supported Habib are being held there. We could use—"

Mirza's SAT phone beeped to let him know a call was incoming. He tried to answer it, heard Finn's voice, but the connection was poor and the line cut out.

"I'm going to find better reception," he told Omen.

She nodded. "I saw a series of windows five or six corridors to the left."

Mirza followed her directions and, once he had a stronger signal, dialed Finn back. "Tell me you're on the road."

"I am. I just don't know exactly where I'm going."

"You're coming to Mahmi. It's big. You won't miss it."

"If all of King Nimir's horses and all of King Nimir's men are headed there, and they have a lead on me, then I can't just drive up to them and wave hello, can I? We need a different rendezvous point. Are there any other landmarks nearby?"

"It's all desert. Just keep driving in this direction. Once I get these people to a safe location, I'll . . ." Mirza trailed off, frowning.

"Irfan? Still there, mate?"

"Hold. I heard something."

He crouched, set the SAT phone down on the ground, pulled out his SIG pistol, and thumbed the safety, all his senses straining, searching for a threat.

There.

He heard it again. Someone moving. Footsteps approaching.

Then four things happened almost at once.

Mirza saw a red dot from a laser sight on a wall near him.

He threw himself sideways, across the hall, in the direction the laser was coming from.

Dina Malik jogged around the corner and stood right in front of where Mirza had been a second before. "There you are. Ren wanted—"

A shot was fired.

Mirza's eyes searched for a shooter even as his body flew through the air. He saw the muzzle of a rifle, aimed for it, and emptied his magazine, landing hard on his shoulder. Then his gaze went to Dina.

The young woman's chest erupted like a volcano, spurting her liquefied insides all over Mahmi's ancient walls. She was dead before her brain could register what had happened. That's what a .50-caliber BMG did to you.

The .50 Browning cartridge was designed for use in machine guns in World War I. It was meant to be used against matériel. It could take a plane down on a tarmac. It could be used to hit light armored vehicles on the field of battle. And, yes, it could be used to destroy the children of Adam and Eve.

When it struck a human target, the massive energy of the projectile shattered bone and turned organs into mush. There was no surviving a clean hit. It was like having a blast go off inside you.

Dina was shot near her spine, on the left side of her mid-back.

She fell to the ground in a heap.

Mirza scrambled for cover, managing to duck behind a corner just as a barrage of bullets opened up behind him.

He listened carefully. The rifle that had killed Dina was no longer being used. These were smaller weapons. An AR-15 and a pistol, he guessed, both of which could leave you nice and dead. But these were hydras, not leviathans, so that was something.

He saw two shadows on the opposite wall approaching. One was holding a handgun, the other an assault rifle.

The SIG was out of ammo.

He dropped it and reached for his CZ 75.

One bullet. Two targets. Both armed.

Not a great equation.

Mirza moved out of cover to line up a shot. Unable to get a look he liked, he drew back a split second later without pulling the trigger. A fresh hail of fire zipped past him at impossible speeds.

He drew in a deep breath, centered himself, and tried again. This time, he put a round through the rifleman's center mass. Then, dropping his gun, he raced at his second attacker at full speed.

It was a woman, and she was holding a revolver.

She brought her weapon to bear and fired.

Mirza staggered back like he'd taken a battering ram to the gut.

Time slowed.

He knew he'd been shot. It had happened before.

He couldn't help marveling, as he always did, at how something so little could hurt so much.

He heard her pull the trigger again and figured this was his end. He thought back on his life and smiled.

At least it hadn't been boring.

The hammer dropped.

Nothing happened.

Her revolver was empty.

Time sped up once more.

Mirza was within striking distance now. Before he could attack, however, she threw a punch toward the left side of his face. He deflected the blow with his forearm, then landed a savage uppercut to her jaw. She stumbled back. Cursing and dripping red from her mouth and nose, she spat out a couple of teeth.

He hadn't looked down yet, but the burning pain in the left side of his torso told him that's where he'd been shot. When he slipped into a fighting stance, he kept his left elbow by his side to defend his wound.

She wiped her lips with the back of her hand, smearing blood over them.

"Who are you?" she demanded.

"Mirza."

"I am Chike."

"Nice to meet you."

"You're making jokes? You should be begging for mercy. You're dead already. Go to hell in peace."

Mirza chuckled. Death wasn't a reason to give up. It was a reason to fight harder and faster, to win this last battle before God took him. "I think I'd like some company."

She came at him with a roundhouse blow to his chin. He tried to dodge it but wasn't fast enough. It connected hard, making him reel.

Chike followed up with two quick jabs that struck home.

Mirza slumped forward, hands on his thighs.

She kicked at his injured side. He managed a block, but the force of her attack drove his elbow into his wound and he screamed.

Chike pulled back, grinning, then aimed another punch at his bruised face. Mirza managed to sway out of the way this time, then lunged forward, tackling her, and landing on her with the entire force of his body.

It took a second before she realized what had happened.

He pushed off and struggled to his knees.

She looked down at her abdomen.

There was a knife sticking out of her where the two sides of her rib cage met. It was a blade that she seemed to recognize.

"I think that's mine," she mumbled.

"Keep it," Mirza told her.

He'd taken her jabs to lull her into a false sense of security. He'd put his hands on his thighs to get them close to his knives. He'd screamed at the top of his lungs to cover the sound of the weapon being drawn, and then he'd planted it deep inside her.

"You fight well."

"I thought . . . I won," she whispered, blood dripping not just from her wound but also from her mouth now.

"Where is the sniper? The one shooting the fifty cal?"

"Dead. You got him right after he took his shot. That was . . . too good."

With a groan of effort, Mirza struggled to his feet.

"I warned him," she said, "this would happen. I didn't want to die here, like this."

"Who did you warn?"

"Atlas."

"Maybe you shouldn't have worked for a snake like him."

The look in her eyes was distant and far away. They were the eyes of a soul passing.

Blood burbled up from inside her throat, but she managed to say her last few gasping words. "But he burned a village for me."

SIXTY-FOUR

MIRZA PICKED UP THE rifleman's Ruger AR-556 and took his spare magazine. Then he limped across the corridor to where he could hear Finn still shouting his name out from the SAT phone. With a pained grimace, he bent down and took ahold of it.

"I'm here."

"Thank God," Finn said.

"You don't believe in God," Mirza reminded him.

"Have to be honest, I did for a second there. What happened?"

"Well, I have good news and bad news."

"Are you hurt? I heard—"

"That's the bad news," he confirmed.

"What's the damage?"

Mirza looked down at his left side. He was losing a lot of blood, but it seemed like no major organs had been hit. So, it'd be a slow death, which—he thought—is all life is, really, and grinned. The best you could hope for is some time to get a few things done, which he still had.

"That's the good news. I'm not dead yet."

"Yet?"

"I have what I need now," Mirza said.

"What are you talking about?"

"Atlas sent me a key. Very nice of him. Listen, Omen won't have good reception, but try to reach her and when you do, tell her to meet me where Ren and I found Mahmud. I'm going there now."

"No," Finn objected. "Don't move. Tell me where you are, and I'll send her to you."

"I can finish this job."

"Forget that. Just . . . I'm on my way, all right? I'll get you out and—"

"'I know you won't let anything delay your arrival, but I'll be dust by the time you learn I've departed.'"

"What the hell does that mean?"

"Always a good question when someone recites Ghalib."

Finn sighed. "Irfan—"

"I am not going to make it. It's okay. We both knew it could end like this, brother."

There was silence on the other end, then Finn admitted, "Guess we did."

"All right then. I'm going to go to work."

Before Finn could say anything else, Mirza hung up and looked around.

He saw Dina, what was left of her, lying on the floor by his feet. He stared for a moment at the bloody ruin that had so recently been a young woman, his head bowed. Then he limped toward the fallen sniper and retrieved his massive firearm.

He was about to resume his mission when he realized that if he left this spot, he might lose the reliable signal he was getting. He might not get to talk to anyone else.

He thought about Maya, about his habit of calling her whenever he took on a mission from which he thought he might not return. He hadn't done that this time, after his conversation with Omen, who'd told him how much the tradition distressed his daughter. He'd wanted to spare her.

312

But surely this was different.

Was he really strong enough to bear never hearing her voice again?

He dialed her number.

She didn't answer.

He was about to disconnect with the intention of trying again, when he remembered that Maya never answered calls from numbers she didn't recognize. No matter how many times he rang, she wasn't going to pick up.

Teenagers.

He waited for her voicemail.

He closed his eyes and listened to her tell him to leave her a message.

Mirza cleared his throat before speaking. He didn't want to sound like he was in pain. "Maya. This is Dad. I . . . I wanted to . . ."

What had Omen said?

I was with her when you called to let her know you might not come back. I saw what it puts her through.

"I wanted to check in. To see how you are. And . . . uh . . . I just . . . I love you, M&M." He paused, not sure what to say as a final good-bye. Then they came to him, the words with which Finn had been bidding him farewell for three decades now. "Stay out of trouble."

SIXTY-FIVE

MIRZA SET UP THE sniper rifle in the Greeting Room and got down on the floor next to it, gritting his teeth against the pain. He tried to steady his shallow breathing, then aimed at the interior wall he'd shot at already.

A massive chunk of rock blew off the wall as a 5.45-inch .50 BMG round, capable of traveling miles, moving at nearly three thousand feet per second, tore into and then burst through sandstone like it was barely there.

He pressed the trigger, reloaded, and pressed the trigger again repeatedly until he'd emptied two magazines, focusing his fire so that one section of the wall, large enough for him to squeeze through, would break open.

Having shot twelve times, he struggled to his feet, leaving the rifle and a pool of blood in his wake. His ears were ringing, and they hurt from enduring what had sounded like blasts of thunder right next to his head.

Just as the dust settled, Omen and Renata rushed into the room.

Ren gasped when she saw the state of him.

Omen froze.

Then she said, "Fuck. Fuck, fuck, fuck. Okay. Just . . . it'll be okay. I can do this. I'll stop the bleeding. You'll be fine."

"I'm not done here," he said when he realized that she was carrying one of the first-aid kits they'd packed.

"Damn straight."

He shook his head. "No. Omen. I'm talking about the wall. It's still standing."

"Forget that. You need—"

"I need it to come down. Ren, do something for me?"

"Of course."

"The Komrad shotgun I picked up earlier. Get it for me. And bring our flashlights, too."

"Now?"

He nodded.

Renata bit her lower lip, placed a quick, comforting hand on Omen's shoulder, then limped out of the room as fast as she could.

"What are you doing?" Omen asked, her voice shaking.

Instead of replying, he took a deep breath, rolled his shoulders like a boxer loosening up for a fight, took stock of his target, and charged at it.

Omen shrieked for him to stop as he ran into the wall at full speed, his right side slamming into it. He howled in agony as his battered body lit up with pain, warning him that it couldn't take much more, that soon it would have to stop, that he would have to stop.

The stubborn wall held.

Mirza stumbled back. He was sweating, his vision felt a little blurred. His mouth tasted like iron. He spat. It came out red.

"Enough," Omen begged. "You've done enough. It's too strong, Irfan."

He exhaled, then ran at the wall again.

Again, it hurt.

Again, he screamed.

But this time, the weakened sandstone bricks gave, and he crashed into the passage beyond, landing in a heap of dust and rocks.

Omen rushed forward to help him out of the rubble.

Groaning, he regained his feet, stumbled, then steadied himself with her aid.

"You're fucking insane."

"You love it," he said. As she shook her head, he pulled her into his arms. She held him tight. He endured the discomfort without complaint. He could feel her tears soaking into his clothes. He stroked her copper-red hair, kissed the top of her head, and inhaled the scent of vanilla and lavender, a little tinged with sweat now, but beautiful all the same.

After a moment, she gathered herself and pulled away. "Let me look at it."

Groaning, he peeled off his pullover and then the thin compression shirt underneath. He rubbed his right shoulder as she knelt in front of him and examined the damage.

"There's an exit wound. That's good. I'll patch you up as best I can, but you need a surgeon."

He let her get her medical supplies. He'd take whatever time she could steal from Death for him. Besides, he wanted to let her know his revised plan. "I'm going to take a flashlight. That'll leave you with one. Use it to get to the West Tower. These rifles I found, take them with you. Give them to the soldiers there."

"I'm not leaving you," Omen said, not looking at him.

"Once they have weapons, they can break out and help you take the wall. Then you can lead everyone to a safe location outside Mahmi. Finn can pick you up."

"I am *not* leaving you," she repeated.

Mirza reached down and tipped her chin up. Her shining green eyes met his dark ones. "Don't let this be for nothing."

She looked away but nodded.

Renata returned with the flashlights and canteens of water. Mahmud followed behind her, cradling more than carrying the Komrad. He was holding it like a newborn. Despite everything, the sight made Mirza smile.

For his part, when Mahmud saw Mirza, he blanched, and his eyes went wide. "Are you okay?" He paused, seemed to realize that was a stupid question, and was about to say something else when he caught sight of the shattered wall behind Mirza. "How did you—"

"Ballistics," Mirza said, reaching over to take the Russian weapon he'd asked for, "is the best science."

"Stand still," Omen snapped.

He looked at what bandaging she'd managed to do so far. His bleeding hadn't stopped, but seemed to have slowed a little. "That'll do, thanks."

"It's not good enough," she whispered.

"It'll have to be." He unclipped his SAT phone and handed it to Ren. "Omen will bring you up to speed. Follow her lead."

"Where are you going?"

Mirza checked the Komrad's magazine. There were three shells left. "To hell if God is not merciful. But I'm going to make a stop first."

SIXTY-SIX

RENATA WATCHED AS OMEN stared first at the darkness into which Mirza had disappeared, then at his blood, which still stained her hands. Ren understood her anguish, but there was no time to grieve. They had to move.

Walking over to Omen, she twisted open the cap off a canteen. "You okay?"

"Yeah."

"Let's wash your hands." As she was pouring out water, Ren asked, "Why didn't you say good-bye?"

Without looking at her, Omen said, "He's Irfan Mirza."

Renata glanced at Mahmud. He didn't seem to know what to make of that answer or what to say in response either. So, as she had been trained to do as a child, she decided to focus on the mission. "What's next?"

"We take all the weapons we can to the West Tower," Omen said. "We arm the soldiers there, break them out from the inside."

"Makes sense."

"Let's go."

"Hold on," Ren protested. "What's the rest of Irfan's plan?"

Omen used the clean parts of Mirza's discarded pullover to dry her hands, leaving pink streaks behind. "Straightforward as usual. We take the North Tower and then we take the exterior wall. That'll be all she wrote."

"Easier said than done."

That earned Ren a tight smile. "Always is. Come on. We have to run."

"I can't." Renata gestured to her leg. "Remember?"

"Shit."

"Mahmud can't either. We—"

"I'm going to go get the soldiers solo," Omen cut in. "You put him somewhere safe and go north—not through the passages, the regular way—and distract the guards there. Take the assault rifle. It'll help. You don't have to take them out. Just hold them off. Can you handle that? I'll join you as soon as I can."

"What's my objective?" Ren asked.

"How subtle do you think Irfan is going to be when he gets inside the North Tower?" Omen countered.

"Not very."

"Yeah. He's gonna make a ruckus. When the guards at the entrance hear it, they'll go upstairs to investigate."

"And in doing so they'll end up flanking him," Ren finished. "He needs their attention to be elsewhere. I get it."

"There is one more thing," Omen said.

"What?"

"Irfan's going to be pissed at me if you die . . . so, maybe don't."

Renata smiled. "I'll try my best."

After Omen walked through the Mirza-sized hole in Mahmi's wall, Mahmud turned to Ren. "Let me come with you. I can help."

Ren walked over, put a hand on his cheek, and asked, "Have you ever even fired a gun, habibi?"

"I've played a little *Call of Duty*."

Renata chuckled. "The video game?"

"It's supposed to be very realistic."

"Right. Listen, I appreciate the offer," she said, "but I'll be more ef-fective if I don't have to worry about you when I'm fighting."

He exhaled, clearly miserable. "I just wish—"

"What?"

"Sometimes I wish I were more like Irfan," Mahmud admitted. "You wouldn't have to ditch me, then."

Ren leaned forward to kiss his cheek, then took his hand and started to lead him out of the Greeting Room, guiding him back to where the other prisoners were. "You are a lot like him, actually."

Mahmud snorted.

"It's true. Think about it. Why are you here?"

"Because I couldn't keep my mouth shut," he joked.

"When you saw oppression," Ren said, "you stood up. You didn't have to. You could've gone along with Nimir and enjoyed a ton of power like so many of your cousins do. Or—and this would've been easiest—you could've stayed out of Aldatani politics altogether and lived a comfortable life somewhere in Europe. You chose this instead. That's what Mirza would've done. You two are made out of the same stuff."

"Except he can break through walls like . . . like a sledgehammer."

"There's no denying the fact that he's a freak. I'm just saying, you're pretty great yourself in a . . . more understated way."

"How come you're being so nice, señorita? It's not like you."

Ren squeezed his hand. "What can I say? I guess prison changes people."

SIXTY-SEVEN

"IN POSITION," RENATA WHISPERED into Mirza's SAT phone. "Looks like there are just two hostiles at the base, like at the other towers. They're Leopards this time though. Still, I've got this."

"Be careful," Omen replied. "We'll head your way as soon as we're out. I'm not expecting any other calls. Are you?"

"Uh . . . no?"

"Then let's keep this line open," Omen suggested.

Ren shook her head. She liked the woman, and Omen seemed like an interesting fit for Mirza, but that sense of humor needed an off switch.

Lowering the volume of the speaker so noises from it wouldn't distract her, Ren crouched down, placed her phone on the ground, then raised the AR-556 Mirza had left behind. With the rifle's stock resting firmly against her shoulder to help her maintain control, she aimed at the Leopard closest to her.

She inhaled.

She'd exhale when she fired, releasing her breath at the same time as the weapon expelled its bullets.

For a moment, Ren waited.

Then she pressed the trigger in the same smooth, steady, controlled manner she'd been taught ages ago.

The burst caught her target in his chest. His body jerked, tottered, then fell.

She tried to take down the second Leopard as well, but he was already scrambling. He managed to get off a volley with his rifle before opening the tower door and taking cover behind it.

Renata figured she'd be able to keep him pinned until Omen arrived with the cavalry. The situation was well in hand.

Safe back behind a wall, she was about to tell Omen to take her time, when more fire came in her direction. She could tell instantly that the muzzle report and caliber didn't match the weapon the Leopard had used.

Ren peeked out to see what was happening.

She gasped and had to pull back as more lead came in her direction, but not before she'd caught sight of two additional enemy combatants taking cover. They were Dandarabilla operatives.

Just like that, she was hopelessly outgunned.

Another storm of bullets flew in her direction.

Ren waited for it to subside, then responded with a few shots of her own, though they were pretty much blind. She wasn't able to get a bead on either one of them. As she was ducking back down, an unexpected bit of movement caught her eye. It took her a second to process what it represented.

An advance.

Her adversaries weren't staying on the defensive. They were moving toward her.

She reached for her phone. "Omen, where are you? Omen?"

There was no response.

SIXTY-EIGHT

MIRZA'S FLASHLIGHT CUT THROUGH the old darkness of the hidden royal corridors of Mahmi Castle. If it were brighter, and if it weren't for the uncomfortable sense of being closed in on all sides by stone, it wouldn't have felt all that different than the rest of the fortification. He ignored the dust, the cobwebs, and the chittering of rodents unused to having their domain disturbed as he moved.

It was harder to ignore the cold he was feeling, though he was still sweating, or the fact that his strength was fading. The long trek across Mahmi was taking a lot of the little life he had left out of him.

Every so often, he passed by a set of empty copper brackets on the side of the passage, no doubt meant to hold torches when these secret ways were in use. They had remained empty for a thousand years, their purpose fulfilled long ago. There wasn't anything left for them to do.

As he moved north, toward his destination, the floor sloped upward and his path began to wind around a cylinder. Mirza came to a set of stairs and began to climb. He glanced at the watch Omen had gotten him. Its face shone in the darkness.

Fifty minutes until the reinforcements from Gozel would arrive.

He hoped the soldiers in the West Tower were capable. If they were important enough to imprison in this place, they were likely senior officers, no longer used to the field. If they didn't have one last battle in them, his entire tenuous plan would fall apart. But there was no other way to go about this that he could see.

He turned around a bend and nearly walked into solid rock.

He stared at it, trying to make sense of the unexpected dead end. Then he realized that there was a decaying wood ladder built into the wall to his left that he hadn't noticed. He frowned, trying to judge if it'd hold his weight.

It led to some kind of ledge, which was too low for him to stand up on. It was too low, in fact, even for someone of average height. He'd have to crouch. Not something he was looking forward to doing in his current condition.

Still, Mirza climbed up. He gritted his teeth. He could hear them grinding against each other, his body's way of coping with pain.

At least he didn't have to go far. Around four yards in, he discovered another ladder, this one made of rope, and he finally understood why no one had been able to discover Queen Arwa's secret.

Access points to the passages were overhead, perfectly camouflaged into the ceiling.

Mirza saw two iron handles embedded into what looked like an otherwise ordinary slab of rock in Mahmi's construction. When he pulled at it, it came away relatively easily.

He lay down and peered out of the opening he'd created. Below him, he saw the landing of the North Tower's highest floor. It wasn't a large drop, maybe eight feet or so, and he had the rope ladder to help him with it.

Mirza climbed down, wondering if he would've ever solved the mystery created by the architects of the castle without having to resort to destruction.

He doubted it. He'd have assumed, like everyone else probably did, that the entrance to the passages—like the passages themselves—were built into the structure's walls. He wouldn't have thought that there might also be secrets overhead.

He would've also focused on important rooms, like those belonging to the queen. Searching the corridors wouldn't have occurred to him, nor would it have been easy to do given the area he'd have to cover.

Once he was on the landing, only a simple wooden door separated him from the topmost chamber in the North Tower. It was a good bet that's where Atlas was.

Mirza started to move toward it, then stopped, listening. He thought he heard gunfire. It sounded close. That didn't make sense. Yes, his progress hadn't exactly been swift, but he didn't think Omen could have liberated the West Tower already. Even if she had, his instructions had been to take the exterior wall next. No one would leave Mahmi alive so long as the enemy controlled it.

He shook his head. Maybe he'd imagined it or maybe the famously eccentric acoustics of the castle were playing tricks on him. There was no time to stand around worrying about it.

As he considered his next move, he noticed that some of the light coming from under the door was getting blocked by a shadow, a shadow that wasn't entirely still. Someone was standing there, fidgeting a little.

Mirza imagined a person of average height on the other side, aimed his Komrad at their center mass, and opened fire.

SIXTY-NINE

AS MUCH AS OMEN loved her chosen line of work, she had to admit that it did have a few fairly significant drawbacks. The ever-present threat of police encounters, state prosecution, and lengthy prison sentences, for example, wasn't great. There was also the less than thrilling possibility of grievous extrajudicial bodily harm, which became exponentially more likely when she did a collab like this one with Mirza.

She shook her head. No. She wasn't going to think about him right now. It was not her habit to worry. The universe would unfold how it would unfold. Letting the future gnaw away at the present was not wisdom, so far as she could tell. It was best to focus on where you were and what you were doing, and what she was doing was the worst part of her job. She was experiencing the ick of it all.

As much fun as being on your hands and knees could be in the right circumstances, crawling through the cramped, poorly lit, dusty, vermin-shit-filled parts of the world was very much not her idea of a good time.

Omen grimaced as her left hand grazed the rough fur of a deceased rodent's corpse and took stock of the situation. On the whole, she had made excellent time, but the end of the journey, which had required that she climb a dilapidated wooden ladder while carrying three MAC-10s and a giant sniper rifle, had slowed her down considerably.

Sweating, cursing, and a little out of breath, she reached the faux section of the West Tower's ceiling. She tried to lift it away. It took her a few tries, but she eventually got the access panel to move. When she looked down, she realized she had a problem.

A guard was standing eight feet below her.

He'd been talking to someone, had cut himself off midsentence, and was staring up at her like her existence was impossible.

As his brain caught up to his eyes, he cried out in alarm and began reaching for his weapon.

Omen jumped.

In midair, she reached down and yanked both her knives out of their sheaths at her thighs.

Bending one of her knees, she dropped it on the guard's face.

Her right hand smashed the point of a blade into the soft skin just above his clavicle.

Instead of tumbling dead to the ground beneath her and breaking her fall, which was how Omen had imagined this playing out, he staggered back, away from her, and remained standing, his weapon still coming to bear.

She crashed into the stone floor hard, landing on her side, and heard a loud crack, then felt a sharp pain by her hip. Had she broken something? It took her half a second to realize that she had. Her SAT phone.

Ignoring it, she slashed up blindly with her left hand in the direction of the guard, and it came away wet. She'd definitely done some damage.

She rolled into a crouch and examined her handiwork.

The guard was crumpling to the ground, his nose broken, red spurting from near his neck. His eyes were wide, apparently still not believing that any of this was real, while his hands were clutching his groin, where she'd inadvertently done something rather gruesome.

"Oooh." She winced sympathetically. "Sorry, dude. Totally didn't mean to do that. But, hey, pretty sure you're going to be dead soon, so it's not like you were going to use any of that . . stuff."

The guard pitched backward and fell over.

"That's what I thought."

Now that she finally had a moment to look around, Omen realized she had an audience.

Around twenty or so men, who had been in the process of eating, were staring at her, looking rather green. She'd landed in a room functioning as the prisoners' mess at mealtime.

Omen gave them a bloody little wave. "Hello, boys."

SEVENTY

THE TWO DANDARABILLA OPERATIVES who had emerged from the North Tower, along with the Leopard who'd been stationed outside it, had stopped advancing for the moment. They had moved to take up defensible positions, then stopped and assessed the tactical situation. They'd figured out that they could outlast Ren.

At the outset of the engagement, she had responded to their barrages with matching volleys of her own, but that wasn't sustainable. She'd had one spare magazine—which she was now using—and nothing else. So, she'd been forced to stop shooting almost entirely.

Unsurprisingly, her opponents had figured out the cause of this reticence. Now, they were being bolder, staying out of cover for longer, goading her into spending what few rounds she had left.

Under normal circumstances, Ren would have tried to withdraw, but Mirza was still in the North Tower. If she pulled back and the hostiles retreated, they'd discover him, just like Omen had predicted.

He hadn't abandoned her to her fate. The least she could do, she figured, was return the favor.

Besides, with her compromised mobility, she wasn't sure she'd get very far.

The operatives fired at her again.

Sitting on the ground, her back to a wall, holding her rifle close, Renata focused on her breathing. That was one of the first things she'd been taught at the orphanage when she'd gotten there nearly two decades ago.

She'd been seven.

All she'd wanted since then was to be like everyone else in the world, to live an uneventful life, to find a little love, a small measure of happiness. After all that struggle to be normal, she was going to die in this wretched, extraordinary place.

It was almost funny.

The question she had to answer now was how she wanted to die. Did she want to go quietly, out of ammo and hiding in a corner, or did she want to take as many of her enemies with her as possible?

Taking a deep breath, Renata rose to her feet and waited for the next barrage from the men she was facing.

It came.

As soon as it was over, Ren stepped out of cover, spraying lead, screaming as she tried to down her opponents.

She couldn't be sure, but she thought she hit one of them.

Then her clip was empty, her weapon useless.

She closed her eyes.

Ren heard running footsteps nearby, then a maelstrom of bullets, and felt . . . no pain?

Frowning, she looked to see why that was.

Omen was standing in front of her, six soldiers at her back. On the ground behind them lay the Leopard and Dandarabilla men.

Renata blinked. "Good timing."

"What the fuck were you doing?"

"I figured this was it and I didn't want to die cowering and afraid. I thought I should choose my end."

Omen stared at her.

Ren shrugged. "It seemed like a good idea at the time."

"Your whole family is nuts."

"Yeah."

Omen shook her head. "Just . . . never mind. We have like thirty minutes before the bad guys get reinforcements and we turn into pumpkins. I'm going to find Irfan. You up for taking these guys to win back the wall?"

"Absolutely," Renata said. "Let's get this done."

SEVENTY-ONE

MIRZA FIRED TWO OF his three remaining rounds.

The first bore through wood and tore into the stomach of the Dandarabilla operative standing behind the door. The second sailed through the fresh corpse's hair and shattered the hip of Atlas's second guard.

That last bit was sheer luck, but it wasn't really surprising. If you fired enough bullets, things you wanted to have happen did eventually happen. It was the Law of Truly Large Numbers in action.

Kicking the now splintered door open, he stormed through.

Atlas was there, standing behind a desk, a silver Mossberg shotgun pointed right at Mirza. The two men locked eyes, both ready to fire.

The second guard was valiantly crawling on the ground, trying to get to a firearm himself.

Mirza stepped on his neck and crushed his windpipe without looking away from Atlas.

"Brutal," Atlas complimented.

"Nice gun."

"Yours too."

Mirza shrugged. "It's all right. But semiautos aren't my thing. There's something about a pump action like yours that I just like."

Atlas's pale-gray eyes shone. "I know precisely what you mean. There is a drama about it. A romance. An ineffable quality that a gas-powered firearm can never truly capture."

"Right."

"Well, against all odds it seems like we're kindred spirits, you and I."

"I wouldn't go that far," Mirza said.

"Well, at the very least, we're both killers. That calls for a certain level of professional courtesy, don't you think? Tell me. Who are you? I know you claim you are Death. I have to grant that you look like it, but let's be serious. Give me a name before I kill you."

"I'm Irfan."

"Irfan," Atlas drawled, drawing the syllables out. "It has a certain something to it, I suppose."

"Glad you approve."

"I must admit that meeting you has been a more pleasant experience than I anticipated. You came across as being a lot less . . . civilized in our earlier communications." Atlas lowered the barrel of his Mossberg to point at the mercenary's side. "It seems like bleeding out agrees with you."

Mirza's dark eyes were locked on Atlas's weapon.

They did not move when it moved.

But they did narrow.

"Normally, I'd happily sit here and watch you die slowly," Atlas told him, "but you did kill Chike, didn't you?"

Mirza nodded.

"That cannot be forgiven. She was . . ." Atlas hesitated, as if almost surprised by the words coming out of his mouth. "She was my friend. I feel like I must avenge her."

"You can try," Mirza told him.

Atlas laughed. "Such bravado in the face of hopeless odds. It's . . . well, you're rather like my shotgun, aren't you, Irfan? Dangerous with an old-school charm. You both have the hint of a bygone barbarity about you that I enjoy. This is a poetic thing to kill you with."

"There's one important difference between me and your gun," Mirza said.

"Really? What's that?" Atlas asked.

Mirza pulled the trigger on the Komrad and then let the now empty gun drop.

Atlas saw it coming enough to move a little.

The slug slammed into the right side of his chest.

Atlas shrieked and fired his own weapon.

Nothing happened.

Mirza grabbed the Mossberg and yanked it forward, tearing it from Atlas's hands. Then he spun it around and smashed the stock into Atlas's face like it was a baseball bat.

Atlas's teeth shattered as his jaw broke.

He couldn't even scream right as he fell to the ground.

He managed to stay conscious, though. Getting to his knees, he looked up at an advancing Mirza, his confused gaze fixed on the firearm that had betrayed him.

"Your gun's safety was on," Mirza said.

Atlas mumbled that this was impossible, that he never engaged the safety. But then he remembered.

He had last used his shotgun when he'd killed three prisoners with it, when he'd gotten Habib to whip Mahmud. That had been just before Mirza had arrived. Chike had come to get him. He'd handed her the Mossberg. She must have engaged the safety for him.

He hadn't bothered to check it because he wasn't in the habit.

"Chike," he managed to spit out.

"I keep telling people friendship is a dangerous business. Look where it's gotten us."

Atlas held up his hands in a gesture of surrender as best he could with the hole in his chest.

"Put them down," Mirza said. "We're both dead. Let's just—"

Atlas's legs darted out, and he swept Mirza's feet from under him. The big mercenary stumbled and fell, his head hitting the side of Atlas's desk on the way down.

Mirza's world swam.

Then he felt Atlas climb on top of him. He expected the Dandarabilla man to hit him. Instead, he felt Altas tear away at the bandages on his abdomen, undoing what little aid Omen had been able to administer.

When Mirza's wound was exposed, Atlas drove an elbow into it.

Mirza roared and nearly blacked out from the hurt of it.

His face went purple because he couldn't breathe.

He couldn't see. He couldn't think. All he knew was pain.

He felt Atlas's hands around his neck, squeezing with all the force he could manage.

Mirza opened his eyes.

His black gaze met Atlas's gray one.

Atlas's eyes were bulging out, full of hatred and fury and, inexplicably, joy.

Mirza struggled to find the strength to try to counter him.

His vision started to fade.

Desperate, he took a trick out of Atlas's own book.

He managed to get his left hand up to Atlas's chest.

He punched repeatedly at the hole the Komrad had left there.

Then as Atlas pulled back, reeling, Mirza slipped his fingers inside the bloody wound, wedged them under Atlas's shattered ribs, and pulled outward like he was trying to rip the man's chest cavity open.

Wailing, Atlas rolled off of him.

Mirza turned himself over so that he was on his stomach next to Atlas, who was writhing on his back.

Mirza reached over and closed one of his massive hands over Atlas's face.

He pulled the man's head up, then slammed it down on the stone floor of Mahmi Castle as hard as he could.

Then he did it again.

And again.

He heard Atlas's occipital bone fracture.

Then it caved.

When blood and brains began leaking out of Atlas's wrecked skull, Mirza finally stopped.

Breathing hard, he growled, "How's that for old-school barbarity?"

Atlas, obviously, had no response.

Mirza tried to stand, but he couldn't.

Instead, he dragged himself across Atlas's office to a window that looked out over most of Mahmi Castle. Propping himself up, he could see that there was fighting happening on the walls. His mind couldn't make out who was winning.

He slumped against the wall of the ancient fortress and looked up at the ceiling. But he was looking past the sandstone and the secret passages and the sky and the heavens up to God.

He'd agreed to help Ren get all the prisoners out of Mahmi.

Whatever happened from here on out, it was indisputable, he thought, that he had tried to keep his word.

"What more could I have done?" Mirza asked.

In the silence, his own proud words from a few days ago came back to him.

Let the Angel of Death come for my soul if that is God's command. Inshallah, he will not find me unprepared.

"Where are you?" Mirza called out, hysteria-laced laughter in his voice, a snake-eating grin on his face, and his end at his door. "I'm waiting."

———

The scent of vanilla and lavender made Mirza force his eyes open. He saw Omen hovering over him, her eyes bright and sparkling with tears, and smiled. The sunlight, filtering through the North Tower window, seemed to make her copper-red hair glow.

She said something to him. Mirza heard it but couldn't make sense of it.

He tried to respond, but he wasn't sure he got any words out.

He felt her leave soft kisses on his forehead, his cheeks, his mouth—frantic, desperate, prayerful. His lips moved against hers and he finally managed to whisper, "This is a good death."

EPILOGUE

IRFAN MIRZA WOKE IN a hospital. He recognized the heavy smell of aggressive antiseptic chemicals and the muted beeping of medical equipment, which never seemed to want to disturb you but did want to make sure you couldn't forget it was there.

As was his habit whenever he was injured, he lay still and took inventory of the damage he'd suffered.

His head hurt. His throat hurt. His shoulders hurt. His abdomen felt like it had been shot, which it had. A deep, persistent ache burned there, but it was bearable, likely because of painkillers.

Finally, and most important, he was still breathing.

He vaguely remembered Omen being with him at what he'd been convinced was the end. He'd said something to her. He had the dreadful feeling it had been emotional.

Now he was going to have to live with the horror of having been sentimental, a fate worse than death.

Groaning, he tried to sit up. The ache in his torso intensified tenfold.

"Irfan."

It was Omen's voice.

He smiled.

"You're awake," she said, coming over to his bedside. "Hold on. Let me get a doctor." She turned to leave, but he grabbed her hand. She looked back at him. "What?"

"No need," he croaked. "I'm fine."

Omen stared at him.

Then she started to laugh, and she kept laughing until she began to cry.

Irfan Mirza's hospital room was busy the next day. Propped up in bed, he'd just spoken to Maya, who didn't know he was hurt. There was no reason to worry her. Now, he was being plied with pills and news, both of which people were eager to give him.

They were all in Yemen, thanks to Sister Elira and Finn. Omen, sitting beside him, holding his hand, was bringing him up to speed.

"Hold on," he said, interrupting her story. "You brought the officers from the West Tower to the North? I thought I told you to use them to retake the outer wall."

"You did," she agreed. "But I don't take orders from you. Not a soldier, remember?"

"Yeah."

"Good. Anyway, the rest is pretty straightforward. I found you. Ren helped retake the wall, and Finn drove in for the rescue."

Mirza shook his head. "And reinforcements from Gozel really never arrived?"

"Nope. Not sure why, but that's what saved your life. You would've bled out if it had taken much longer for Sister Elira to get to you."

Finn, who had pulled up a chair to Mirza's right and was devouring his Jell-O cup, said, "You're a right jammy bastard, mate. That God of yours loves you."

"Or it's like Omen said," Renata joked, "and he just doesn't want to miss the show."